ocona shouted, while he was still two hundred
rds away.

Black Snake shook his head and waved a hand
front of his face as if to chase away words he'd
ther not speak.

Nocona felt a chill then. It froze his spine and
emed to spread into the deepest recesses of his
ody.

"Something's happened. What is it?"

Again, Black Snake flailed with his hands. He
wallowed hard.

"Tell me," Nocona said gently.

"The village . . . Osage . . . they . . ."

"How bad?"

"Bad."

Black Snake looked at him then, his eyes suddenly
welling up. "White Heron," he said. "Little Calf . . ."

Nocona tilted his head back just a little. Then he
nodded.

"Both of them?" he asked.

Again, Black Snake nodded. "Both of them."

Shaking his head slowly, then faster, Nocona said,
All right. Bring the horses. I'm going on ahead."

"You can't. The Osage might be . . ."

"I hope so," Nocona said.

By Bill Dugan

Duel on the Mesa
Texas Drive
Gun Play at Cross Creek
Brady's Law
Death Song
Madigan's Luck

War Chiefs
Geronimo
Chief Joseph
Crazy Horse
Quanah Parker
Sitting Bull

Published by HarperPaperbacks

Quanah Parker
WAR CHIEFS

BILL DUGAN

HarperPaperbacks
A Division of HarperCollinsPublishers

HarperPaperbacks   *A Division of* HarperCollins*Publishers*
10 East 53rd Street, New York, N.Y. 10022

Cover illustration by Jim Carson

First printing: March 1993

Printed in the United States of America

HarperPaperbacks and colophon are trademarks of HarperCollins*Publishers*

❖ 10 9 8 7 6 5 4 3 2

Chapter 1

Summer 1832

VIEWED FROM HIGH up on the ridge, the camp looked more like an anthill than the habitation of human beings. The conical structures, dun and buff colored, here and there darker brown, some painted with brilliant swirls of color, others left the same unadorned shade of tan they had been under the skinning knife, were scattered for nearly half a mile along the valley floor. The river, which curved in the bright sun, seemed poised like a blue-bladed scythe about to harvest the tipis. The specks of children darted in and out among them, their headlong turmoil as confusing as that of a swarm of gnats.

On the far side of the shallow river, two thousand or more horses grazed contentedly, sometimes snorting, sometimes dashing in short sprints, flexing muscles that hadn't been used for several days. On the ridge, the heavy heads of hollyhock waved in the breeze, bees darted in

1

and out among the taller stems, and a thick carpet of flowers in reds, blues, and yellows followed the gentle curve of the slope all the way down to the village.

Standing just outside his tipi, Peta Nocona surveyed the hillside, glanced up at the sun, so hot it was almost white, bleaching the sky of its blue and threatening to parch everything for as far as he could see. Even the flowers on the hillside seemed pale under the brilliant glare. He watched a handful of young boys race toward the riverbank and splash out into the current. Their sun-brown feet kicked up curtains of gleaming silver as they waded in until the water was waist deep and it was no longer possible to run. Then they pushed out still deeper, their chests generating lengthening vees of blue water out behind them until, almost as one, they dove under the surface, disappearing in a sudden jungle of calves and ankles.

Nocona remembered when he had been young enough to play like that, when he didn't have to worry about where the next buffalo would be found, when the next Osage war party would swoop down on the horse herds and the tipis, when the next hunting party would fall prey to Apaches. It hadn't been that long, maybe twenty winters, but so much had happened in that time that it might as well have been twenty lifetimes.

He walked through the camp, nodding to friends, smiling at children who stopped what they were doing to watch him pass. The attention came with being someone everyone knew would one day be a chief, and there were some who thought that's all there was to it—smile, spread your arms wide, and gather in the glory. But those who thought that way couldn't have been more wrong. Being chief was like living under a cloud, a cloud so dark it obscured even the most brilliant sun, so heavy it threatened to crush the air from a man's lungs, make pulp of flesh and bone, grinding him to paste and then to powder, as if he were no more than a handful of corn between two great stones. They should only know what I know, he thought.

They should only know for one day what it was like to have the lives of so many people closed in your hand. Keeping them safe was like trying to hold a fistful of water. No matter how tightly you squeezed, drops managed to slip away, to land in the dust and disappear as surely as if they had never been. Try to save one, snatch it from the air as it fell, and you lost another and another. All you could do was watch, and try to keep the others safe. If you were naive enough to believe in the Great Spirit, you could pray for his guidance, but Nocona had seen too much to think it did any good. But still, he knew that one day those problems would be his, and he would accept them because the people demanded it, and a man did what his people asked of him. And he would ask the Great Spirit for help, with no great expectation of an asnwer.

After all, he thought, it was not just the Comanche who asked for His intercession. The Osage prayed, too, and the Apache and the Mexican. He had heard that even the Texans and other white men prayed to the Great Spirit. And it seemed to Nocona that the Great Spirit had a sense of humor of sorts, and a cold detachment that allowed him to stand by and watch while men struggled against one another the way a child stood by and watched armies of ants make war on one another, sometimes even egging the contenders on, not out of malice so much as just to see what might happen if this were done, or that were changed.

And later that day, he knew, he would be leaving the camp behind again, most of the warriors with him, and riding across the Rio Grande and into Mexico, where there were horses to be had for the taking. Others would try to stop the Comanche, of course. There would be Mexican soldiers, who were little trouble, and Apache, who were too much trouble. He wished there were some other way, not knowing what that other way might be, but he was wishing away a thousand years and more of history, trying to change what had always been, and substitute nothing more than the vague notion that another way might be better. He said so around the council fire, but the chiefs always laughed because when they asked what he proposed to take the place of life as they had always known it, all he could do was shrug his shoulders. But he knew they had to change, because a change was coming, and it was better that the matter be decided by the Comanche than by others.

He reached the water's edge and looked up at the sky once more. The sun was still there, watching him, patient, emotionless, the unblinking eye of a teacher who knows that a mistake will be made, if only he waits long enough. Nocona watched the boys swim for several minutes, feeling a pull to join them, as if somewhere deep inside him he carried some tenacious remnant of the boy he was in that time so long ago he barely remembered it now.

Without thinking, without even being aware of what he was doing, he waded out into the water, feeling the silky glide of the current as it pressed against, then swept past, his calves. The water was cool and clear, the blue color gone now that he was so close. He looked at the surface, like a sheet of silver one moment and the next as transparent as if it weren't there at all. He saw a school of small fish, darting a few inches at a time, then stopping, their fins fluttering like rags in a stiff breeze. He half expected to hear the flap of cloth snapping, but there was nothing but the burble of water against his legs and, across the river, the shouts of the boys, to break the stillness.

Nocona leaned over, watching the fish, staring at them intently, as if he hoped to mesmerize them with his stare. Unblinkingly, the fish stared back, hanging there suspended, frozen, only the pulsing of the gills and ragged wave of the fins to prove they were living things.

He let his hand slide into the water, then cupped the fingers. With a movement so sudden it startled him, the fish darted and he reached for them almost instinctively, his forearm throwing off a great wave that obliterated the transparency in a flash. He felt the tickle of a single fish against his palm for an instant as he closed his fingers, but knew that he had missed it even before he looked.

Withdrawing the hand, he stared at it for several seconds, conscious that there was no squirming in the closed fist. Slowly, he uncurled the fingers to find his hand empty of everything but the water which lay in a small pool in the bowl of his palm. He watched the water as if not quite sure it was as empty as it seemed. The hand moved, and he saw the sun staring back at him from its center. Tilting the hand, he watched the sun vanish and the water trickle like liquid silver back into the river, each drop sending out a circle that disappeared within a few inches.

To himself, he whispered, "That's all we are, a few drops of water in a great river that doesn't know whether we are there or gone. And doesn't care."

He took a couple of steps out into the current, feeling the coolness climb past his knee to midthigh. Turning, he looked upriver for a long time, only dimly aware of the raucous laughter of the boys. Turning again to stare, this time downstream, at the water that just a moment before had not yet reached him and now was already past and moving away as certainly as if he had never stood in its way, he shook his head.

A shout reached him then, and he turned to see several of the boys waving at him, their thin arms churning the air, beckoning him to join them. He smiled, wishing he could. One of them was his son, Little Calf, and the boy took a few strokes toward him. He wanted to say that he couldn't, that he was too busy to join them, that he had things to do that were more important than flopping onto his belly and drifting like an otter on the sluggish current.

But before he could shape the words, he realized it would be a lie. He could do what he wanted, not because he was a great warrior, but because he was one of the people, and what was the point of being a man if he couldn't do what he wanted when he wanted?

He dove then, landing with a slap that sent great waves in every direction. Digging in, he stroked rapidly across the river, until he sensed the boys in a school around him, darting just like the fish. He stopped then to dogpaddle, spitting a shining feather of water high into the air, then using his palms to send sheets of water like Mexican swords slicing just above the surface.

The boys squealed and used their own small hands to fight back, sending a dozen daggers for every saber. Nocona rolled onto his back and stroked toward them, provoking squeals of fright that were half simulated and half real. Rolling back onto his stomach, he felt for the bottom with his feet and only then was conscious that he was still wearing his moccasins. He would be in trouble for that one.

The moccasins were nearly new, and his wife would surely skin him alive for his carelessness. He smiled at the thought. He could see her now, hands on hips, a skinning knife jutting out from one clenched fist, as if she had grown a steel spine. But in the end, he knew, she would shake her head more in amazement than resignation that such an influential man could also be such a fool. Then, in the manner of all husbands since Adam, he shrugged and turned back to his fun. She might not understand, but she would forgive, in a day or two. It was too late, in any case, to undo the damage.

During the brief period of inattention, the boys had rallied, quieted down enough to sneak closer and when he turned back to the business at hand, he found himself surrounded. With an earsplitting shriek, the boys charged ahead, most of them too short to stand on the bottom, treading water as they flailed their arms and sent sheets of water cascading over him from every direction.

With a roar, he swept his arms in a broad half circle, setting off a tidal wave that pushed the boys back, and he dove under, heading straight for the legs of his son, Little Calf. Sliding under,

he rose to the surface, with Little Calf on his
back. Then he lifted the boy high in the air and
tossed him away.

Little Calf landed like a huge stone, and sent
another wave across the current. Spluttering and
laughing, he surfaced, raised a fist, and charged
back into the fray.

Nocona, knowing when to retreat, stroked for
the far shore, and hauled himself out dripping
and laughing. Instinctively, he glanced at the
new moccasins, shook his head and took a deep
breath. He swept his gaze from one end of the
camp to the other, and it seemed as if the river
was a kind of screen, one that gave him some
detachment. It didn't matter for that moment
that it was his village and that its people were
his people, people who depended on him to
make decisions and who, if they chose, one day
would follow him, but *only* if they chose. It was
only by making his decisions wisely that he
would keep his authority.

And at the moment, the prospect of that
authority seemed like a burden, instead of the
gift it was meant to be. Still dripping wet,
Nocona walked away from the river, toward the
huge herd of horses. It was a motley assort-
ment—large American horses stolen from
Texans, wild mustangs run down on the Llano
Estacado, the smaller, more delicate Mexican
horses.

Looking at the animals, Nocona wondered
how it came to be that the Comanche could

have become so dependent on an animal they had first seen not that long ago. In less than three hundred years, the horse had revolutionized a way of life that had persisted for four times that long. The old ones were full of stories handed down from grandfather after grandfather, and no one knew exactly how many winters it was that the first Comanche had climbed onto the back of a horse—but it was a long time, everyone agreed on that.

And now, the slender ankles of the animals were all that kept the Comanche from starvation or, worse, death at the hands of the Osage or the Pawnee or the Apache. It was hard to know whether the gift of the horse was a blessing or a curse. But it no longer mattered which. The Comanche were hooked, and that could not be undone.

Pushing through the herd, Nocona climbed the gentle slope all the way to the wooded ridge beyond it. When he reached the crest, he sat down, his back against a cottonwood, and thought about the coming war party. Everything he saw spread out before him could be wiped out in one blinding flash. He might ride into Mexico never to return. He wasn't afraid, he was too much of a warrior for that and, too much of a fatalist. But the thought made him sad all the same.

He wondered if he were to die whether he would still be able to see the wonders of this world. Would he be able to watch Little Calf grow to manhood? Or White Heron take off her dress and wade out into a pool draped in willows to bathe, the way he had first seen her? Would he be able to warn his people if danger threatened to take them by surprise, or kill a buffalo for a starving old grandmother who had no one to care for her?

He wanted to think so, but he just didn't know. Dying didn't frighten him, not anymore, not like it used to. But the thought that he would never again be part of his people's lives filled him with a thick gloom shot through with streaks of terror, like lightning flashes in a winter storm.

And he closed his eyes to listen to the wind in the leaves high above him.

Chapter 2 ===

NOCONA EXAMINED A FISTFUL of arrows, checking each shaft to make certain it was straight and true, ensuring that the heads were sharp and secure and that the fletching was smooth and tight. Satisfied, he slipped them into a quiver that glittered in the firelight, elaborate beadwork catching the flames and scattering them in every direction.

His wife, White Heron, watched him quietly, looking up now and then and letting her hands rest in her lap, an unfinished moccasin under them. She didn't like it when Nocona was away for long stretches of time. She understood it, realized that it was what he did, how he supported his family and also that it was expected of a great warrior. But knowing all that didn't make the long, lonely nights any easier to bear.

She was not alone in her distaste for the long separation. Nocona himself had told her once, lying awake long after their son was sleeping, the fire crackling as it died, and the walls of the tipi shivering in a cold wind from the north. "I wish there could be another way," he'd said, "another way to live. But this is the only way I know. I don't want to be like the Mexicans, tied to one piece of land, bending my back over a plow and trying to scratch a living from stones."

At first, unsure whether he meant for her to hear, she said nothing. He turned toward her then, rested a hand on her forehead and brushed a lock of jet black hair aside. "What do you think?" he'd asked then.

"I think you do what you have to do. I think that you know what is best for you. And what is best for the people. One day you will be a chief, and these are things that you must think about for their sake."

He'd laughed, almost bitterly. "I wish you were right, but . . ."

And that had been it. He'd never mentioned his doubts again, and she'd never raised them on her own. What was would have to be enough. But every time he prepared for war, or got himself ready for a raid far to the south or west, she thought about that night, heard his words as plainly as if he had spoken them again. And she worried. She worried because she knew that uncertainty was as deadly an enemy as any Apache or Mexican, could snuff out Nocona's life in a twinkling. He had to believe in what he was doing, do it with all his heart in order to do it well. If he were unsure, he would hesitate, and one day that hesitation would get him killed.

Now, hearing the whisper of the arrrows as they slid into the soft deerskin quiver, she heard the words again. And this time, like every other time since that night, she chewed on her lip rather than mention that conversation, hoping that it had slipped his mind. She would not risk reminding him and perhaps giving him reason to question what he was about to do.

"Will you be gone long?" she asked. It was what she always asked, always quietly, as if she hoped he didn't hear her. But he always did. This time was no exception.

He shook his head. "Not long. I'll be back just as soon as I can."

"You go to Mexico?"

"Of course. Mexico. That is where the horses are. You know that."

"Don't we have enough horses?"

"You can never have enough horses, you know that, too. We can trade most of them to the Kiowa and the Shoshone, anyway. It is much easier for us to get them from Mexico than it is for them."

"What do the Kiowa have that we don't have already? Why do we need anything to trade with them? Is their buffalo meat better than ours? Do their children have moccasins while ours do not?"

"You know that's not it . . ."

"What, then? I want to understand . . . I know

you have told me before, but I still don't think I understand."

"They have guns, white man weapons they get from the north and the east."

"Your arrows are deadly enough, are they not?"

He laughed. "Yes, they are. But I can't shoot an arrow as far as a gun can shoot a bullet. And there will soon come a time when our enemies have enough guns that they will not be afraid to attack us. And when that day comes, we had better have guns of our own."

White Heron took a deep breath. She didn't want to argue with him. Not now, not when he would be leaving so soon, and maybe not coming back. That was no way to send him off to Mexico. So she turned back to the unfinished moccasin, her practiced fingers working the rawhide lacing through another hole and another and a third. She became aware of the silence then, stopped once more, and looked up at Nocona. He was watching her intently, his eyes wide.

"What is it?" she asked.

"Nothing." He continued to look at her, and his expression seemed to be changing from one dark mood to another.

"Tell me . . ."

"I like watching you do that. There is something comforting in it. It is nice to have such control over something that you can start and know just what it will be like when it is finished."

"Don't make too much of it."

"Or what?"

"Or I might put sleeves on your next moccasins."

He laughed then, lightheartedly this time, and dropped to one knee beside her. "You would, too, wouldn't you?"

"If you don't go soon, yes. The warriors are waiting for you. You can't disappoint them, or when it comes time they will look to someone else to be chief."

He sighed. "There are times when I wish they would do that."

"Don't talk like that. You know you don't mean it. You would not hate being chief."

"Probably not. But I wonder if I would not hate it as much as I would not hate *being* chief."

"It is what you wanted ever since you were a little boy. I used to watch you, then. Remember running around with your face all painted up, sneaking into tipis and scaring the life out of the old women with your shrieking? You even stole my uncle's horse one time."

"That was nothing. Just something I did so you would notice me."

"How could I not notice you? You were everywhere. No matter which way I turned, there you were. And everybody teased me about it."

"That isn't why they teased you." He knelt closer, his eyes on her face, as if searching for something.

"Why, then?"

"Because they knew how much you wanted me to follow you, and you all the time complaining when there I was, doing exactly what you wanted me to do. They saw through you. They knew just what you were up to."

"Who? Who knew?"

"Everyone." Nocona reached out and cupped her chin in one hand, then leaned forward and brushed her forehead with his lips. Then he straightened up and got to his feet.

"Be careful," she said. "And come home as soon as you can."

He didn't answer. Bending to retrieve the quiver, he pushed aside the entrance flap and slipped out of the tipi into the bright sunlight. He grabbed his war shield from its stand beside the tipi, took a lance and swung up onto the back of his favorite war pony. He had already cut a second horse from the herd for the long trail into Mexico. The rest of the warriors were already on their mounts, some even sprinting them back and forth on the edge of the village to give them a second wind. They would ride hard for the first day, then make a more deliberate pace all the way to the Rio Grande.

Pushing his pony with his knees, the war rope coiled in his fist, Nocona made his way to the raiding party. The warriors saw him coming and started waving their bows and lances in the air, shaking their shields and yipping. They were anxious to get on the move. Or so it appeared. He

wondered whether any of the others were as
ambivalent as he was.

He had never discussed his own concerns
with any of the other warriors, not even with
Black Snake, his closest friend. It wasn't because
he was afraid Black Snake would think him a
coward, but because it was a chief's responsibility to lead his men, and you could not lead men
who knew you were uncertain about where you
were leading them, or whether you ought to be
leading them at all. So he had swallowed his
doubts, let them chew at his insides, and kept
his own counsel. Even when he became chief, he
knew, it was not something he would discuss.
Perhaps especially not then.

Black Snake, riding a pinto daubed with
stripes of bright red and yellow, rode forward to
meet him.

"White Heron didn't want to let you go?" he
asked, grinning broadly.

"You're only saying that because you wish
your wife tried as hard to keep you at home,"
Nocona said.

"If my wife looked like White Heron, she
wouldn't have to try hard at all to keep me at
home. She would have to drive me out of the
lodge with a lance."

Nocona waved a derisive hand. "You love
raiding the Mexicans more than you love life
itself. You wouldn't stay at home willingly, even
if you had a handful of White Herons in your
tipi."

"A handful of White Herons would send me off to meet the Great Spirit." Black Snake smiled. "That would be the only place I could sleep."

"Are we ready?"

Black Snake nodded. Like Nocona, he was a subchief, and highly regarded by most of the warriors. "We're ready. Are you all right?"

"Yes, why?"

"I don't know. It seems like you have something on your mind. Something heavy. Are you angry that I teased you about White Heron?"

"It is not the first time you have teased me about such things. Why would it make me angry now?"

Black Snake shook his head. "If you're sure you're all right, then we should go. It is a long way to Mexico, and the warriors are anxious to get moving."

"They are always anxious. Always they want to count coup and swagger around like no one has ever touched an enemy before."

"They are young. They will get used to it, and then it will not seem like such a big thing to them. You and I were like them once."

Nocona sighed. "I know. It wasn't that long ago that I don't remember."

"Then you should be more patient with them. Let them have their fun. It doesn't last that long. One day they will be old and toothless, if they are lucky, and will wait at home while others go and bring back horses and buffalo."

"I am worried about the Osage."

"There hasn't been any sign of them. Not since they attacked the Kiowa village and that is almost a year ago. What is there to worry about?"

"It is not like they have dried up and blown away, like the husks of old corn. And they haven't made peace with us. Why would I not worry?"

"Because the Osage would not dare attack a Comanche village. They know what would happen if they did."

Nocona looked up at the sun rather than answering his friend. "You are right. It is time to go."

Holding his lance high overhead, Nocona let out an earsplitting wail, shook the lance, and prodded his pony into a gallop. The women and children and the few warriors left behind to defend the village all raced out of the camp and down to the river, where Nocona plunged in, barely slowing his pony. They were shouting and waving, the individual words lost in the din.

As he came out of the river on the far side, Nocona turned to watch the others, most of them still well out in the current and some even on the far side yet. He scanned the crowd for White Heron, but knew that she would not be there. She never was. It was for others to scream and yell and rattle whatever came to hand. She preferred to stay in the tipi, her mind on her work. Nocona had always come home, and she was not about to do anything that might change that. Not now.

Urging his pony up the ridge, he turned once more at the crest and watched the last few warriors straggle out of the river and spurt forward, streaming water like silver ribbons in the bright sun. It was time to turn his mind southward.

Chapter 3 =======

WHITE HERON WAS UP earlier than usual. When the sun came up, normally she would already be preparing the morning meal, or sitting quietly by the newly made fire, doing beadwork. She enjoyed the quiet time, when the camp was silent, and she could follow the trail of her own thought without interruption. But when Nocona was away on a hunt, which might not bring him back for two or three weeks, or a war party, which might not bring him back at all, sleep was hard to come by.

At such times, as often as not, she would hear something in the dark, an owl or the yip of a coyote, even the snorting of a restless pony across the river, and she would awaken, knowing even as her eyes snapped open, that sleep was gone for the rest of the night. And this time, having sensed Nocona's restless foreboding, sleep was more elusive than usual.

Brushing aside the entrance flap, she stepped outside, then held the leather in her fingers as she lowered it back in place. She stood there for a long moment, her back to the tipi. Painted by the light of a nearly full moon, the whole village seemed to have been made of Mexican silver. In its stillness, it looked to her almost like a collection of toys, as if the pale light somehow diminished everything, shrank it all down to a size more appropriate for children's playthings.

Moving toward the river, she watched the horses across the sluggish current, most of them quiet, some standing with bowed heads, others twitching tails and ears to catch the first hint of danger which could come at them at any moment, from any direction. Everything seemed so fragile to her, so precarious, as if the life she lived were balanced on the edge of some yawning abyss, one into which it could all vanish in the twinkling of an eye with one false step.

At the water's edge, she sat down, her back to the village, and watched the placid surface. The water murmured softly. Almost instinctively, she turned her gaze skyward, toward the cold moon impassive in its stare. It was almost unfriendly, as if it wanted to force her to use its light to see things she chose not to see. Out near the center of the river, an image of the moon, like a second, colder eye stared back at her as unblinkingly as the original, or the eye of a rattlesnake.

She was worried about Nocona. He seemd to be struggling with some heavy burden. No one else seemed to be aware of it, but she could sense it in the sag of his shoulders, in the grudg-

ing way he laughed now, so unlike him. He was
a young man, not even thirty winters behind
him, but he carried himself like one of the old
ones, as if he had seen things no man should
have to see, or knew things one was better off not
knowing. Even the children, who normally could
make him smile in the middle of a towering rage,
no longer seemed to brighten his mood. When he
looked at them now it was with a silent sadness,
as if he feared for them some fate he could sense
but not understand.

Things were changing rapidly. White Heron
knew that. He was soon to be a chief, and she
understood that being chief in such a time was
no easy thing. But that was always true. Being
chief was never easy, and things were always
changing, sometimes rapidly, sometimes not.
The perils were constant, the pressures unremit-
ting. The Osage were as bloodthirsty as always,
the Apache as rapacious, the Texans as greedy.

But those were not new concerns.

White Heron grabbed a fistful of grass and
slapped it against her thigh as she watched the
surface of the river. Almost as if the moon read
her mind, it exploded into a shower of silver
droplets, a dark shadow arcing into the air where
the white disc had been, then crashing with an
audible slap that sent ripples in every direction.
Startled, it took her several seconds to realize
that a trout had leaped after a bug, destroying her
tranquility in its hunger.

When the reality finally sank home, she

thought how appropriate it was that the stillness should be broken by a need that respected nothing, not even tranquility. It is, in some ways, a perfect emblem of the Comanche life, she thought. She smiled ruefully, embarrassed that she had been so frightened by something so ordinary. Almost as if she expected that someone would be there, she looked over her shoulder, hoping no one had seen.

Getting to her feet then, she moved east, along the riverbank, heading away from the village, as if it were too solid a presence, despite its apparent fragility. A stand of willows marked the eastern edge of the camp, and she headed toward the trees. A single dog drifted toward her from the tipis, falling in behind her, hanging at her heels as she kicked at the sandy shore.

The trees were dark against the pewter of the grass and the brighter shine of the water where the river curved around behind the willows. A cluster of boulders jutted out into the river just past the trees. She would be shielded from the prying eyes of early risers there, and since sleep was out of the question and it was too early to disturb the others with morning chores, she decided to spend some time in total isolation.

Brushing aside the trailing branches of the first willow, she ducked under its umbrella into deep shade. Turning for a moment to peer back through the thickly leaved branches, she could barely see the tipis, even under the bright moonlight. It seemed almost as if the village had ceased to be. Part of her wished that it would, that she could just walk off into the rising sun to see what life might be like where the white men were in control.

She knew that Nocona hated the whites, and feared their coming. And she knew, too, from years of living under the dangling sword of Mexican soldiers, that he was right to be concerned, but that didn't dampen her curiosity. In her heart, she understood, like Nocona, that things were changing. Unlike her husband, who imagined some all-consuming confrontation that would leave all the whites or, far more likely, all the Comanche, to rot in the sun, she hoped that some sort of accommodation was possible. But deep inside, deeper than she was able to go, she knew it wasn't possible. There was too much hatred, and too much greed. Even for the land that most whites called a desert, the trackless plains of the Llano Estacado, there was too much white greed.

Ducking through the far branches of the willow, she slipped back into the moonlight and climbed up onto the rocks, easing in a crouch over the rough stone until she could stare down into the river. The dog, suddenly attached to her, followed her out, stood for a moment until she ruffled the fur on its neck with an idle hand, then curled into a ball and lay down just out of reach.

It was so quiet, she could hear her own heart beating if she listened. She could see part of the village now, at the far end, where the river curved to the south. The near end was hidden completely by the willows. The stillness seemed to squeeze her like a giant fist, and she felt frightened for the first time, as if the thickening air meant to do her harm.

Shuddering, she wrapped her arms about her, feeling a sudden chill. She glanced at the willows, but the branches were motionless in the still air. The river continued on, its surface undisturbed. Looking toward the village, she caught a glimpse of something, movement perhaps, she wasn't sure, out beyond the last tipi. She was not the only one who had difficulty sleeping, she thought.

She got to her feet, still staring at the end of the camp, hoping to catch another glimpse of whoever it was who felt the urge to get out into the quiet and the dark. The dog, too, seemed to sense something, and got to its feet, its tail down and motionless. It woofed once, then took a couple of tentative steps toward her, as if for protection.

She saw the movement again, a quick darting of shadow barely outlined against the grass beyond the village end. Then another, and a third. These were not movements of a single shadow, she thought. Three shadows, maybe more, but who . . .

She started to run then, dashing off the rocks and turning an ankle. She nearly fell, but managed to keep her balance as she swept through the willow branches and into the shade. Her feet were silent on the soft mulch of willow leaves. Reaching the far side, she carved a hole through the overhang and peered intently. She could see the near end of the village now. Three dogs got to their feet and headed toward her. One fell to its stomach almost immediately. The other two stopped, turning to the fallen dog as if to see why it had stopped.

She could hear a whimper now, but wasn't sure whether it came from the fallen dog or one of the others. About to step through the willow curtain, she pulled the branches aside then stopped, one foot poised in the air. More shadows, these moving furtively, darted toward the tipis from her right, dashing out of the meadow behind the village then disappearing into the tall grass.

Instinctively, she let the branches fall back to shield her. Something awful was about to happen, but she didn't know what. She wanted to shout, but knew that the shadows would silence her before anyone heard. Moving quickly now, she went back the way she'd come, scrambling back onto the boulders and out over the water.

On her knees, she turned her back to the water and let herself down over the sheer face of the rock until she felt the cool water around her ankles. Letting go, she plunged in up to her neck with a splash that seemed like thunder to her. Holding her breath, she waited for some indication that her entry had been heard and, when she was sure that it had gone unnoticed, she pushed out away from the rock, floating on her back.

Stroking quietly, she pulled herself away from the shore and headed upstream. The current was not strong, but it made the going strenuous. Keeping to deep water, she knew she was taking a risk, because if she were spotted, she would be helpless, an easy target. Still not sure who the invaders were, she kept sweeping the shoreline, hoping to catch a glimpse. The village seemed to retreat a little with every stroke, and she quickened her pace, fighting the pull of the river while trying to remain silent.

She saw one of the shadows then, standing erect, a man, his head shaved clean. In the moonlight, it looked almost as if he had been cast from some dark, heavy metal, lead or iron. But there was no mistaking what he was—Osage. She thought of the Kiowa village the summer before, and her blood went cold.

The dog had followed her, dancing along the shoreline as if she were playing some sort of game with it. Once, it ducked into the water, then bounced back out. Finally, it barked, short, sharp yaps, almost angry, as if to demand that she return to shore.

She held her breath, hoping the dog would not call attention to her. It barked again, this time trailing off in a short yelp. She looked again, and the dog was dragging itself with its forepaws, its hindquarters hugging the ground. It whimpered once, and then went still. She had heard the sharp thud of the arrow this time as it pierced the dog's slender body. Squinting in the moonlight, she could see the shaft jabbing at the sky. And the angle made her turn her head. She saw more shadows, maybe as many as a hundred, sprinting toward the river from the far side.

She started to shout then, knowing that any further delay was pointless. Pulling toward the shore, she saw the first splashes as arrows landed all around her. She could hear the hum of bowstrings, like great unseen bugs among the willows, and more arrows rained into the river, one grazing an outstretched arm.

The tipis seemed to echo her feeble cries, and she reached water shallow enough to stand. Once again, she shouted, and this time, one of the entrance flaps moved. She saw a face appear and shouted, "Osage, Osage, Osage!"

The face disappeared, then reappeared, and she recognized Blue Bear, an old man who had been friendly with her father. Blue Bear's voice joined hers in shouting the alarm. The Osage warriors, knowing that further stealth was pointless, began to yip and shriek, shadows exploding out of the grass all around the camp and darting toward the tipis.

Comanche were spilling out into the night now, as the sky began to turn gray, as if the sun were in a hurry to see what all the rumpus was about. Stumbling out of the river, her feet slippery on the muddy bank and short grass, she tried to run toward her tipi.

Sensing something to her right, she turned as a shadow hurtled toward her. Still shouting to raise the alarm, she turned, dodging the leaping Osage, but a heavy forearm slammed into her knees and took her legs out from under her. She had a knife in a sheath on her hip, and grabbed for it, feeling a thick leg fall across her own. Without looking, she jabbed once, then again with the knife, and felt the softness of flesh end abruptly as her knife struck bone. The Osage grunted, then a fist crashed into her stomach as she flailed with the blade again and again.

Getting to her knees, she threw herself on top of him, and saw then that he was young, not even twenty. But there was no time and this was no place for pity, and she brought the knife down sharply, catching him in the chest just below the heart. She put all her weight into the blow, and felt the knife slide in between ribs. The Osage mumbled something, his voice surprised and almost gentle, then a burble escaped from his chest and she felt blood welling out around the hilt, smearing her fingers as she pulled the knife free.

Getting to her feet, she looked back toward the river. The rest of the Osage were scrambling onto the bank now, and she knew that there were too many. She started toward her tipi again, surrounded by figures darting in every direction. But all she cared about at that moment was her family.

Some of the tipis were already knocked on

their sides, the heavy buffalo skins pulling the poles to the ground and flattening them like cast-off toys. Her own lodge still stood, and as she raced toward it, she saw three Osage warriors slicing at its side, and she screamed. One turned and smiled as he charged toward her with a lance braced on his hip. She saw the point gleaming in the moonlight, then felt the dull blow as it glanced off her hip. The warrior kicked at her and she went down. He stood over her, the lance raised high, one foot pinning her to the ground. For a split second, she saw the lance poised high overhead, then looked away, past him, toward her tipi, as its side was torn away. She heard the whimper of a child, not sure whether it was her own.

The lance stabbed through and into the ground beneath her, and she closed her hands around it gingerly, almost tenderly. The warrior grunted as he placed a foot on her stomach next to the lance and started to tug it free. The last thing she saw was his gritted teeth, shiny in the moonlight, as he started to pull.

Chapter 4

THE RAID HAD gone well. Peta Nocona rode at the head of the returning raiding party, his face impassive. The Comanche had taken nearly three hundred Mexican horses, and they hadn't had to go that far over the border to get them. In the past, they had gone as far south as Durango, through rough country where food was scarce and water scarcer still. It had tested their determination and their endurance, and the pickings had been slim. Even the few horses they had managed to capture then had found the return trip too strenuous and almost half of them had been lost. But that had been a hard summer, when the water holes had shrunk, leaving thick layers of salt crystal in rings to mark the slow dwindling. More often than not, what water had been left was unfit to drink.

But that was the past. Now, three hundred head of prime Mexican stock to the good, there was every reason for Nocona to smile, but it seemed too taxing for him. His face sat like a stone carving on his shoulders, and even Black Snake was reluctant to ask him what was wrong. But that was what friends were for, and the warrior eased his pony close to Nocona's mount. He thought it best to start with idle chatter.

"We have done well for ourselves, old friend," he said.

Nocona grunted. "So it seems."

"You get first pick. Is there one that catches your eye?"

Nocona shook his head. "No. I think White Heron is right. I think I have enough horses. I don't need any more."

"But it is your right to choose before anyone else. It is the way it has always been. You know that better than anyone. It was you who taught me everything I know about horses. How to geld them, how to choose a pony that would run all day and all night without breaking down, how to choose a good mare for breeding. You love horses as much for what they are as for the honor their ownership brings you. How can you say you don't want any more?"

Nocona shook his head. "You're right. In the old days I knew a good deal about horses. I thought I knew everything."

"There are some who say you do."

"They are wrong. Besides, as you said yourself, that was the old days. That was the old way.

I think maybe the old way will not be our way for too much longer."

"Why? Why should anything change? Why should not things go on as they always have? We can defeat anyone who comes against us. We go where we please, to follow the buffalo or to trade horses. We have everything we need. The *comancheros* come to us with anything we can't make for ourselves. It is a good way. I don't see why we should change."

"We should change because we will be forced to change. I think maybe it would be best if we decided for ourselves when and how."

"Maybe you are tired. I think you will feel differently once we get home, and White Heron makes you new moccasins and a new shirt. Gray Fawn says she has been working on something special for you. I think maybe it will be ready by the time we get back to the village."

"I have enough shirts, too," Nocona grunted.

"Is there anything you don't have enough of?"

"Time," Nocona said. "There is never enough time. The days slip by so quickly, like a sidewinder on the desert. They make no noise as they move. They are in front of you and then they are behind you before you even knew they were there at all."

"You talk like an old man. My grandfather says things like that all the time, but I expect it of him. It is what the old ones do, because it is all they *can* do. But you are young yet. Your best days are ahead of you. That should be reason enough to smile, but you pull a long face today. You pulled a long face yesterday, as if you were carrying a heavy stone on your back."

"I am. I am practicing. That is what being chief is like. A heavy stone, many heavy stones. Sometimes I think there is one for each of the people and the chief has to carry them all. I want to be ready."

"You always wanted to be chief. Now it sounds like you have changed your mind."

Nocona nodded. "Yes, I did. But that was before I knew just how hard it was . . . and how little anyone else understood. I knew nothing then. And now that I am soon to be a chief, I know things that no one else knows, things I can't teach them, and things they can't understand if I talk about them. Even you, my oldest friend. You don't understand. You *can't* understand. I look at you and want to tell you what it is like. Sometimes I wake up in the middle of the night and I think, 'Maybe this is something I can tell Black Snake.' But I know right away that it would be no use. I don't blame you for that, but it makes me very lonely. Any burden is less heavy when you can share it with someone. The only one who understands even a little is White Heron, and she doesn't understand much."

"So, what are you saying? Are you saying that you don't want to be a chief any longer?"

Once again, Nocona shook his head. "No, I am not saying that. I would not wish any man to carry the burden I will carry. I don't mean to sing my own praises, as if I were someone special. I'm not, and that is the one thing that being chief has made me see me more clearly than any other; but measured against the burden I will carry, no man is special. One ant under a great stone is like any other."

Black Snake didn't really know what to say, but he had the feeling that he had to keep his friend talking. "Have you discussed this with any of the old ones? Red Owl might understand. He was a chief. It was a long time ago, but . . ."

"Yes, it was a long time ago. Times were different then. Red Owl understands the old ways better than anyone I know. But he knows nothing of the new ways, the new troubles. He would want to do things as they have always been done, but that is not possible. Not anymore. Knowing how to deal with the new troubles requires new ways of thinking. I am not sure anyone is ready for that. I know I am not."

"You don't give yourself enough credit. You have always done well. No matter how difficult the problem, you have managed to deal with it. There is enough to eat, more than enough, even. We have all the horses we need. We don't have to worry about the things that really matter. You have done well."

"Yes, so far. But it has made me tired."

"Maybe in the council, we can discuss these things. Maybe there is some way to . . ."

"No! If I bring it up in council, it will be an invitation for some young hothead to challenge me. He will not know what he is getting into. It will tear the people into pieces, force them to choose sides. Now, more than ever, we have to think as one man. There are too many who would use that confusion for their own purposes."

"Inside?"

Nocona nodded. "Yes. Inside. And out. But if you work against the people, it makes no difference whether you are inside or out. The result is the same. I can't let that happen. It will probably happen one day soon anyway, but I don't want to make it easier for anyone."

Nocona lapsed into silence, and it seemed to Black Snake that it was permanent. He had nothing to say that could help, and he realized that, rather than helping Peta Nocona as he had intended, he succeeded only in blackening his friend's mood still more. He didn't understand what Nocona was concerned about, but thought maybe that one had to be a chief to see far enough into the future, where troubles moved like shadows at the bottom of a deep well. One needed sharp vision to distinguish the shades of darkness. It was all well and good for him to be cheerful, and to tell Nocona there was nothing to worry about, but he didn't have to make the decisions Nocona had to make. All he had to do was keep his arrows sharp and his arm strong. The rest would take care of itself.

Reluctant to let the conversation end on such a bleak note, he said, "At least we will be home tomorrow. We can rest. Maybe things will not seem so bad when you have had time to be with White Heron and Little Calf. A man's wife and son help him forget about things he can't control."

Nocona laughed. "Maybe you are right, my friend. Maybe what I need is something I already have."

Just then they heard a shout, and Nocona stiffened. Black Snake pointed toward a high ridge far ahead, where the silhouette of riders could be seen heading toward them. The riders were moving fast, kicking up a cloud of thick dust from the dry ground.

"Apache?" Black Snake wondered.

"No," Nocona said. "If they were Apache, we would not know they were there until it was time for them to spring their trap."

"Maybe it is a trick."

"I don't think so. Those people are in a hurry. And they are heading right for us. They must have seen us, must know who we are. I wonder . . ."

Others in the Comanche raiding party had spotted the riders now, and started yipping, jabbering excitedly and stabbing at the oncoming riders with the tips of their bows. Nocona realized he had better do something.

"Take three men," he said, "and see who those people are. And be careful!"

Black Snake dug in his heels and peeled away, shouting to the nearest group of warriors. Three of them waved their bows high overhead as their ponies leaped forward. Black Snake led the small band at a full gallop, the sturdy Indian ponies making good time as they raced downhill into the broad shallow valley between the Comanche raiding party and the advancing newcomers.

Nocona slowed his own pony to a walk, then turned and shouted for a halt. It was best, he thought, to wait and see what Black Snake learned before heading down into the valley. If trouble were coming, better to face it from high ground.

He saw the small advance party closing rapidly on the distant strangers. In a matter of minutes, Black Snake had reached them, pulled up and held a hand overhead for the three warriors with him to stay quiet. He saw Black Snake turn then and look back up the hill toward him. He squinted, trying to read his friend's features, but at that distance they were just a copper blur in the sunlight.

But there was no mistaking the urgency as Black Snake wheeled his pony then and broke back across the valley floor. He left the three warriors with the newcomers, and charged back the way he'd come, glancing back over his shoulder once or twice, either to make certain his orders were being followed, or as if he feared something unseen on his trail might be gaining on him.

He was yelling long before his words were intelligible. Nocona knew now that something was wrong and told the raiders to stay put while he headed downhill to meet Black Snake in the middle of the slope.

"What is it?" Nocona shouted, while he was still two hundred yards away.

Black Snake shook his head and waved a hand in front of his face as if to chase away words he'd rather not speak.

Nocona felt a chill then. It froze his spine and seemed to spread into the deepest recesses of his body.

"Something's happened. What is it?"

Again, Black Snake flailed with his hands. He swallowed hard.

"Tell me," Nocona said gently.

"The village . . . Osage . . . they . . ."

"How bad?"

"Bad."

Black Snake looked at him then, his eyes suddenly welling up. "White Heron," he said. "Little Calf . . ."

Nocona tilted his head back just a little. Then he nodded.

"Both of them?" he asked.

Again, Black Snake nodded. "Both of them."

Shaking his head slowly, then faster, Nocona said, "All right. Bring the horses. I'm going on ahead."

"You can't. The Osage might be . . ."

"I hope so," Nocona said.

Chapter 5 ═══════════

NOCONA FELT THE WIND in his hair like a pair of ragged claws, tugging and scratching at him, as if it meant to tear his scalp from his head. It seemed as if all his fears, everything that had haunted his late nights, had gathered up ahead of him like some deadly flock of predators, and he plunged headlong toward it, knowing that it was too late, and not caring. He had to see for himself if each of those fears had come to roost.

He rode without regard to anything, even the gallant pony beneath him. If the horse played out, he would run, and when he could no longer run, he would walk, and then he would crawl on bloody knees, if that's what it took. But somehow, no matter how, he would reach the village.

Twice, he passed bands of stragglers, but skirted them rather than stop and learn another few bits and pieces of the horror that awaited him. He knew the fury of the Osage, how terrible their vengeance could be. He had seen the ruins of the friendly Kiowa camp the year before, and knew that what awaited him would be every bit as bloody and as terrible as that slaughter.

His heart was hammering at his chest in unison with the pony's hooves, and when his heart would race ahead, he would lash the horse with a rawhide quirt, sometimes even pounding on its chest with a fist to squeeze every last bit of speed from the laboring animal. And sometimes, taking a deep breath to try to still the pounding beneath his ribs, he would hear a drumming in his ears as his blood raced through him looking for some way out, some way to vent the unbearable pressure, the way a raging flood will find the tiniest crack and begin tearing at the walls that tried to hold it in.

It was near sundown by the time he entered the valley of the Arkansas River. The village was not that far away now, but he raced on, as if the carnage ahead were some kind of giant magnet, pulling him faster and faster the closer he came to its irresistible force. The sun had paled, its waning orange seeking refuge behind a haze that spread from one end of the valley to the other. He glanced up at it, telling himself he could not be sure whether it was natural or the residual smoke from a village laid to ruin. But that was a lie. He knew.

He was following the river now, the pony keeping to the sandy bank where the grass was thinner and the rocks were more easily seen. The

sluggish current was dyed orange by the sunlight, stretching two hundred yards to his right, a
sheet of cloth broken here and there by the leap
of a trout, its own back a darker orange as it
spasmed in a violent arc before landing with a
slap like that of clapping hands.

In the back of his mind was the thought that
the Osage could be haunting the riverbank,
waiting to pick off stragglers. It was a remote
possibility, because even the fearsome Osage
knew the fury of the Comanche, and would
likely not wish to linger too near the flames of
that rage.

Deep inside him, a voice kept whispering,
repeating over and over the wordless hope that
the report was wrong, that some mistake had
been made, that it was all a horrible joke. But
there was another voice, this one trapped in his
skull, that screamed again and again that there
was no mistake, that it was all true and that it
would be better he cut his own throat and tore
out his own eyes than look on the ruins.
Nocona knew which voice to believe, and he
knew which one he wanted to believe. The
warring voices shouting each other down were
like two mad women fighting over a man. The
louder one screamed, the louder the other
responded, until words were useless, and furious volume was the only communication left
them.

He saw smoke now, not much, not enough to
suggest a peaceful village, but certainly not left

from the slaughter of a week before, either. The sun was darkening, turning the river to blood, as if the village lay prostrate, hemorrhaging the last precious drops of its life into the current. Dead ahead was a steep rise and the village lay beyond it, not more than a mile away. He pulled up then, feeling his sides heaving, the frenzied hammering of his heart almost audible in the sudden silence. Taking a deep breath, he dismounted, grabbing the war rope and curling it securely in his hands and tugging the pony toward the rise.

The thick grass looked dark, almost gray in the fading light, and felt it crush under his moccasins as he started uphill, the pony jerking its head behind him, as if reluctant to accompany him.

He felt the urge to run, to let go of the horse and sprint through the long grass the way he had as a child, but it struck him as unseemly, and he shook his head, as if baffled by such a treacherous impulse. The grass seemed to cling to his buckskin leggings, as if trying to persuade him not to climb the rise, to stop and stay where he was, even to go back. But he trudged on, the horse still bucking him with every step. Near the top of the rise, he stopped and turned to look at the sun setting now far behind him. The trees were all tinged with red, bright ruby auras surrounding the crowns of the tallest, as if they were just about to burst into flame. The dark shadows of the trees speared up the rise like so many charcoal snakes.

He let the pony go, and it shook its head, nickered once, then backed up a couple of steps. Shaking its mane, it turned away from him, but moved no further. He collapsed into the grass, his legs folding beneath him by instinct.

He was breathing deeply, each inhalation swelling his powerful chest and taking with it some of the terror as it rushed from his body. His hands trembled in his lap, and he looked at them as if they were live things that crept up on him unawares. Lifting them, he held them overhead, blocking the sun and watching as the fingers turned ruby red at their edges. He curled the fingers into fists, shook them once, and let a great shout rush from his lungs. He heard the wordless bellow come echoing back from the hills around him and looked toward the loudest echo as if someone else had shouted to him.

Shaking his head, he doubled over. A hand closed over his shoulder, and he gave a start, reaching for his knife as he tried to rise, but the hand held him down, and he was too drained to struggle.

He glanced up then, and found himself staring into the face of Red Owl, the oldest man in the village, a man who had lived more winters than anyone could count, more winters even than Red Owl himself could remember clearly.

"My son," he said, "you have come back."

"Too late," Nocona mumbled. "Too late."

"You've heard, then?"

Nocona nodded. "Yes, I've heard."

"It was terrible, terrible. I think maybe you should not see."

Nocona shook his head sharply. "And what should I do, then, Father? Should I forget what has happened? Should I pretend that I never lived here? That my family never was?"

"No. Of course not. But some things are better not seen."

"This is not one of them. This I must see for myself. I want to carve it into my memory to scar it, the way a knife scars the skin."

"Then I will go with you. We should go now, in the dark, when these terrible things you will see will not blind you."

Nocona nodded his assent. He got to his feet and looked then at Red Owl. The old man looked as if he had aged fifty winters since the last time Nocona had seen him. It must be horrible, he thought, to make this old one so much older still.

"Let's go," he said.

Red Owl turned and looked toward the crest of the rise, not more than fifty yards above them. He nodded. "We will go," he said. He started walking, and Nocona made a move to brush past him, to take the lead. Red Owl reached out and closed his bony fingers around the younger man's wrist. "No," he said. "I will lead you."

"There is nothing there that can harm me," Nocona argued. "I don't need your protection."

"Everyone needs protection from such things," Red Owl insisted.

"And what then, will the dead be less dead because you see them first? Will their hearts still beat, will breath still be drawn?"

"No."

"Then what difference does it make whether you go first or I do?"

"It is better. Trust me. It is better so."

"All right, but get on with it."

Once more, Red Owl nodded his head, the long white Sioux-styled braids he favored draping his shoulders and seeming to wriggle like snakes with the movement. He started forward again, this time more purposefully, his short legs whispering in the tall grass with every step. Nocona fell in behind him, leaning forward against the increasingly steep incline. At the crest, Red Owl raised his hands to the sky and mumbled something that Nocona didn't catch.

"What did you say?" the young man asked.

"Never mind, my son. That is between me and the Great Spirit."

Nocona moved up alongside him and stared down into the broad valley. The river still had a trace of color, its rippling surface dark red at the center and shading to nearly purple near the banks. The valley was full of shadows, the willows on the far end of the village masses of black as the sun disappeared behind boiling black clouds. Nocona looked up at the spears of

blinding light for a moment, half a dozen of
them lancing out from behind the gilt-edged
clouds and, one by one, vanishing.

Peering down into the gathering darkness,
Nocona could see that it was worse than he had
feared. Most of the tipis had been burned, leaving heaps of ash and burned goods, sometimes,
too, leaving charred lodgepoles like the rib cages
of great beasts. Mounds of shadow lay scattered,
and he knew without seeing the details, that they
were the bodies of his people, slaughtered like
buffalo and left to rot in the sun.

He started to run then, breaking away from
Red Owl, his voice roaring from his lungs of its
own volition. His feet were flying through the
tall grass and he had the sensation that if he tried
to stop, they would go out from under him.
Halfway down, he stumbled, fell headlong and
rolled over and over, then spread his arms out
like wings to arrest the fall and popped to his
feet again as if he had meant to fly.

On the flat, he picked up speed, stumbled
once more and this time sprawled on his face,
the wind knocked from him by the fall. He
turned to see what had tripped him, and realized even as he crawled toward it that it was a
body. He closed his eyes, screwing them tightly
shut, hoping that he would never have to open
them again. But he knew that was no answer.
Slowly, he opened them, his hand hovering just
over the back of the prostrate figure. The smell
was overwhelming and it hit him with all the

suddenness of a bird flying into a stone wall.

The smell of death was everywhere, thick in the air, like a mist that seemed to be coating his skin. He covered his nose, scrambling away from the corpse and getting to his feet. Nocona pinched his nostrils shut. In the last lingering dark gray of twilight, he could see mounds of shadow everywhere he looked. Heaps of belongings lay scattered everywhere, bits of cloth charred at the edge, broken arrows, dried meat in piles in the dust.

Here and there, Nocona saw the body of a dead horse, its belly bloated, its legs stiff as driftwood. And the flies were swarming around every bloated corpse, dog, horse and human being. Moving toward the ruins of a tipi that lay on its side, its buffalo skin covering charred to wavering sheets of ash, he bumped against a food basket. It fell on its side, and something moved. He thought for a moment that a scavenger of some sort had been hiding in the basket, but whatever it was stopped and lay still only a few inches from the overturned basket.

He dropped to one knee for a closer look, leaning over the basket and peering at its contents. It took him a few moments to realize it was a human head, the black tongue swollen like rotten fruit in its mouth, the eyes hidden under a pulsing mass of insects.

He gagged then, and his stomach emptied itself before he realized what was happening. He lay there in the dust, his body wracked by convulsions, and he knew that he had to find his own tipi, knowing that there was no point, knowing that any hope White Heron or Little Calf might have survived was foolish, but still, he had to see for himself. Getting to his feet again, he staggered toward the center of the village, his eyes darting this way and that, fixed dead ahead rather than on the wreckage all around him.

He found where his tipi had been, and saw that it, too, had been overturned and burned. The hide covering was charred ash, the lodgepoles like black bones in the fading light.

He found her almost at once, lying on her back. Her head, at least, had not been severed, but her buckskin dress had been torn, and her legs were splayed wide. Her throat had been cut, and her fists were clenched in the agony of her dying.

He knelt beside her, his head falling to his chest. He didn't want to look at her, but he couldn't not. Steeling himself, he opened his eyes again, brought his fingers to his lips then reached to brush hers with the tips. An angry fly buzzed, landed on his hand for a second, and he swiped at it with his other hand, the sharp crack of the slap echoing off into the night, the mocking buzz of the unharmed insect darting past his ear for a moment then disappearing.

He looked at the sky then and knew that everything he feared was becoming real. Things had to change, and kneeling there next to the body of his wife, the wreckage spreading around him all the way to the edge of the world, he no more knew how to change them than he knew how to fly.

He would learn.

But not before the Osage were made to pay.

Chapter 6

May 1836

ELDER JOHN PARKER STOOD on the rough wooden porch, his hands already dirty from morning work, although it was not yet eight o'clock. He looked at the sun a moment, then turned to holler back through the open door behind him.

"Looks like another scorcher of a day, Granny. A little hellfire to keep us honest."

Mrs. Parker joined her husband on the porch, drying her hands on an apron. "Sometimes I wonder why we came here, John. The weather can be so unbearably hot. Lord knows, there's not a whole lot to recommend this place."

"Never easy doing God's work, Granny," he said. "You ought to know that by now, if you know anything at all. Nobody ever said it would be easy work bringing the Good Lord to the heathens."

"And we have precious little to show for all that hard work," she said. "You haven't made one convert in the year and a half we've been in this godforsaken place."

Parker shook his head. They had had this conversation a thousand times before. And deep down, he was almost as discouraged as his wife, but there was no way he was going to let her know that. "Come on with me a minute, Granny," he said, reaching back and closing a big fist on her apron, then tugging her gently but firmly toward the single step down to the hard-packed ground.

Already, the sun was heating things up, its silent hammer blows flattening everything in sight, like a berserk blacksmith venting his rage on whatever came to hand. Once on the ground, he turned to make sure Granny was following him, and let go of the apron.

She had a stiff back when she wanted to, and John Parker knew better than to take her compliance for granted. It was a hard life he had chosen, not just for the two of them, but for a couple of dozen others, including his sons, Benjamin, Isaac, and Silas, and daughters-in-law and their children. And if he could be said to have learned one thing in the last eighteen months, it was that Texas was nothing like Illinois, and Kiowa or Comanche nothing like Papists or Presbyterians. But he wouldn't give up because giving up was no more a part of him than a third eye or a pointed tail.

Moving toward the tall gate mounted dead center in the wooden palisade surrounding their settlement, which, by default had come to be known as Fort Parker, he quickened his pace, glancing once or twice over his shoulder to make sure her resolve hadn't kicked in.

When he reached the tall gate, he slid the heavy log that served for a bolt aside, and backed away, grunting, as he tugged the gate open. The sun came pouring in through the widening gap and when the gate was all the way open, it rode almost dead center, as if the gate had been positioned like some primitive temple entrance to greet its rising.

"John, what in tarnation are you doing?" Granny shook her head watching the stubborn old man she'd married so long ago as he strode confidently out through the open gate and spread his arms wide.

"Come on out here, Granny," he said, turning smartly on his heels and waving impatiently. "Come on, now, come on out here and have a look."

Reluctantly, she wrapped her hands in the apron once more, even though they were already dry, then, when she could delay no longer, she stepped through the gate.

He walked back to meet her, dropped one thick arm heavily over her broad shoulders and swept the other in a wide arc, like a salesman with a fish on the line. "Just look at that," he said. "Look at all of it, not just the fields, but the wildness, the trees and the river, the flowers across the valley. The lilies of the field. And if you listen, you can hear the birds singing, Granny."

As if to give her the opportunity to verify his claims, he lapsed into sudden silence. "All I hear is bugs," she said. "Flies and beetles wondering when we're gonna leave them be and let them eat everything we planted."

Parker laughed. "It's not that bad, Granny. We got a good-sized crop of corn in, and beans and peas and potatoes. We got some livestock, not much right now, I'll grant you, but it'll increase, just like the good book says."

"And you think we'll be here to see that, do you, John Parker?"

"I don't just think it, Granny, I know it. I have faith in the Lord, and He won't let us fail."

Before Granny could answer, she heard footsteps on the hard ground behind her, and turned to see Michael Frost and Hiram Hardee shuffling toward the gate.

She nodded to Frost, and he returned the acknowledgment with a nod of his own. When the two men were close enough, Hardee said, "You folks are up mighty early this morning. Anything the matter?"

Parker shook his head. "Just trying to get Granny out of her funk, is all. She woke up with gloom in her eye this morning, and I was just trying to show her the bright side of things, cheer her up a little, that's all."

"Well, Mrs. Parker, I'll allow that I sometimes get a little testy my own self. Especially out there bent over a hoe when that sun starts to feel like a great big hot rock sittin' on my shoulders. But all I do is take a look around and see how far we come in so short a time, and I get to feelin' better pretty quick."

"And what about your Sarah, Hiram? She feel better then, too, does she?"

"I don't reckon I ever discussed it with her, to tell you the truth."

"Maybe you ought to. You men are all alike. You see what you want to see, and the rest of it might as well not even be there. A lot of foolishness, I think."

"Those are some pretty hard words, Granny," Parker said. "I don't think Hiram come out here to get a lecture from you *or* me. I figure he's got some work to do, and we ought to let him get to it."

Frost grinned. "From the looks of that sun, John, I don't think I'd mind listening to Granny all day long, if it meant I could stay in the shade to do it."

Parker smiled. "You underestimate her. Granny can flay a whole herd of cows when she gets that tongue of hers to flappin'."

"You hush up, John Parker," she said, snapping his leg with one tail of her apron. "I was just saying what was on my mind, is all. I'm a little scared. It doesn't seem like to me that the Indians around here have much use for us. Seems like to me they'd as soon see us under the ground as tilling it, if you ask me."

"Now, you know that's not true, Granny. They've been friendly enough."

"The two or three we ever see, maybe. But what about the rest of them? Why do you think they haven't been here pounding on the gate to get in? Did you ever stop and think that maybe they aren't particularly interested in the white man's God? 'Cause it sure has occurred to me. More than once."

"You have to have faith in the Lord, Granny," Hiram Hardee said.

"I have all the faith I need, thank you, Hiram. I just don't see that it's made a whole lot of difference to the Comanche, is all."

"That'll change. You just wait, Mrs. Parker. They'll come around."

"There isn't anything else to do here *except* wait, Hiram. So, I suppose I'll have to do that. But I don't have to feel good about it. Or do I?" She turned when she heard a familiar voice calling to her.

"Granny, Granny!"

It was her granddaughter, Cynthia Ann, who came racing toward her, followed in succession by her grandson, John, and her son, Benjamin. Cynthia Ann's little legs were pumping as she dashed across the open plain of the compound, a rag doll flopping in one hand, its arms and legs flailing every which way as it dangled just above the ground.

The woman got down on her knees to take the onslaught, and Cynthia Ann hurled herself into her grandmother's arms, followed almost immediately by little John.

"What are you children doing out here?" she scolded. "You know you shouldn't be out of the gate like this."

Benjamin smiled. He was holding a musket, and brandished it with a certain pride. "My turn to watch the gate, Mother," he said. "I told them they could come out to see you."

"We'd better get to work," Hiram said. "The sooner we get finished, the sooner we can get inside and out of this infernal sun."

Granny straightened up, then took the children by the hand, and started back toward the house. "You come on with me, now. You can keep me company on the porch. I've got peas to shell. If you're good, you can help. You'll see your Uncle Ben later on."

"I can't shell peas," young John said. "I don't know how to shell peas."

"Sure you can, Johnny," Granny said. "You just watch me, and you'll catch on in no time. You're already five years old. 'Bout time you started earning your keep."

She was teasing, but the boy looked uncertain. Turning to Cynthia Ann, she asked, "What do you think, Cynthia? Shall we teach your brother how to shell peas?"

Cynthia Ann, at nine, was rather self-assured. "I already know, even if he doesn't," she said. "I can do it better than anybody."

Elder John followed in their wake, nodding to

Peter Wilhelm and David Jason, two more of the members of their small community. "Going to be hot out there. You boys ought to bring some extra water along today," he said.

"I'll just run down and drink me some of that river water, if I get thirsty," Wilhelm said.

"I been here eighteen months, Peter, and I ain't seen you run for nothing yet, except maybe for dinner, that is," Jason joked.

"You may have seen me hungry, but you never seen me thirsty, David."

Ben Parker watched the men drift on out to the fields, until they were little more than blurs under the early morning glare. He liked gate duty, because it gave him a chance to be alone with his thoughts. He admired his father, but there was something a little too stiff and unyielding in the older man, especially when it came to matters of religion.

Ben was a believer, Elder John had made sure of that, but it was not an unquestioning belief, nowhere near as certain as his father's. He leaned against the wall, the musket near at hand, and tilted his hat forward to protect his eyes a little without interfering with his ability to scan the surrounding land for Indians.

There hadn't been any trouble in the eighteen months they'd been in the Navasota River valley, but Ben knew that vigilance was most necessary when it seemed least important. Bands of Kiowa and Comanche, usually small hunting parties, had visited the fort and Elder John had tried to make them understand the purpose of the fort. In every case, though, the Indians moved on, and as far as anyone in the fort knew, none had ever come a second time.

There hadn't been any hostility, but the skepticism of the Indians had been apparent. And the Comanche, especially, had a fearsome reputation for bloodthirsty cruelty, although it was by reputation only that any of the Fort Parker inhabitants knew them at all.

Two more of the men moved on out to the fields, waving to Benjamin as they left the safety of the palisade and trudging across the baked ground and through the tall, sun-brittled grass. Ben watched clouds of insects mushroom with every step, and for a while he could hear the whisper of the dry grass against the rough cloth of the men's pants.

Soon, they joined the others, and were reduced to shadows bent over hoes, scratching at the ground. Even at that distance, he thought he could hear the sound of the metal blades on the hard ground, but knew it was just his imagination. It was backbreaking work, he thought, but not as hard as trying to change a heathen's mind about God. And Benjamin smiled ruefully at the thought, knowing that of the two dozen souls at Fort Parker, only his father had a faith unwavering enough to believe that they would triumph. It might take a while, Elder John argued, but the Indians would come around. It was, after all, the Lord's will.

Under the scalding sun, though, Benjamin was inclined to doubt it. He knew that agriculture was not in the least appealing to people who made their living off the land as they found it, instead of trying to transform it through sweat and determination. And he couldn't blame the Indians, because there had been precious little reward for eighteen months of backbreaking labor.

Chapter 7 ═══════════

BENJAMIN LOOKED BACK through the gate and watched his niece playing in the shade of the front porch. He could just make out the bulky figure of Granny, an apron spread wide on her lap, her hands busy in the capacious hollow between her knees. And for a moment he envied the children. They didn't miss Illinois so much because they had never had time to get attached to it. And it seemed to make little difference where you played with a doll or a toy soldier. Texas was the same as Illinois.

But, soon enough, that would all change. When Cynthia Ann was old enough to work, her childhood would vanish in a twinkling, and the choices available to her here were few and unattractive. He thought about school and wondered how his brother Silas would ever be able to send John to college. He talked about it all the time, as if it were just as easy as snapping his fingers. As it was, what little schooling the children were getting had to be crammed into those few precious moments when neither work nor prayer had prior claim on the adults. Free time was nonexistent.

And there would be no money. They would have their hands full scratching enough to eat from the ground. The river bottom was fertile enough, and there was plenty of water and, God knew, more than enough sun. But there was no market, no place to sell what little excess they would be able to raise, and without money, college for John would be nothing more than a dream tucked away in the back of his father's skull. They were growing food for themselves, and at least they wouldn't starve, but beyond the next day of stultifying field work, and the one after that, there wasn't a lot to look forward to.

He turned back to the fields, glancing involuntarily at the sun until his eyes watered and he was forced to turn away, rubbing at the brimming sockets with his knuckles. Shaking his head, he wondered how the men could endure their work. It was one thing to believe, like Elder John Parker, or to be the son of such a man and willing to endure out of a sense of filial obligation, and quite another to dig down inside yourself and find enough faith of your own to pack up everything you had and follow a man already full of fire and brimstone to the very doorway of hell itself.

But that's exactly what Hiram Hardee and Peter Wilhelm and David Jason had done. And they had dragged their families along in the bar-

gain, imposing on them, at one remove, the same
sense of duty that John Parker had imposed on
him. But, willing or not, they were here, and
they would all have to make the best of it.

Benjamin was feeling restless, and turned his
eyes to the distant edge of the pine forest that ran
along the river bottom, spearing dark green
tongues toward the sun and shimmering in the
glare like green flames. It looked cool, even
pleasant, but he knew the same oppressive heat
that choked him there against the wall would
clamp him in its viselike jaws under the trees.
The tang of the pine needles would make it more
pleasant, perhaps, but not much.

He looked at his musket and started to reach
for it for some reason, then changed his mind
and allowed himself to slide down along the
rough bark of the palisade wall. The ground was
dusty, in some places the dirt so fine it felt like
talcum powder under his fingertips. It was
smooth and almost slippery. He hefted a palm-
ful, then tossed it into the air and clapped his
hands together to rid them of the residue.

The first hint of movement near the edge of
the trees almost slipped past him unobserved,
but for some reason he could not quite put his
finger on, he glanced up. At first, he saw nothing out of the ordinary, but squinted away the
bright sun and finally spotted what had drawn
his eye. A figure on horseback, then another
moved away from the dark mass of pines. As he
got to his feet, he spotted a third, moving quickly

out of the trees and closing on the first two.

He could tell at once that they were not white. Grabbing the musket, he turned to yell back into the fort. Granny heard him and came running. The Indians were holding a makeshift flag of some sort, gray or beige as near as he could tell through the glare, and waved it once or twice, then stopped their ponies as if to wait for him to come meet them in the middle of the open field.

Granny reached the gate, with Elder Parker right behind her.

"What is it, Ben?" John asked.

Benjamin edged back toward the open gate. "Indians, three of 'em. Over there," he said, jabbing a finger in their direction.

Parker looked for a moment. "Why, them Indians has got a white flag! See there?"

Instinctively, Benjamin glanced toward the fields where the others were working. It was a long run, and he didn't want to call attention to them if he could avoid it. Some of them had guns, but there wasn't a soul at Fort Parker who was much of a marksman. If there were trouble, he thought, they might be unnoticed as long as no one directed attention their way. They'd be safer than trying to shoot it out.

"What do you figure they want, Pop?" Benjamin asked.

Elder Parker shook his head. "Can't be sure, son. I suppose they want a little food or something, like the others. I wish I knew enough of their lingo to talk to them. I can't even tell what kind they are."

"They're Indians," Granny snapped. "That's all you need to know. Come inside and close the gate, Benjamin."

"They're why we come here," Elder John corrected her. "How can we bring them the Lord, if we turn them away when they come calling?"

"I think maybe it would be best if we went inside and closed the gate," Granny suggested again. "They can receive the Lord another day."

"That would be unfriendly," Elder John said. "Not to mention shirking our responsibility."

"I'm not feeling any too friendly," Granny said. "And I don't much know what our responsibility to heathens is."

"Maybe if I go on out there, I can find out what they want," Benjamin said. "They're carryin' a white flag, so they must have had some contact with white men before. They must know what it means."

"Knowing what it means and doing what it says are two different things, Benjamin," Granny said. "Don't you go out there."

"The boy's right, Granny," Elder John argued. "You go on ahead, Ben, but be careful. The first sign of trouble, you scoot on back here."

"You'd best take your gun, Ben," Granny added.

"No, that'll just give them the wrong idea."

"You go ahead and take your gun. Most likely they have their own weapons. I'd feel better."

Reluctantly, Ben snatched at the musket and started slowly away from the fort. As he approached the Indians, they seemed to be whispering among themselves, the ponies shifting nervously beneath them. Ben could hear the snuffle of the ponies, and the swish of their tails as he closed the gap. He was conscious of the rustle of tall grass against his clothes and tried to ignore it as he listened intently.

The Indians started forward then, and he realized that something was amiss. It didn't dawn on him right away. But when all three of the warriors were arrayed in a row twenty yards away, it struck him—despite the white flag, they were wearing war paint, red and yellow bands that arced across their cheeks and bridged the broad, flat noses, and gave them a malevolent appearance, despite the fact that they were grinning at him.

"Howdy," Ben said, not expecting an answer. He shifted the musket nervously from hand to hand, then curled his finger through the trigger guard. He thought about cocking the hammer, but decided it might be too provocative a move.

The warriors moved into a circle around him then. Suddenly, the white flag fell to the dirt and the warriors started prodding him with their lances, counting coup, which Ben knew was one method of attaining honor among their people. The jabs of the lances got more forceful, and Ben adjusted his grip on the musket. He wanted to say something to them, distract them from the game, if it was a game, but the language barrier was unbridgeable.

Unconsciously, he moved his thumb to the hammer and started to cock it. Abruptly, one of the lances was raised high overhead and stabbed down in a vicious arc before he could do anything to protect himself. He lost his grip on the musket, and realized that his forearm had been cut by the sharp point of the lance.

He turned and tried to break out of the circle, looking back at the fort and its open gate that now seemed so far away. More prods with the lances, sharper and harder, and he fell to his knees. Something struck him in the shoulder and he felt the sharp thrust of the lance as it pierced his chest and struck bone. He was driven over backward. He saw the gates starting to close, his mother standing there with her hands to her mouth, and heard a yip. The thunder of hooves erupted then, and what seemed to him like a hundred ponies dashed out of the pines and rumbled past him on the way to the fort.

Once more, he saw a lance high overhead, its blade glittering in the sunlight, then saw it plummet toward him. He heard the sound of the lance hitting home, felt the pain as a warrior leaned his weight into the thrust, then saw the jumble of pony legs as the other warriors leaned over to stab at him with their own lances.

At the gate, Elder Parker struggled to get it closed, but the first warriors reached it and shoved it aside, knocking him to the ground before he was able to move the heavy log into place.

The warriors were shrieking now, racing their horses around the inside of the small palisade. Elder John got to his feet and grabbed at a warrior as he rumbled past, dragging him from his mount. Furious, he leaped on the Indian, but felt something slash at him from behind and turned to see that another warrior had dismounted and come to the aid of his unhorsed comrade.

He saw Granny running toward the house, calling to the children. He never even felt the slice of the blade as it slit his throat. Granny, too, was knocked to the ground. Scrambling on all fours, she saw the Indians leaping from their horses and swarming around the houses. Already, smoke was beginning to spew out of the buildings as Comanche rousted the inhabitants. A few gunshots rang out, but the muskets were too difficult to load for close fighting, and soon the defenders were reduced to using the heavy guns as clubs, wielding them by the barrels and lashing out with the heavy wooden stocks.

Granny felt something strike her in the back, and she collapsed on the ground. A moment later, she heard the rasp as the lance was pushed all the way through her shoulder and driven into the dirt beneath her. Desperately, she clawed at it, but her strength was ebbing quickly. She saw Sarah Hardee running from her log house, several Comanche in pursuit. The children were running aimlessly, crying and trying to hide.

Once more, Granny tried to get up, but she was too weak, and lay there pinned like a butterfly on velvet as the chaos she feared, and that her husband had refused to acknowledge, swirled around her. The houses were all in flames now, and the Indians seemed to be tiring of their sport.

Several sprang back onto their mounts and raced out of the fort, nearly trampling her as they thundered past. The air was filled with a thick pall of smoke. She heard shouts in English, and the report of a musket, as the men from the fields raced, too late, to defend their homes and families.

She kept looking around, trying to see through the smoke. Weakly, she cried out for Cynthia Ann and John, but no one answered her feeble cries. A moment later, she saw an Indian racing toward one corner of her house. Flames were already licking up the front wall, and smoke billowed out of the broken window. The door had been shattered and dangled from a single hinge. Tongues of flame lapped at it through the opening, and she saw Cynthia Ann then, darting from the house and rushing toward the stable. But a Comanche saw her, too, and raced toward her, leaning far over the side of his pony. The warrior snaked an arm around the girl's waist and hauled her up into his lap.

Wheeling the pony, the warrior dashed past, and Granny reached out a hand toward Cynthia

Ann's flailing arms, but a moment later pony, warrior, and grandchild all were gone. A few seconds later, John was captured. He was crying for his mother as his captor dangled him by his arms trying to get him draped over the pony's neck. As soon as he felt his captive secure, the burly warrior dug his heels in and the pony broke into a gallop for the open gate.

Granny lay there, her hands curled into fists full of dust until the clouds of pain drifted over her. Soon, she was conscious only of the horrible pain in her shoulder. Then that, too, mercifully faded.

Chapter 8

CYNTHIA ANN CLOSED HER EYES hard, until she thought the pressure would squeeze them so tightly she would never be able to open them again. She felt the hands on her back, the rough hair of the horse under her. All around her, she could smell the tang of pine needles. She could tell by the sound of the pony's hooves that it was in the pine forest near the fort. And under the smell of the pine, she smelled sweat, both of the pony and of the wild man who held her.

She kept seeing things in her mind's eye, things she didn't want to see, things that terrified her and made her scream, and only when she realized that did she understand why her throat was so raw. She could see Granny, the lance stabbed through her shoulder, pinned to the ground the way Elder John had once pinned a kingsnake. Only the kingsnake had wiggled and curled itself into a ball, then straightened out as it tried to squirm away. But Granny just lay still. There was blood on Granny's dress and her hair was a mess, the pins undone, the long strands of gray spread out around her like a string mop.

And Cynthia could see her father, his body all bloody, his arms and legs lying loose, limp, like a shattered doll. And he had been bloody, too, his shirt soaked with it, his face pale and his eyes staring up at the sky like he was looking for a bird. Smoke from the burning buildings swirled all around him, and he disappeared.

But worst of all was Uncle Ben. She had just caught a glimpse of him as they raced past, but his body was all torn, chunks of skin laid open and blood everywhere. His shirt had been torn to ribbons and she couldn't even tell what color it was, there was so much blood. And his eyes were the color of the sky, as if they had become two pieces of glass that had no color of their own, and could only reflect what they stared at.

She didn't want to see those things, but knew she couldn't not see them, whether her eyes were open or squeezed shut. She knew, in fact, that she would see them for the rest of her life, and at the moment it didn't seem likely that would be very long at all. She tried to stop screaming, to rest her throat, and she felt the hands on her back patting her, almost stroking her, as if trying to calm her down, the way Grandpa John had done when her first and only dog had died. They were rough hands, like Grandpa John's hands, but not unkind.

Her screams died away to whimpers, and finally to occasional sobs. She felt things she couldn't see and didn't want to look at ripping at her arms and legs. Thorns tore at the skin of her exposed arms and snagged in the cloth of her dress sleeves. Her legs kept battering against things that first resisted and then gave way, and she knew without looking that the pony was moving deeper into the forest. She kept telling herself that it would be all right, that the Indian who had taken her did not mean to harm her, but then those pictures of Granny and her father and Uncle Ben flooded back, and she knew that the man could have meant nothing *but* harm.

She could hear a wail off through the trees, and it took her a moment to realize the voice was familiar, that her little brother had been taken, too, and was not far away. Her first instinct was to call out to him, to tell him not to be afraid, but she didn't want the Indian to know she was awake and alert. Better he think she had closed up like some slimy snail, gone deep inside herself where things couldn't reach her.

Trickles of blood ran down her arms and legs from the tears and scratches, and mixed with sweat that kept dripping from the man who held her. The sweat was salty and made the cuts and scratches sting, but she didn't try to wipe it away. The burning sensation gave her something to think about. If she could keep her mind on something simple, something ordinary, maybe she could forget all about the horror that swirled around her now like a tornado.

Now that she had stopped crying, she felt the

hands holding her relax a little. They lay there, spread on her back with the fingers splayed wide enough to balance her. If the Indian thought she meant to escape, he showed no sign, and she thought about trying to wriggle free.

To do that, though, she would have to open her eyes, and she didn't want him to know. Letting her head hang and wobble, as if she had fallen asleep, she tried just peeking, but all she could see was a blur a couple of feet beneath her, where the carpet of pine needles flashed by, little spouts of brittle needles geysering with every hoofbeat. That was good, because the needles would cushion her fall.

But wriggling from even so casual a grasp would not be easy. She sensed that without really thinking about it. She might have to grab hold of something to pull herself free, maybe a tree limb or a sturdy vine. But she would have to choose carefully, because she knew she would get only that one chance. Once the Indian knew she meant to escape, he would be much more careful. And the more she thought about it, the more unlikely it seemed that she might succeed. If she found just the right branch, at just the right height, she might be able to grab on, but that would throw her back into her captor, and he would react immediately, grabbing her with both hands. And it would probably make him angry. Instinctively, she seemed to know that if she were going to survive this terrible ordeal, the most important thing was to make no trouble,

none at all. The less attention she called to herself, the better her chances of living long enough
to find a way to escape.

Then, when she thought about John, the idea
of leaving him seemed an impossible thing to do.
He would be terrified as it was, and she would
have to help him. If she stayed, maybe they
could find a way to get away together. But John
would never be able to escape on his own. He
wouldn't know how to go about it, and even if he
found a chance, he would be too scared to take
it.

No, it was better for both of them if she waited. The longer she stayed still, the more careless
the Indian would become. Maybe. And if she
was right, and he dropped his guard, maybe then
she could get away, tugging John by the hand the
way she dragged him home to supper.

She could see the trees flashing by her, and
as she watched, her eyes bare slits, she realized
the forest was thinning. They were reaching the
edge of it, she thought, maybe going back to the
fort. Maybe it was all a joke, maybe the Indian
was taking her back, and her father would be
waiting at the gate, laughing, tears rolling down
his cheeks at such a great trick. Granny would
be there, too, her hair pinned up again, a big
bowl of bread pudding on the table, with brown
sugar sprinkled all over it, just the way she
liked it.

Maybe that was it. She allowed herself to
relax a little at the thought, not quite believ-

ing it, but not wanting not to believe it, either. It would be . . .

But it was too hard to think that way. It was no joke. She knew that, deep down inside. And finally, she allowed herself to open her eyes wide. She turned her head then, partly to protect her face from the lashing pine branches and partly to sneak a look at the Indian.

She saw that his face was painted with red and yellow, and that his eyes were narrowed against the pines and the swarms of gnats that swirled around them. The broad nose was bridged with the garish paint, and his lips were set somewhere between a smile and a snarl.

And she screamed again. The sound went on and on in her own ears, and she thought it would never stop.

Unable to close her eyes, she saw him glance at her, then felt one firm hand pat her back as if she had hiccups. He said something she didn't understand, and nodded as if to reassure her that he meant what he said.

Suddenly the sky exploded and there was sunlight all around her. It took her a moment to realize that they had come out of the forest and she tried to raise her head to look around. The dark wall of pines was falling away behind her, and she saw ponies erupting all along the tree line. Some of the Indians howled and shook their bows and lances overhead as they converged on the man who held her across his lap.

Cynthia Ann looked for John, but none of the

ponies seemed to be carrying double, and she
squirmed some more. The Indian seemed to
know what she was trying to do, patted her
shoulder and pointed. Once more he said something that sounded like a grunt, and she tried to
look, but it was too difficult. Realizing it, the
Indian grabbed her under the arms, swung her
high in the air, the way Grandpa John used to do,
then lowered her over the pony so she could sit.
He wrapped one arm around her waist, and she
looked down at the copper skin, the swirls of
war paint that ran from the shoulder all the way
to the middle of the muscular forearm.

Again the man pointed, and this time she was
able to follow the extended arm. She saw John
then, hanging like a sack of flour over another
pony. He seemed to be sleeping, and for one terrible moment she thought he might be dead. But
then she realized that there was no point in carrying dead weight, and the Indians would have
no use for him, and would have left him behind,
if he were not alive.

She almost smiled then, able for a second to
forget about where she was and how she had
come to be there. She raised a hand timidly,
until it was just a little above her shoulder, and
curled two fingers in the smallest of waves. But
John didn't see her, and so she waved the hand
back and forth, still keeping it below her head.
Again, John failed to respond, and she knew
then he was probably unconscious or sleeping.

Sensing what she was trying to do, the Indian

nudged his pony toward the one which carried her brother. The pony moved in very close, so close that she could reach out and touch John's blond locks, full of pine needles and the husks of seeds. She couldn't see his face, but she noticed the bloody scratches on his arms. Instinctively, forgetting for a moment where she was, she gasped, "Is he all right?"

Only when she turned to wait for the answer did she remember, and she started once more to wail. The Indian shook his head and put a finger to his lips. He made a shushing sound and took the extended finger from his own lips to hers. She trembled as the fingertip approached, and shrank away for a moment when she felt it touch her lips.

She shushed because she was afraid not to, but continued to sob, her hands extended toward her brother. The Indian raised a hand and the others all stopped. She realized then that he must be somebody important, maybe even a chief. He shouted something and one of the warriors moved closer. Some of them, she noticed, were followed by riderless horses. One of these was brought close and the man who had captured her slipped from his pony so easily that she didn't even hear him land on the ground. He picked her up then, his large hands encircling her waist, and placed her gently on the riderless pony. Then, he walked toward the Indian who carried her brother.

Taking John in his arms, he rocked him almost

tenderly, then tickled the boy's nose with the tip
of a finger. She saw John's eyes open then, the
bright blue almost glowing in the harsh sunlight.
The boy started to cry, and the Indian rocked
him again, one hand patting the boy's sob-
wracked shoulders. Then, spinning the boy high
overhead, as he had done with her, he brought
John down on the pony in front of her.

The Indian barked something, and one of the
warriors tossed him a sack of some kind. The Indian
she had already begun to think of as the chief
opened the sack and took out a length of rawhide.
He jerked a knife from a sheath on his hip, and John
screamed. The Indians all laughed, and Cynthia
leaned forward to coo in the boy's ear, trying to
calm him.

Working quickly, the Indian secured her feet
under the pony, did the same to John, using one
continuous length of the rawhide, then cut it,
sliced a short piece from the remainder, and
brought her hands in front of John. He tied her
hands together with her arms around John's
tiny waist, taking care not to cut off her circula-
tion. Then, without a word, he swung up onto
his pony, nudged it close and leaned over to
snag the lead rope attached to her pony's
rawhide bridle.

Once more, he barked a command, flapped his
knees against the pony's sides, and the flight
resumed.

She saw now that they were heading out into
the plains. As far as she could see, tall grass

waved in the hot sun. She glanced over her shoulder at the trees for a moment, as if trying to fix the place in her memory.

From time to time, one or another of the warriors would ride close. Mostly they said nothing. But occasionally one of them would grunt something at her, then smile. One even reached out and took some of her long blond hair in his hand and draped it across his wrist, then made several rapid clucking sounds and backed away, shaking his head.

By noon, her terror was giving way to thirst and hunger. She hadn't had breakfast, and her stomach was grumbling. John snuffled from time to time, tilting his head to wipe his nose on the sleeve of his shirt, but he calmed down enough that Cynthia was able to concentrate more on their surroundings. The trees were long gone behind her, and the sun hammered relentlessly down.

The sun was past its zenith before the crows of some cottonwoods appeared on the horizon. The whole band swung toward it as if they had known it would be there, and then she realized that of course they had. They were Indians, after all.

It took nearly a half hour to reach the trees, and they were almost within a stone's throw when she saw the gleam of water through the tangle of underbrush. A spring, she thought. Maybe now they'll give us some food. The Indians dismounted, except for a handful who

spread out in all directions to stand watch while
the rest watered their animals.

When they had dismounted, the chief and one
of the warriors opened a buckskin bag and
offered her some dried meat. It was chewy and a
little too salty for her liking, but at least it was
food. She thought they might let her and John get
down, but so far there had been no indication
they would.

All she could do was watch. And wait.

Chapter 9 =========

WARRIORS SPURTED AHEAD of the main body, driving horses stolen in their raids far to the east. Cynthia didn't know it, but the raid on Fort Parker was just an afterthought. The fort was there, and the Comanche just happened to be passing by. A few miles to the north, and they wouldn't have bothered. The pickings at the fort had been pitifully slim, and Peta Nocona was already wondering whether it had been worth the trouble. He thought about the people left bleeding on the ground, some dead before the Comanche had ridden away, some to be dead before the dust of the Comanche flight had settled. They were white, and that was reason enough to hate them, given how the whites had come into land that wasn't theirs and started to act as if the Comanche were the interlopers.

Looking at the two children, he wondered why he and Black Snake had taken them. They had captured the children of enemies before, but things were changing fast, and now he wondered whether it might mean trouble of a kind they had never seen before. It was common practice for the Comanche, as for most plains Indians, to take captives, almost always women and children, and as often as not, they were taken into a tipi and adopted by the tribe. There were such people even now in the main camp of the Noconi Comanche. Three Mexicans, all of them taken long ago, so long that it seemed to all but the very oldest, that they had always been part of the tribe. There were whites, too. Two men who were warriors now, more Comanche even than the real Comanche, and a woman who had been with them for fifteen winters. Maybe, Nocona thought, Black Feather can help. He knew the children were terrified, and he didn't blame them. But, he thought, better to be frightened and alive than dead like Little Calf, just a memory now, a little boy who had never hurt anyone fallen victim, like so many other children, to the brutal reality of Comanche life.

As the first of the tipis came into sight, Nocona moved alongside Black Snake, who was grinning from ear to ear, delighted with the captives. Nocona wanted to ask him what he planned to do with the boy, but now was not the time. That would have to wait until they were alone, maybe on a hunt. They could go off together, just the two of them, as they had done so many times before. Then, alone in the center of the universe, the campfire swallowed by the dark night around them, he could ask, and Black

Snake would answer, because they were the best of friends, and had no secrets from each other.

Shaking his head, he urged his pony forward, slowly gaining on the leaders of the band, soon passing them and, as the village took shape before his tired eyes, mustering the energy to lead the triumphal procession into the village. All around him, the warriors were yipping and howling, waving feathered lances and racing their ponies pell mell, cutting in front of one another and showing off, especially the young warriors, who were more interested in catching the eye of some young woman they fancied than the number of admiring glances from the old squaws or the subtle nods of approval that seemed to be the best the old men could manage.

As the people closed around the returning warriors, Nocona stayed close to Black Snake. For some reason he didn't understand, he felt protective of the young captives. He had watched the girl, particularly, and admired the way she had kept control of her emotions. She had seemed to realize what she could do and what she couldn't do. Once she had regained her composure after the initial terror, she had kept still, and he thought he could see her watching, learning, even as they rode.

And he admired the way she had tried to protect the boy, whom Nocona took to be her brother. That took courage out of the ordinary. This was a brave little girl, of that much he felt certain. With the celebration swirling like flood

water around him, he dismounted in front of
his lodge, propped his shield on the stand,
then his lance, and gave the horse to one of the
boys to feed and water.

Immediately, he moved toward Black Snake's
lodge, and got there just as Black Snake was cutting the rawhide binding from the little girl's
hands. Black Snake hefted the little boy and as
he set him on the ground, Nocona moved past
and helped the girl down. She looked up at him
uncertainly, her eyes wide, her hands, face, and
legs ragged with scratches and laced with dried
blood, the whole covered with a thick paste of
trail dust mixed with sweat and blood.

Holding the little girl's hand, he turned to
his friend. "What will you do now? With the
children?"

Black Snake shrugged. "What we always do, I
think."

"They need a woman to watch over them, to
teach them how things are here."

"And . . . ?"

"And I was thinking that maybe Black Feather
would be the right woman for the boy."

"Why Black Feather?"

"Why not? She will understand what he is
thinking and feeling. She might even remember
some of the Anglo language, which will make it
easier for both of them."

"But she doesn't have a husband. It is enough
that the rest of us have to hunt for her. How will
she feed the child?"

"It is time she had a husband."

"But there is no one who . . ." Black Snake stopped in midsentence and backed away a step. "You're not suggesting that I . . ."

Nocona shook his head. "Yes, I am suggesting that."

"But who will speak for her? She has no family here, now that Blue Buffalo is gone. He took her in, he raised her, he . . . there is no one to speak for her."

"I will speak for her. As the chief, it is my right, even my duty. I will speak on her behalf."

"But I don't . . ."

"You think she is pretty. I know that. I see you making sick calf eyes at her at the dances. After each hunt you give her so much buffalo meat that no one else has to give her anything. When she makes moccasins, she gives you the best pair. When she goes down to the river to bathe, sometimes you sneak into the willows and watch."

"How did you know . . . I never . . . but, I am not ready to be married. There is . . ."

"There is nothing left for you to accomplish that you cannot accomplish with a wife. And if you have a family, I think maybe you will even live longer. As a friend, that is something that is important to me. You know how the hot-blooded young men are. They are so busy trying to impress one another that they don't stop to think. They think war is a game."

"It *is* a game."

"No. Nothing which leads to death is a game. Life is too important for that. You are a great warrior. Everyone knows that. There is nothing left for you to prove. I think maybe it is time that you paid more attention to how long you live and less to how close you can come to dying."

"I don't know. I . . ." He stopped again and tilted his head, looking at his friend out of the corner of his eye. "She is pretty, isn't she? She is a good woman. But she is a little older than . . ."

"Not so old. Only twenty-two or twenty-three winters. Younger than you are. It would be a good match. You know that, and so does everyone else in the village."

"Do you think that she knows it, too?"

"Yes, I think she knows it. But if it will make you feel better, I will ask her."

"You can't just come right out and ask her something like that."

"Why not?"

"What if she says no?"

"Will that hurt your pride so much? Besides, who will know? Only you and me and Black Feather. I will tell no one, and neither will she. So, if anyone learns about it, it will be because you pull a long face and mope around. But I don't think she will say no."

"Maybe you could . . ."

"What?"

"What about the marriage gifts? She has nothing. How will it look?"

"I will take care of that. Since I will speak for

her, I will take that responsibility. It is the custom, and you know that. You are just looking for excuses. The great Black Snake, who eats Apache for his morning meal then cuts the heart out of a Pawnee for his evening meal is afraid of a woman, a white woman at that. Now *that* I will not keep to myself, and you will have no one to blame."

"Sometimes," Black Snake said, laughing in spite of himself, "I wish I were chief, so I could make you do things that make your skin hot and the women laugh at you behind your back."

"No, my friend, you would not really want to be chief. Not if you knew the things I have to worry about. Arranging a marriage for a friend is an easy thing. But it might be the only easy thing."

Suddenly, both men were aware of the jubilant chaos around them, and the press of women and children on all sides. Nocona knew that meant that the thing was settled and that they were free to think about other things.

"I will ask her about keeping the boy right now. I will speak about the other thing later."

"When?" Black Snake sounded eager, in spite of himself.

"Tonight. Unless you want me to do it now."

"No!" The answer came so quickly, Black Snake was embarrassed. Nocona smiled, but didn't make the obvious observation that his friend was more terrified of the woman than of any foe.

"Come with me," Nocona said.

Black Snake shook his head. "No, I think it . . ."

"He is your captive. You should be there when I talk to her."

"You won't mention the other thing?"

Nocona smiled. "No. I won't mention the other thing. I promise."

He glanced down then, as if aware for the first time that he held a small white hand in his own. He saw the girl looking up at him, her face apprehensive but composed. It was, he thought, as if she knew what we were talking about, knew that it concerned her and the boy. Then, as if something had been settled permanently in his mind, he tugged on the hand and started toward Black Feather's lodge, pushing through the crowd and turning back to see Black Snake hoist the small boy onto his shoulders and start after him.

Black Snake was smiling, and Nocona thought he knew why. When he reached the lodge where Black Feather lived by herself, he announced himself, and heard her invite him in. He ducked through, pulling the suddenly reluctant girl in after him. He waited for Black Snake to come inside before he spoke.

Black Feather was sitting by the fire pit, but there was no fire in the oppressive heat. She had the sides rolled to let in light and to try to find some relief from the sweltering air. She looked at Nocona, then at Black Snake and only then did she permit herself to glance at the children.

Nocona thought it was because she was afraid of what she would see. She averted her eyes quickly, and he started to speak, but then saw the silver glistening on her cheeks, and he stopped.

She swallowed hard before asking, "What do you want?"

Nocona indicated the boy with a nod of his head.

"What about him?"

"I think it would be a good idea if he stayed with you."

"Why?"

"Because you need someone to help you. And he needs someone to help him."

"That is what a family is for," she snapped. "He probably has a family. Why don't you take him to them?"

Nocona cleared his throat, embarrassed at the impeccable logic of her question, and more than a little intimidated by the anger straining to break through her clipped speech.

Black Snake started to say something, but Nocona held up a hand. "Maybe you should leave us alone for a while," he said. "Take the children outside."

When Black Snake was gone, Black Feather stood up and turned her back, as if she were afraid to say what she had to say while facing Nocona. "A long time ago, I was taken from my family. Now you come here with other children, taken just as I was taken, and you think that makes it all right, because I will understand what they are going through. And you would be right. I *would* understand. What I don't understand is why they *have* to go through it. Why didn't you just kill them?"

"Has it been that terrible for you?"

She whirled around, then. "What do you think? How do you think it's been? You knew your parents. You sat in your mother's lap. You learned to hunt with your father."

"I saw them grow old and die."

"Is that why you did this? To spare them the pain of watching the people they love and who love them grow old and die? Then why don't we give away all our children, let someone else heal their wounds and quiet their fears? Maybe we shouldn't have children at all. Maybe it would be better if . . ."

"You don't mean that."

"Don't I?"

"No. But you are right, and I am sorry. I just thought that . . ."

"You thought that I would take the children because I have none of my own. That they would be my family because I have none, and I would be their family because you saw to it that they have none."

"No! I brought the boy to you because I thought you were one of us. It is what we do. I thought it would be what you would do, because you *are* one of us."

"You're right. I am one of you. But not by choice."

Nocona smiled. "I am not a Comanche by choice, either. But I *am* a Comanche. And so are you." He turned then. "I am sorry. I will . . ."

"No, wait . . . I . . . of course I'll take care of the boy. I just . . ."

"I understand," he said. "I had a family of my own, once. But no more. . . ."

"Bring in the boy," Black Feather said. She turned to look at him, saw that his back was turned, and walked over to rest a hand on his shoulder. "There are enough orphans," she said.

Chapter 10 ═══════════

GRANDMOTHER WALKS ON WIND was appalled at the condition of the child. She grabbed Cynthia around the waist and started peeling off the mud and sweat-soaked clothing as she carried her toward the river. By the time the old woman reached the sandy bank, Cynthia was naked, squirming like a fish, her arms and legs flailing in every direction. As Walks on Wind held her out over the water, she thought for one terrified moment that the woman meant to drown her. It seemed unfair to be taken all this way just to have it end so cruelly and suddenly.

But that wasn't what the old woman had in mind. Letting Cynthia down rump first into the water, she kicked off her moccasins and waded in after the girl. Grabbing her by one arm, as if to reprimand her, she collapsed into a sitting position and started scooping water with one hand. Gently, trying to avoid contact with the worst of the cuts, she washed away most of the dirt, then moved into deeper water.

The river felt cool, its water taking some of the sting from her body and making the deepest of the scratches sting even more. The old woman's hands were rough, but not unkind. Her no-nonsense approach quelled whatever impulse Cynthia might have had to resist, and when the woman crooked a finger at her and nodded her head downstream, Cynthia followed.

Leaving the girl in water to her chest, Walks on Wind moved toward the shallows, bent over as if looking for something lost in the current. Finally, spotting what she sought, she moved to the shore, her arms pumping, doing something Cynthia couldn't see. When Walks on Wind turned around, she had both hands full of some sort of plant. She was already crushing the leaves and stems as she started back to where Cynthia stood shivering as much from the cool water as from fright. She started to smear the pulpy green mass over the child's head and face. The smell was pleasant, and as the woman's hands worked, a thin lather started to appear, trickling down over Cynthia's forehead and into her eyes. It didn't sting like her mother's soap, but she knew it was meant to cleanse her matted hair.

Forced under for a moment, she came up spluttering. Picking her up under the arms, Walks on Wind hoisted her overhead until only her toes were tickled by the current. Turning her this way and that, the old woman

made sure her new charge was clean, then
grunted, let her down and held out a hand.
Not knowing what else to do, Cynthia took the
offered hand, letting her fingers rest in the cal-
lused palm.

Walks on Wind turned then and started
toward the riverbank, tugging the girl in her
wake. Cynthia felt embarrassed, naked in front
of a thousand pairs of savage eyes, but Walks
on Wind didn't seem to notice. When they
reached the shore, she picked up the girl, rested the weight on one hip, and started back to
her tipi.

Once inside, Walks on Wind turned her
attention to the scratches and cuts. She rum-
maged in a basket in one corner, found what
she was looking for with some difficulty, then
moved close to the small fire at the center of
the tipi and patted her lap as she sat down.
Cynthia understood and walked close, enjoying the feel of the soft buffalo robe beneath her
bare feet. Some sort of greasy ointment was
applied to her cuts, and Walks on Wind,
whose eyes were not the best, kept leaning forward, gesturing for the girl to turn so that she
could scrutinize every square inch of ravaged
skin.

Satisfied that she had missed nothing significant, the old woman then moved into the dim
light at the edge of the tipi once more, returning
with what appeared to be a ball of skin. Only
when she shook it out was it revealed as a

buckskin dress. She held it up, shook it again, then brought it close to Cynthia. The firelight played on an elaborate beadwork design on the front as the old woman moved it this way and that.

Then, handing it to the girl, Walks on Wind mimed donning the dress. Grateful for a chance to cover herself, Cynthia wasted no time slipping the soft leather over her damp hair and tugging it down. It was too large, but that was no wonder. Walks on Wind measured the fit with a long-practiced eye, then pinched the dress here and there, suddenly a seamstress.

Once more, she moved away, this time returning quickly, a pair of moccasins in her hand. They, too, were too large, but close enough to a proper fit that they would stay on her feet as long as she didn't move too quickly. Then it was time for her hair. Even wet as it was, it was much lighter than the old woman's hair, which was thick and black, and hung over her shoulders in a thick cloak, decorated with beaded bands.

Using her fingers to get out the tangles, Walks on Wind worked swiftly and expertly, then took a bone comb and raked the long tresses into a thick cape that hung down over Cynthia's back. The fingers moving nimbly fashioned braids, then tied them off with pieces of buckskin. Finally, satisfied that her transformation had done as much as it could, Walks on Wind sat back, holding Cynthia at arm's length and turning her once, then again to admire her handiwork.

She reached into a basket and handed the girl a cheap mirror with a wooden back. It was old, its silver crazed and laced with a network of oxidized veins, but it was still good enough for the girl to see herself, clouded in the glass and, even if the mirror had been perfect, all but unrecognizable.

But she smiled.

The old woman grunted again, took the mirror and tucked it back into the basket, and stood up. Her ancient knees cracked in the silence, sounding like logs on a fire, and she was breathing heavily, as if the morning's work had drained her. Holding up a finger for Cynthia to stay put, she went outside, and returned a few moments later with strips of dried buffalo meat, which she held out, smacking her lips, telling Cynthia she should eat. The girl took the offered food reluctantly, even though she was famished. Chewing greedily, she downed the meat, then bent to wipe her hands on the dirt near the fire, smacking them together to clean them.

She could hear voices outside now, one deep and curt, the other, a woman, higher pitched and impatient. Then a shadow darkened the open entrance flap and a young woman entered. She said something to Walks on Wind, and then moved closer to the girl, circling her and the fire at the same time. She kept shaking her head, and

Cynthia noticed that her cheeks were wet, as if she were crying.

One brown hand moved up to wipe away the dampness, and she moved close to the girl with the suddenness of an attack, gathering her in her arms and nearly crushing the air from Cynthia's lungs.

She sat down then, still holding onto Cynthia's hand. "Name . . ."

It sounded odd, like the Stebbins boy, who wasn't right in the head, and mumbled a pidgin English that was somewhere between human speech and animal grunting. It sounded almost as if the words were stuck in her throat, coated with thick phlegm and refused to come out.

Again, the newcomer said, "Name . . . ?" This time, it was apparent that it was a question, and Cynthia, her own lips trembling, said, "Cynthia Ann Parker. I want to go home. . . ." Then, in spite of her resolve, she started to sob.

The woman reached out to her, but Cynthia turned her back. She felt hands then, tugging at the hem of her buckskin dress, and the old woman moved in front of her, placed her hands on the child's shoulders, and pushed, gently but firmly, until the newcomer's lap caught her when she stumbled.

She looked up then, and saw that the woman was crying once more, this time making no effort to wipe away the tears. "Black Feather," she said, less tentatively, tapping herself on the breast. "Black Feather." Then, one quivering finger reached out to touch Cynthia's nose and the woman smiled as she said, "Cynthia Ann Parker."

Cynthia nodded. Black Feather pointed to the old woman and said, "Walks on Wind. . . ."

"Walks on Wind?" Cynthia said.

The younger woman nodded her head. "Name," she said. "Walks on Wind. She is your mother, now."

"No, she's not my mother. I want my mother, my real mother." It was nearly a scream, the voice shrill, sharp, the words almost enough to slice the tipi walls to ribbons, but Black Feather held her tightly and said, "Walks on Wind is mother now."

Walks on Wind leaned over her and reached down. Cynthia took the old woman's hand, and followed her out of the tipi, Black Feather right behind them. As soon as they were out in the open, children gathered around, the girls rushing in close, the boys, perhaps shy, hanging back a bit. A hum started then and soon Cynthia realized the whole village had gathered to see her. She felt almost proud and a little bit like a prized heifer as the old woman led her around, pointing things out rapid fire, and turning each time to Black Feather, who had to rummage around in the misty attic of her English to find the right word or words, then giving Cynthia the Comanche equivalent.

Walks on Wind was determined that Cynthia's education would be rapid and comprehensive. The girl wondered that the old woman's legs didn't give out as she darted here and there, jabbing a crooked finger at a horse or a tipi or a bow or shield. Half the village, mostly women and children, trailed like a comet's tail in the wake of the trio. The Comanche words were difficult for her, some of the sounds being totally alien to her. But she was quick-witted, and seemed to realize that if she were to get along, she would have to go along, until such time as a chance for escape presented itself.

Occasionally her mind would wander, and she wondered whether John were in some other village, getting the same treatment. He would be terrified, so much younger than herself and with no one to turn to. She found herself being grateful for the presence of Black Feather, but started to wonder how the woman had come to speak English. The more curious she became, the closer she watched her interpreter, and it began to dawn on her, not only how she had come by the language, but why she had been crying—she was a captive, too, Cynthia thought. Just like me, she had been taken from her home and forced to learn the Comanche ways, the Comanche language and, with her skin sun-bronzed and her dark hair, seemed almost to have become a Comanche herself.

And now the reality of her future began to gather in her mind, a storm cloud far off on the horizon, blackening, thickening, growing more and more turbulent as if rushed unopposed into the center of her consciousness. Black Feather had been here a long time, years, maybe even most of her life. And if that were true of Black Feather, it would likely be true of Cynthia herself. She began to cry then, letting the water seep from the corners of her eyes, but soundlessly, trying not to call attention either to her tears or to herself.

She wanted to go home, and she kept seeing that awful image of Granny Parker pinned to the ground, Grandpa John dead, and Uncle Ben a bloody pincushion with glazed button eyes, and she knew she would never see home again.

Black Feather kept one hand on Cynthia's shoulder, squeezing it from time to time to reassure her, but it made no difference. Nothing would make a difference, nothing would ever be the same again, and she let the truth wash over her like a huge wave, not struggling against it, but letting it sweep her along. Her eyes darted every which way, following the sharp jabs of the old woman's finger, and she tried to take in the words, but it was all just a buzz now, a distant hum, as if some hive of great bees were getting angry, beginning to swarm out and defend itself. It rose to a roar until she could barely hear the words of the white woman who was a Comanche, and when she could hear them they sounded as if they had come from a great distance, maybe under water, sounds without meaning.

And bow, arrow, lance, and shield surrounded her on every side. Tipis stabbed the sky, the children swarmed like gnats and all of it was just a blur through the waterlogged slits her eyes had become. She stopped paying attention to the words altogether because she didn't want to know anything, thought that knowing how things were here, what things meant would make it all the harder for her to go back.

Then, a shadow spilled over her and she opened her eyes wide. She looked up into the face of a man who stood smiling, one hand hidden behind his back. He squatted down in front of her, reached out to tickle her under the chin. She pushed the hand away, but it kept coming back, hovering like a hummingbird just out of her reach.

He looked familiar somehow, but she wasn't sure why. Then imaging the scrubbed and gleaming face striped with red and yellow paint, she understood. This was the man who had stolen her away. And now he wanted to be friends, as if he had done no more than take her for a walk in the park. He was teasing her, playing with her, the way an uncle or grandfather might.

And she hated him. She flew at him suddenly, her small fists pounding on his chest. The suddenness of the onslaught had taken him by surprise, and he fell over backward. In an attempt to keep his balance, he had brought out the hand that had been hidden, and she saw something in it, stared for a moment, suddenly powerless to move.

The people all around were laughing, saying things that made the man smile broadly. Slowly, he brought the hand close to her, and she saw that he held a small doll, an animal, probably a buffalo. He held it out, shaking it once or twice until she understood that it was for her.

She turned away, and he said something that made the others laugh. Then, looking at Black Feather, she asked, "What did he say?"

Black Feather smiled. "He said you have the heart of a panther."

"What does . . ."

"Take the doll," Black Feather said. "He wants you to have it."

"I don't want it!"

But, in spite of herself, she turned back. Once more the buffalo was dangled in front of her. "I want to see my brother," she said.

"I'll take you," the woman answered.

Then, slowly, Cynthia Ann reached for the gift. She stopped with her fingertips just grazing the stiff hairs of the doll. Then, gently, he pressed it into her hand. Her fingers closed reluctantly. And then it was hers.

And she knew that in that moment she had turned a corner. Life would never be the same.

Chapter 11 ══════

Summer 1845

CYNTHIA WOKE UP EARLY, as she had been doing for as long as she could remember. Leaving the tipi, she walked to the top of a hill behind the village, enjoying the chill in the predawn air. It made her shiver, raised little bumps on the skin of her arms and legs. Even in the chill, the air was heavy with the smell of hollyhock and lupine, their blossoms just masses of charcoal against the darker mass of the hill. It was too early for the bees to be about, and passing through the tall flowers, she allowed them to swish against her. Once or twice, she bent to sniff deeply of one of the blossoms, letting the cool dew tickle the tip of her nose.

When she reached the hilltop, she sat down, tucking her legs primly beneath her, even though there was no one about. She watched the village, heard a dog bark, and the distant nicker of a nervous horse. Where once such sounds would have raised the hair on the back of her neck, they were so much a part of her life now that she found them comforting, for reasons she could not explain.

She was worried about Walks on Wind. The old woman seemed almost indestructible, but Cynthia, now called Naudah for so long she barely remembered her old name, couldn't shake the feeling that she was beginning to slow down. Her hair had whitened in the last couple of winters, and the hands which had been so strong that morning so long ago when Naudah had first been taken to her, now trembled so much that beadwork was no longer possible for her. The simplest things seemed to give her trouble, things she had done almost as long as she lived, which, as near as Naudah could figure, had to be about sixty years, maybe even older.

More and more, Walks on Wind looked to her to do things. Almost all of the skinning, except on those very warm days in the middle of the summer hunt, when every hand was necessary, now fell to Naudah to do. And even when Walks on Wind tried to help, she often spent hours on a single hide, trying to conceal her frustration and the inevitable tears it prompted. Walks on Wind was a proud woman, and she hated for anyone to see the weakness that was catching up to her.

As often as not, even the cooking fell to Naudah. She didn't mind. In fact, she even took some pleasure in it. It was one of the few things she felt comfortable doing. So much of what Walks on Wind had taught her had come with difficulty. She tried, partly because she knew it would make her life easier, and partly because she took pride in doing things well, but she suspected that deep inside her was a frightened ten-year-old unable to get out.

On her solitary walks, she would try to remember how things were before her life had been turned inside out, to imagine what they would be like if that one horrible day hadn't happened. She didn't blame the Comanche anymore. She had seen too much to do that. Their lives were hard, suspended between the earth and a heavy stone that might at any moment fall, crushing them like so many bugs. But she felt cheated.

Lying back in the tall grass, feeling the beads of dew seep into the collar of her dress and send shivers down her spine, she closed her eyes for a moment. When she opened them, the sky above was full of fireflies, hard, white points that seemed to shimmer. Once, a blade of brilliant yellow lanced across the black skin of the night, so fast she thought she might have imagined it. But it was there even when she closed her eyes, and lingered for several seconds, slowly fading. Only when it was gone, did she open again, as if to see whether it would come back.

Looking down on the village, the place she

now thought of as home because it filled the
vacuum in her heart left by the loss of her real
home, she saw a dark figure moving away
from the tipis. For a split second, her blood
went cold. The thought crossed her mind that
it could be an Osage or an Apache. But the figure was walking too easily, unconcerned
whether or not it was observed, and a warrior
scouting for a war party would never have
been so casual.

She relaxed then, watching the figure as it left
the camp circle behind and reached the bottom
of the hill on which she sat. It was a man, but
she could not tell who. He came up the hill then,
his steps tentative, as if he weren't sure he wanted to make the climb. Probably someone restless,
maybe River Walker, who had a fight with his
wife that evening, one that made everyone laugh,
which only succeeded in making River Walker
still angrier. Maybe he had been unable to sleep
and come out for some quiet thought. Or maybe
his wife had thrown him out. Naudah smiled at
the thought.

As he drew nearer, she started to worry that he
might see her and, worse yet, that someone else
might see the two of them and jump to the wrong
conclusion. Only when he reached the crest did
she recognize him. Peta Nocona. This time, she
closed her eyes again and refused to open them.
He was a chief now, no longer just the subchief
who had wrapped an arm around her and carried
her away.

She knew that he worried about many things, and that he seemed hardly ever to sleep. But why was he up here? she wondered.

She didn't want to say anything, partly to keep him from knowing she was there and partly because he intimidated her. Not that he was ever rude or abusive. But there was something about him, some majestic chill that seemed to insulate him from the rest of the people. She wondered whether it was like that for all chiefs, whether kings and queens were as isolated on their thrones.

"You couldn't sleep?" he asked. Just when she thought he hadn't noticed her.

At first, she debated whether to answer. Perhaps she could pretend she was sleeping, and he would not speak again, leaving her to her dreams. But she couldn't do that.

"No," she said, her voice cracking, almost catching in her throat.

"I couldn't sleep either." He wasn't looking in her direction, and the words were soft, almost inaudible, not like the terrible thunderbolts he delivered when around the council fire.

"You have been with us a long time, now, Naudah," he said.

"Yes."

"Ten winters."

"Yes."

"I have thought about it a great deal in the last few days."

Emboldened by his candor, she was moved to ask, "Why?"

"Because I have often wondered whether it was the right thing to do."

"It doesn't matter now."

"Doesn't it?"

"No."

"I think it does."

"You did what you do. It is what Comanche have always done, is it not?"

"Yes. Even when we were not Comanche but Shoshone. So long ago that no one remembers exactly when we stopped being Shoshone and became Comanche. But because a thing is always done, does that make it right? This is what I have been asking myself."

"It doesn't make it right, no. But it doesn't make it wrong."

"You lost family that day, people who were close to you, people who loved you and whom you loved. That was painful. I know that."

"People say that Peta Nocona had a family once, too. That he lost them, just as I lost my family."

"They were taken from me, yes. But they are dead. You don't know whether your family is alive or dead."

"My father and his brother are dead. My grandfather is dead. My grandmother is probably dead."

"The old woman with white hair?"

"Yes."

"She was a very brave old woman. She tried to save you from me."

"Was it you who . . . ?" But she stopped herself. She didn't really want to know the answer.

"No. It wasn't. But that doesn't make the loss any less painful. It doesn't mean . . ." He trailed off, his voice confused, as if he weren't sure what it didn't mean, any more than he knew what it meant.

"As I said, it no longer matters. I couldn't go back now, not even if I wanted to."

"Since that day, we have never taken a white captive into the Noconi village. Do you know why?"

"I wondered about that."

"Because I realized that it wasn't fair. War is one thing, but that was something else. If I were dead, I would want to know that my family was well cared for. But I could not stand to be alive and not know where my son was, whether he had enough to eat, whether he was cold in winter or thirsty in summer. I would hate not knowing."

"So it was because of your son that . . ."

Nocona shook his head, the movement just a blur of shadow in the starlight. "No. It was because of you. Because of you and your family. We still make war with the whites because we have to defend our lands and because they make war on us, even though the old chiefs once signed a paper saying that there would be no war. The Osage signed, too, and the Kiowa. The Kiowa are our friends, so we don't make war on each other, but the Osage are our enemies still, and still they make war and we make war. It is like that with the whites. The paper means nothing. Not to anyone. It is just paper."

"What, then?"

Nocona tapped his chest. "What I felt in here . . . that means something. And I feel that you have been done a great evil. For this I am sorry. I would undo it if I knew how. But . . ."

He sighed heavily, and Naudah felt bad for him, knowing that he meant what he said and knowing, too, that what he said was true, that it could not be undone. Even if she wanted it to be.

"I no longer blame you, as I once did."

"It would be all right if you still did. I would understand."

"But I don't. Walks on Wind has been good to me. She didn't have to be. In the beginning, Black Feather told me stories of what happened to some . . . captives. I was lucky."

"Lucky?"

"It could have been worse. Much worse."

"Yes," he said. "It could have been worse."

"I wonder about my brother."

"So do I. But I have never heard word of him. Every time I meet someone from another band, I ask. Black Snake has too, and Black Feather. I don't know what happened to your brother. You may not believe that, but it's true."

"I have no reason not to believe it."

"You think he is dead, don't you?"

"Yes."

Nocona grunted. "I think so, too. I am sorry."

"You are sorry about so much tonight. Maybe you should look at the stars and smell the hollyhock, and try to forget about things you can't change."

"Knowing that I can't change these things doesn't mean that I don't want to."

"I know that. But knowing you want to change them is enough. I don't expect the impossible."

"You are very wise, for . . ."

"For a woman?"

"No, I was going to say for one so young. I was not half so wise when I was your age."

"One does not become a chief without being wise."

Nocona laughed then, an arctic laugh. "And one who is wise knows not to become a chief."

He looked up at the stars then, letting his gaze take in their vast sweep. "So many," he said.

"Yes."

"Good night."

And without another word, he started down the hill. Naudah had the urge to race after him, thinking that she had been too direct, too critical, but he would see through any attempt to change her words, and she thought it better to let them be.

When his shadow disappeared among the tipis, she got to her feet and started down the hill. The sun would be up soon, and there would be a lot to do. Just as there always was.

Chapter 12 ═══════

NOCONA DIDN'T NOTICE THE SHADOW until he almost reached his tipi. As he was about to duck inside, he caught the movement of darkness and turned, his hand reaching instinctively for the knife on his hip.

"You don't need that knife, brother," a familiar voice said.

"Black Snake. You startled me. I thought . . ."

Black Snake laughed softly. "If I were an Osage, brother, we would all be in trouble. As it is, it is just you who are in trouble."

"Trouble, how?" Nocona whispered.

"Let's walk awhile. Get away from the village, where we can speak freely."

"It's late, and I'm tired."

"You are always tired. Because you don't sleep as much as you should. That is a problem for any man, but especially for a chief." Taking Nocona by the arm, he tugged firmly. "Come on. It's important."

The chief gave in to his friend, and followed

him through the silent tipis sitting like huge bee-hives in the darkness, until they were at the riverbank. Impatient to know what was on Black Snake's mind, Nocona reached down to tug at a swatch of dry grass, uprooted it, and slapped it rhythmically against his knee.

"Now, what is this trouble that you know about and I don't?" he asked.

Black Snake sat on the ground, crossed his legs, and patted the sand beside him. "Sit," he said.

When Nocona followed suit, Black Snake leaned back, folding his arms beneath his head and stretched his legs out toward the water. Nocona remained sitting.

Taking a pebble, Black Snake tossed it out over the river, where it landed with a distant splash. "It's been a long time since White Heron and Little Calf," he said. A bold move, since it was custom not to speak of the dead by name.

Nocona realized that, whatever it was, Black Snake was willing to run the risk. "Yes. No one knows that better than I do," he said.

"Listen, a long time ago, we had this same talk, only we were on opposite sides. But you were right. She was the right woman for me, and I . . . it's been a long time since she and the boy . . . but . . ." He stopped for a moment, swallowed hard and rubbed his forehead.

"There, you know the pain. How can you tell me something like this?"

"It is time for you to have a family again. You have been alone for too long."

Nocona snorted. "No. Once was enough. I am content to be alone."

"I know that no one can replace those you have lost," Black Snake said, reverting to a more formal obliqueness. "But I also know that it is not good for a man to be alone, especially a man who thinks so much, who has so much to worry about, as you do. It is important to be able to share those burdens with someone."

Nocona shook his head in the dark. He was too impatient and interrupted, "I don't . . ."

"Let me finish . . . whether you agree or not is not important. It is so, and you will come to realize it too late if I leave you to make the decision on your own."

"You are impertinent."

"That is what friends are for. Someone has to risk offending you by telling you what everyone knows. You should marry again."

"I don't want to."

"You need to and, whether you know it or not, you want to. I am only saying what everyone says."

"Oh, and who is it I want to marry? Or doesn't anyone know?"

"They know. And so do you, very well, even though you won't admit it."

"I . . . and who is it I want to marry then?"

"Naudah."

Nocona snorted.

"Why do you laugh? She is pretty. She is a good worker. She has been good to Walks on Wind. She likes you. It is the perfect match for both of you."

"No, she doesn't. Besides, I took her away from her family."

"That was a long time ago. She is one of us now. You know that as well as I do. Everyone thinks that . . ."

Nocona shut him off. "It doesn't matter what everyone thinks."

"Maybe not. But it does matter what you think. And if you search your heart, you will see that what I am saying is true. You will see that she is perfect for you. And who better than you to give her children?"

"I had a son once . . . I . . ."

"That is not the argument. You can't live in the past. It has been nearly fourteen winters since . . ."

"Fifteen," Nocona said. In the darkness, his voice seemed louder than it was. Then he whispered. "Fifteen . . ."

"It is a long time to be alone. Too long."

"But I am too old for marriage."

"No. You know that isn't true. Older men marry young women all the time. As often as not."

"They are men who take too long to gather the bride-gift. That is not my problem, it is theirs."

"The bride-gift is not a problem. Besides, it is

already set. I spoke to Walks on Wind, and she agrees it is the best thing for both of you. For her, too. She is getting old, and will not be with us much longer. She wants to know that Naudah will be well taken care of."

"You shouldn't have done that."

"Someone had to." Black Snake waited in the darkness for further argument, but none was forthcoming. When he was certain Nocona had been swayed, he said, "You should talk to Walks on Wind soon. Today."

With that, Black Snake got to his feet. "Good night," he said. And walked away.

Stunned, Nocona sat there for several minutes. He kept looking around as if he expected someone to argue for him, but there was only silence and shadows. Slowly, he got to his feet and trudged back to his empty tipi.

"Today," he whispered. "Today, he said, as if I were some gawky boy. He spoke to Walks on Wind! I can speak for myself."

And that afternoon, he did, bringing ten of his finest horses to the old woman's tipi. She heard the uproar as he made his way through the village. Everyone must have known, because people stopped in their tracks to stare at him, grinning and teasing him as he strode by, his eyes fixed dead ahead, tugging sharply at the lead rope and doing his best to ignore the whistles and catcalls.

Walks on Wind was outside waiting well before he reached her tipi. She was not smiling.

"I have come to ask for Naudah," he said, thrusting the lead rope into the crooked hand. "These are for you."

"You are a man of few words, Peta Nocona."

"Words are just wind."

"I see. Then they should be easy for one such as you to make. I am surprised it has taken you so long to make those particular words."

"Don't make this any harder than it is, Grandmother."

She tilted her head back as if to look at the single cumulus drifting high overhead. Rocking on the balls of her feet, she said, "Agreed."

And that was it. Quick, painless, it had seemed like endless torture in prospect, but in execution had flown by like a hawk on the wind.

Naudah, uncertain of just what it was she had to expect, threw herself into her work. Walks on Wind, her fingers no longer equal to the task, let her sharp tongue create the elaborately beaded wedding dress, with Naudah's fingers doing the work.

In the old woman's looking glass, even more faded than it had been ten years before, the young woman looked at herself and tried to see in the murky reflection some shadow of the girl she had been. The long blond hair was not as long, and much darker now. Her skin, exposed to a decade of searing sun on the Llano Estacado, was no longer fair. Burnt brown, she was not as dark as the Comanche women, but almost. Gone were the freckles that sprinkled her face and arms. Angel kisses, Granny Parker used to call them. And at the thought, she stopped looking at the mirror, let the hand holding it collapse into her lap. She found herself drifting back, wondering what had happened to them all.

But the reverie was too seductive for her to succumb to it without a struggle, and Walks on Wind seemed to know when the past was trying to pull Naudah back. She loved the girl who was a girl no longer, and knew that things had been indescribably painful for her, but, like all Comanche women, Walks on Wind lived in the present, because the past was dead and the future was too uncertain. The Great Spirit would provide or not, and, propitiations aside, there was little anyone could do about that. So, whenever Naudah started to drift like a broken reed on the currents of her memory, the old woman waded in, grabbed her by the arm, and hauled her back to shore.

And there was much to do. A wedding was no small thing, a wedding to a chief larger still. And when that chief was the leader on an entire band, as Peta Nocona was leader of the Noconi Comanche, no effort was too great. Naudah would benefit greatly by the match. She was young and strong, she was pretty, and turned more than her share of young men's heads. It was best for her if she were to get on with the business of being a woman.

And Walks on Wind was not disinterested, either. As the mother-in-law of the chief, more than a little benefit would flow to her. But it was the welfare of her adopted daughter which took the central place in her concerns. She had taught her much, perhaps even everything she knew, and that had been considerable. Unwilling at first, Naudah had shown a resilience that was uncommon, matched only by that of Black Feather in the old woman's experience. Now, it was time for all of that wisdom and learning to be put to good use, and the tipi of an old crone was no place for that. Naudah needed a home of her own, a man of her own, children of her own, while she was still young.

Watching Naudah, Walks on Wind knew that it was the best thing, but she understood the uncertainty, the reluctance that was not quite fear but not quite something else, either. More than once, she sailed away, an empty canoe tossed by swirling water, thinking of her own youth, her own husband, long since dead at the hands of Apache, somewhere in Mexico, and her own sons, victims of the Osage so long ago she could barely remember their faces when she wanted to, and could never chase them when they haunted her.

As they were finishing the wedding garment, she watched Naudah in silence for a long time. The beadwork was extensive and elaborate, and Walks on Wind explained the significance of the design, element by element, knowing that Naudah had her mind on anything but the placement of beads and bits of shell.

"You are worried," she said, and only the crackle of the fire answered her at first.

"No," Naudah said, her voice hoarse, the answer almost a question.

"Yes, you are. But that is all right. It is a big thing you are about to undertake. I know you are frightened. I was frightened. All women are. It is one thing to slip out of a tipi at night and lie in the grass with a boy. It is something else again to lie in a buffalo robe with a husband. But he is a good man, and he will treat you well."

"He always has. I'm not worried about that."

"Soon, you will teach your daughter the things I have taught you. And Peta Nocona will teach your son the things his father taught him."

"I don't know enough. I feel so empty, like everything that was in my head has gone away."

"Your head does not matter. It is your heart that matters. And your heart is large and full."

"I hope so."

She let the dress fall to the floor of the tipi and walked to where Walks on Wind was sitting in the shadows. Sitting by the old woman, she let her head collapse and felt the old woman's fingers in her hair. She thought back to the first time Walks on Wind had touched her, and she started to cry.

The old woman patted her back. "It will be over soon," she whispered.

Chapter 13 ═══════

Summer 1846

NOCONA LAY AWAKE, tossing restlessly, Naudah, now pregnant, lay beside him. Reluctant to ask what was on his mind, she propped herself up on an elbow and looked at him. His eyes were closed, but neither the movement of her body nor the pressure of her eyes on him made him aware of her presence. He opened his eyes and looked at her, blinking as if he had just come back from a long way away, someplace where his thoughts had occupied him fully.

"Why are you awake?" he asked.

"Because you are awake."

"You need sleep. It will not be long before the baby comes."

"Is that what you were thinking about? Were you wondering how he would compare to Little Calf?"

"No."

"You can tell me. I know you still think about

White Heron sometimes. It's natural that you would. I would want you to think about me sometimes if . . ."

"Stop!" he said, placing a finger to her lips. "I don't want to think about that. I couldn't bear to lose you. Not now, especially."

"So, then, tell me what you were thinking about."

"I . . . I was thinking that it would be a good idea to move the village. Farther from the Texans. I know a place, very pretty, deep in the Llano Estacado. Not even the Osage come there. It is Comanche land if any land is."

"It is a lot to ask of the people."

He nodded. "I know, but we have done it before. It is our way. You must know that by now."

"Yes, I do. But I would hate for them to think it was because of me."

"It isn't. It is just that I am worried. This war between the Mexicans and the Americans. I am afraid it will spill over into our land. And even if it doesn't, once it is over, whoever wins might decide that it is time to make war with the Comanche. They will have their soldiers and their weapons. They will be spoiling for a fight, and we will be handy. It is a dangerous time."

"Then I think we should move."

"I do, too." He lay back and closed his eyes.

"That was easy," she said.

He swatted her on the hip. "It is always easy to help someone else make a decision. Not so easy when the decision is your own to make."

"Sometimes I think you just like to exaggerate how hard it is to be chief."

He laughed. "I wish it was something I could control."

"I'm sorry, I didn't mean to make fun. It's just that sometimes I worry about you. You have so much on your mind."

"Sometimes I think that is what separates us from the horse and the buffalo. Sometimes I think how nice it would be to *be* a buffalo, and worry about nothing. They roam around wherever they want, and if a Comanche comes along, then the buffalo fights or runs. If the Comanche catches him, that's the end of it. If not, he roams wherever he wants again, until the next time. But in between he doesn't worry. He doesn't even know the Comanche is there when he doesn't see one. But I know the Mexicans are there, and the Americans and the Osage and the Apache. And sometimes I wish they weren't."

"Tomorrow, we will go wherever we want to, and we won't worry about the Mexicans or the Osage. We will worry about the baby. That will be enough to worry about, don't you think?"

He grunted.

And they moved.

The tipis were disassembled, the lodgepoles converted to travois, and everything packed. It took just a few hours for everything the village owned to be loaded, and by early afternoon, the Comanche were on the move. Men, women, and children were mounted, the younger boys given responsibility for the extra horses. The warriors were divided into three groups, one small contingent sent on ahead to scout territory and make sure there were no surprises. Another group was sent to the rear to guard against attack from that quarter, and the remainder stayed with the main band, keeping to the outer edges of the caravan for defensive purposes. Like most plains war chiefs, Nocona also sent men to either flank.

The hundreds of travois gouged tracks in the earth and tore up some sod, leaving a plain track for anyone but a blind man to follow. In addition, the hundreds of horses kicked up a considerable cloud of dust which would hang in the warm, nearly motionless air of early summer. The cloud could be seen for miles, and with enemies on every side, only a fool would think his passage would be overlooked by warriors in the area.

But the move, which took several days, went off without a hitch, and as Naudah crested the last rise before the intended campsite, she saw something that took her breath away. The Laguna Sabinas lay below, its deceptively blue waters bitter with alkali. But the valley surrounding the huge lake was covered with flowers. Even in the desertlike atmosphere, the mingled fragrance of buttercups and violets and bluebonnets was strong, disguising the dryness that smelled of brittle grass and seed hulls.

She looked at Nocona, who smiled. She was

pleased with the campsite, and he was glad.
With the baby coming, her mind would be on a
hundred things, and he wanted the surroundings
to be as pleasant as possible.

Everyone rushed into the valley, eager to
establish the new village. The travois were
unloaded then disassembled, the poles recon-
verted to frames for the lodges. By early
evening, the camp looked as permanent as if it
had been there for a year.

And it was time for Naudah to prepare the
birthing lodge. That evening, she walked in the
meadows above the laguna until she found the perfect spot, a little hill away from the village, grass
covered and overlooking the vast lake.

First thing in the morning, she began to super-
vise construction, several women assisting her. It
was like the other lodges, but smaller, since it
served a single purpose and would not be
required to house anyone once the baby arrived.

Inside, a bed of buffalo skins she had scraped
and prepared especially for this purpose occupied the middle of the floor. On either side, at
the head of the birthing bed, a stake had been
driven into the ground and leather loops
attached. During the hours of labor, she would
take hold of the loops and pull to facilitate the
delivery.

Once her labor began, two women accompanied her to the lodge, to render whatever assistance might prove necessary. There was much to
do. Cloths and warm water to bathe the newborn

had to be readied, drinking water and meals for the attendants had to be brought in. No one knew how long it would take.

Nocona stayed in his lodge, sometimes smoking, sometimes getting up to pace nervously. He had been through this before, but it was as if it were the first time. He tried to occupy his mind with his responsibilities, but at the moment, no responsibility was more important than that of expectant father. Friends tried to keep him busy. Black Snake told stories of Nocona in his youth, amusing everyone but the chief, who seemed too distracted even to hear them.

It was near nightfall when Naudah's attendants rushed in, bearing what appeared to be a ball of fur. Inside it, as everyone knew, was the infant.

"A son," one of the women shouted, handing the bundle to Nocona, who gingerly unwrapped it to see the red face and wrinkled fists of the baby, its eyes squeezed shut.

Holding the baby aloft, its arms waving from the fur blanket, Nocona paid thanks to the Great Spirit. Relieved, overwhelmed, his head swimming, he burst into the most brilliant smile anyone could remember, and handed the baby back to the attendants to return it to Naudah. As soon as they were gone, he went outside to decorate the wall of his lodge with the large black spot that proclaimed the birth of a son.

Now there was the business of a name, and he made arrangements for a medicine man to come to the lodge the following morning.

As the sun rose, Nocona, with the significant chiefs and warriors of the band in a semicircle around the fire and the new baby on a buffalo robe between them, he waited for the arrival of the medicine man. In ceremonial dress, the shaman entered the lodge. He acknowledged the newborn, then got down to business.

Facing the place of the rising sun, he paid meticulous attention to his ceremonial pipe, packing it carefully, lighting it and making sure that it would stay lit. When he was finally ready and Nocona's eternity of waiting had ended at last, the medicine man took a deep drag on the sacred pipe and expelled the smoke toward the east. He repeated the procedure three more times, each time turning to a different cardinal point on the compass before spouting a plume of smoke.

Passing the pipe to Nocona, he bent over the child, lifted him and presented him in turn to each of the compass points, starting with the east. And to each direction he announced, "His name shall be Quanah. One day, like his father, he may become a great chief, with the blessing of the Great Spirit."

The name, chosen by Naudah, meant Fragrance, and he was named in homage to the flower-laden scent of the valley in which he was born. When the ceremony was over, Quanah was taken back to his mother, and the medicine man left the chief and his friends to their celebration.

Nocona, bursting with pride, hosted a feast for

the men, who not only were the elite of the village, but the men on whom he most depended to defend it. Black Snake, as Nocona's closest friend, so close they thought of each other as brothers, had a special place in the feasting, and led the dance of celebration that began at sundown.

Nocona, as was his custom, was sedate, even restrained, at the dance. He missed Naudah, and was counting the hours until she would return to his lodge after the prescribed period of separation.

When the dancing was over, and he was alone in his lodge, he lay awake staring at the stars under the sides of the tipi, rolled to let the cool air circulate. Shadows and memories, the distant echoes of another infant's cries, the murky face of another son, seemed to drift in and out of the lodge.

He remembered what it had been like to play with Little Calf. He found himself reliving the swim they had taken that last day before the raid into Mexico. And he started to cry.

Ignoring the tears, he sat up and left the lodge, walking out into the village and heading to a hill overlooking the lake. When he reached the crest, and felt sufficiently alone, he let it all flood. The tears streamed down his cheeks, and he fell to his knees, his fists clenched and hammering at the ground.

Over and over, in the deepest recesses of his head and heart, the same words kept repeating, until they sounded like thunder. "Nothing will hurt you. Nothing will hurt you. Nothing will hurt you."

He didn't know where the words came from. They were not a promise, because he was too wise a man to think he could deliver such a guarantee. And yet, there was no one else there. The words were his own. He looked up at the stars then, letting his clenched fists relax. Breathing deeply, overwhelmed by the night fragrance swirling around him on a cool, stiff breeze, he rubbed at his temples, then pressed his fingertips against his aching eyes.

Aloud now, he heard the words once more. "Nothing will hurt you." And he realized this time that the voice was his own.

And he meant to make the words true.

Chapter 14

QUANAH SPENT THE FIRST SIX MONTHS of his life in a cradle board most of his waking hours. Wherever Naudah went, Quanah went with her. When she bent over the skins, he was propped up nearby. When she went to the river to swim or bathe, he dangled from a nearby tree. When she went for a walk, he was strapped to her back. And all the while she talked to him, telling him everything she was doing, not knowing whether he understood her or not, but talking all the same, thinking that everything she told him would one day sink in, and shape his life, perhaps even save it.

When he was not away on a raid against the Texans, who were getting more and more aggressive, Peta Nocona spent time with his son. They would play on the buffalo robes on the floor of the lodge. Still given to solitary walks, Nocona often brought the boy with him, hoisting him high into the air and dropping him onto his shoulders as if they were a saddle, holding the tiny feet in his hands as he climbed a hill or ducked under a tree limb in the thick forest of the Cross-Timbers, the tongue of pine forest that licked at the center of Texas, south and east of the Llano Estacado.

Increasingly, the Comanche were pressured by western expansion, and spent less and less time away from the Llano, where they were safe and where their superior horsemanship, endurance, and knowledge of the forbidding terrain gave them the kind of security they could have nowhere else.

The boy looked like a Comanche, his skin copper, his hair black. Only the blue-gray eyes revealed his mixed heritage. But it was in biology only. Naudah was thoroughly a Comanche now, hating the Texans with all the fervor of the other Comanche women. She understood their ways as if she had been born to them, riding as well as any of the squaws. She knew as much about the buffalo as anyone, and knew as well how to prepare the meat for drying, how to pound and soften it, then add ground nuts and berries, pounding them in with stone to make pemmican. She knew what roots were edible, which ones helped to heal wounds, which ones could be stored for long periods of time and which had to be eaten immediately. She knew where the best berries grew and how to mix buffalo marrow and mesquite to make a pleasing dessert.

She was Comanche through and through now,

her language, her Anglo past no more than misty
shadows. And Quanah, as the son of a chief, was
destined to be more Comanche still.

By the time he was able to sit up by himself,
Naudah took him on her horse, sitting him on its
neck as she rode. Like most of the Comanche
women, she had learned early how to ride, partly
out of a spirit of adventure and mostly as a skill
to master because one day it might mean the difference between life and death.

Because Nocona was often away from the village, sometimes for weeks, even months at a
time, much of Quanah's education fell to the old
men of the camp. They were repositories of trib-
al history, and their tales held the boys spell-
bound. Almost every night, summer and winter,
a few of the old men would gather in a lodge,
surrounded by the young boys, who were so
quiet one wondered whether they were even
breathing as they hung on every word. Only
when a story was done did they explode into a
storm of questions, begging for another story or
an amplification of the one they'd just heard.
Quanah seemed even more eager than most of
the others.

They seemed to like best stories about the
ancient days, when the Comanche lived in the
plains of the north, where there were high mountains. They were not Comanche then, but
Shoshone, and they hunted buffalo on the grass-
rich plains where the weather was not so hot and
there was cool water everywhere. But those days

were long gone, and not even the grandfathers of the old ones had been alive when the Comanche lived there.

All that was left was the language. Even now, the boys were told, the Shoshone and the Comanche spoke the same language, no matter where they might meet one another. But now the Comanche lived where the earth was thirsty all the time, where the sun came too close and stayed too long, making even the strongest Comanche sometimes walk with his tongue like a strip of buffalo hide in his parched mouth, and his body shriveling in the heat like an old berry forgotten in a parfleche.

And after every such story, it was always Quanah who wanted to know why the Comanche no longer lived where the Shoshone lived, or why they didn't go back where the air was cool and the grass long and thick. But that was something not even the wisest of the old ones knew, and Quanah was left to wonder until the next time.

Sometimes, during the long summer days, he would seek out one of the old men and beg for a story just for him, and the old man, Blue Cloud, who was the best storyteller and Quanah's favorite, would oblige him, sometimes sitting right there in the open lodge, sometimes taking the boy by the hand and walking down to the river, where they could sit under a cottonwood out of the scalding sun. Then, slowly, choosing his words carefully, Blue Cloud would weave

another fabulous web, a gnarled spider spinning words to catch the imagination.

Quanah would lie on his back, his eyes fixed
on the leaves overhead or a far-off hawk drifting
silently on the wind so high it was little more
than a black speck against the summer glare.

Blue Cloud was careful, because he knew
that Quanah would one day become a leader of
the people, and it was important that a leader
not have his head full of nonsense. History was
a precious thing, the only way one could learn
to avoid the mistakes of the past. And, as both
the Great Spirit and Blue Cloud knew, there
were enough pitfalls and blind alleys to trick
the wisest of men. It would never do to have
Quanah's head stuffed full of milkweed and
dead leaves.

But the best times were those with Peta
Nocona. When he was home, the chief would
take his son on long walks, pointing out the track
of a deer, the small prints of a single rabbit in the
dirt, the trace of a rattlesnake as it slithered
across a patch of dust. There was so much to
learn, Nocona doubted he would ever have the
time to teach it all. When he thought back over
his own life, how everything he learned seemed
to spawn a dozen questions, and each answer a
dozen more, he despaired of teaching it all to
Quanah.

But the boy was a quick study, and the questions he asked showed that not only did he
understand what he had already been told, he

was thinking about the next step and the one after that. He seemed able to connect things together, following the logic of a situation the way many full-grown men were unable to do. It made Nocona proud, and more than a little frightened. The boy seemed to understand things far beyond his years.

But he pushed on, spending as much spare time as he could squeeze out of the clutter of his daily life to be with the boy and, after a couple of years, with Pecos, Quanah's younger brother.

One morning in late summer, when Quanah was six years old, Peta Nocona woke him early. Pressing a finger to his lips, he shushed for the boy to be quiet, then waved toward the entrance of the lodge. The fire was almost out, and there was a morning chill in the air that made Quanah reluctant to leave the warmth of his sleeping robes. But when his father called, he knew better than to drag his feet.

Once he was certain Quanah was awake, Nocona slipped outside, where he waited patiently for his son. When the boy appeared, still rubbing sleep from his eyes with his knuckles, his face was full of questions, but he said not a word, watching Nocona to see what would happen next.

Nocona walked away from the lodge, waving again for Quanah to follow him. The boy hurried to catch up, not sure where he was going but starting to get excited. This had never happened before, and he knew it had to be something special.

Beyond the edge of the village, Quanah saw Nocona's horse, hobbled and ready. Beside it, a second one, smaller, also hobbled, and fitted with a small saddle pad and a third. Running to catch up to Nocona, Quanah grabbed onto his father's hand.

"Where are we going, Father?"

"You'll see."

"Does Mother know?"

Nocona nodded. "She knows."

"Will we be gone long?"

Nocona shook his head. "Not long, I hope."

"Where, then?"

Hoisting the boy up onto the small horse, he bent to unhobble it, then did the same to the other two horses. He climbed onto his mount before answering. Taking the tether rope of the third horse in his hand, he eased in alongside Quanah. "I thought it was time you learned to hunt."

"But I don't have a bow."

"There is much to learn about hunting before you ever get to notch an arrow. You will have a bow in good time. Now, you are old enough to learn the other things, the important things that every good hunter has to learn if he is going to find the game to shoot with his bow. That's what we will do today."

"Why so early?"

"The deer don't move around much under the hot sun. They make their appearance either

early, while it is still cool, or toward sundown,
after the worst of the day's heat has passed."

"Is that what we'll be hunting? Deer?"

Nocona nodded, then broke into a broad grin.
"That's right."

"Why didn't Mother come, too?"

"She has her own work. Hunting is something
men do. They provide food for the village, and
others prepare it. It is a way of making sure that
no one has more to do than he can do."

They moved away from the village in the
predawn gray. The last few stars were all but
invisible, and the air smelled damp. The grass
showered small drops of dew as the hooves of
the three horses moved through it.

"Where do we look for the deer, Father?"

"They will be coming for water, soon. We will
find a creek where they like to drink, and we
will wait for them. The best way to hunt a deer
is to get where he's going before he does. Let
him come to you. If you are very still, and make
no noise, he will come close and you can get an
arrow into him before he knows you are there.
But if he is already at the creek, then he will
hear you coming, unless you creep up on him
from a long way off. That takes time, and it
means you have to be too far from your horse.
No Comanche wants to be far from his war pony.
Even here."

They rode for more than an hour, Quanah ply-
ing his father with a thousand questions, his
quick mind skittering from fact to fact like a

surefooted frog hopping on lily pads.

Nocona reined in as the sun started to come up. It was just a mound of brilliant red on the horizon. In the valley below him, a creek meandered through a stand of cottonwoods and willows. The leaves of the trees were stained a bright ruby color by the first rays of the sun. Here and there through the trees, the sluggish creek was dyed red, the color winking like fireflies as the soft breeze stirred the tree limbs.

Nocona had hunted in the valley many times, and he knew it was a favorite watering hole for deer. Nudging his horse with his knees, he urged the boy to follow him over the hilltop and down toward the creek. Keeping a wary eye peeled for an early deer, he led the way to the water, urged the horse into the creek and out on the far side, then followed the tree line, just skirting the thick brush under the cottonwoods.

He seemed to be looking for something in particular and Quanah noticed.

"What are you looking for?" he asked.

"A good place to leave the horses. We will have to dismount so that we can get close enough. The horses will frighten the deer if we bring them with us."

"But you said a Comanche never leaves his horse."

"I said a Comanche never gets too far from his horse. But if we want to have venison, we will have to hunt the deer on foot."

When he found the spot he was looking for, he swung down lightly, his feet hitting the tall grass without a sound. Quanah slid from his pony, making a small thump that brought Nocona's disapproving gaze to rest on him for a moment. "Sorry," the boy said.

"It's a good thing you are not fat like Black Snake's son, or the deer would hear you in the next valley." But he laughed, and ran a hand through Quanah's hair. "It's all right. Just try to be more quiet, son."

They hobbled the horses again, then Nocona took a bow and a buckskin quiver full of new arrows from his horse and moved down to the water's edge. Quanah followed him, reaching up to take the quiver from Nocona's hand. "I want to help," he said. "If I can't use the bow, at least I can carry the arrows."

Nocona smiled. "You are always thinking, aren't you?" he said.

Quanah nodded eagerly. "Always."

"Good. Our people will need someone who is always thinking to lead them."

"You are always thinking."

"But one day I won't be here. And you will have to take my place."

The boy didn't want to hear such things spoken of, and changed the subject. "Will there be many deer?"

"Probably. But we only want one. Two, if we are lucky. We don't need more than that."

"But there are many people in the village."

"There are many warriors to hunt, too."

"But some people cannot hunt for themselves. Someone has to hunt for them. Grandmother Walks on Wind does not hunt."

Nocona held a finger to his lips. "I'll explain that some other time. Right now, we have to be quiet and start looking for the deer."

Chapter 15

Summer 1851

THEY WERE QUIET for a long time. Quanah was
starting to get restless, and each time he would
start to move, Nocona would tap him on the
shoulder and put a finger to his lips. Leaning
over after the fifth or sixth time, he pressed his
lips close to Quanah's ear. "You have to be still,"
he said. "Or the deer won't come."

Mimicking his father's gesture, Quanah whispered, "The deer aren't going to come anyway.
They will never come. And even if they do, they
take too long."

Nocona laughed in spite of himself. He knew
just how hard won was the patience necessary to
stay and wait for the skittish animals. And he
knew, too, that unless Quanah learned it, everything else he learned would be as good as worthless. Patience is the simplest of things, he
thought, but the hardest to understand.

But Quanah tried hard to be still. And soon he

sensed Nocona growing tense. He wanted to ask what was happening, but knew it was a bad time to ask anything, so he craned his head trying to see through the brush across to the other side of the creek. He strained his ears, but all he could hear was the hiss of the breeze in the cottonwood leaves and the burble of the water where it flowed over some stones.

But Nocona maintained his vigilance, and Quanah struggled with his own impatience. Soon, Nocona reached for his bow, took an arrow from the quiver and notched it, then took a second arrow and clamped it in his teeth, where he could get at it in a hurry. Turning to Quanah, he made the sign for deer, and for five. Quanah wanted to shout, but bit his tongue.

Soon, he heard the dull thud of hooves on the grass across the creek, then the rattle of brush as something pushed through the undergrowth. Twisting sideways, he could see upstream for nearly twenty yards, but there was still no sign of the animals.

Nocona shifted his position now, getting comfortable on one knee. A sharp crack echoed among the trees, and a deer stepped through the brush and stopped, its head cocked. Quanah held his breath and Nocona leaned forward drawing the bow at the same time. Waiting for the deer to expose itself fully, he held the bow at half draw.

The deer looked around, its ears twitching, took a tentative step forward, and a second appeared behind it. The lead animal was a good-sized buck, its antlers sporting eight points. Its eyes were like wet pebbles in the shadows, catching a glint of early sunlight as it swiveled its head, then it stepped all the way into the clear.

The second animal, following its lead, moved into the open, and suddenly two more broke through, a young buck and another doe. Quanah kept looking from Nocona to the deer and back, waiting for his father to shoot, wondering why he didn't.

Finally, as if in response to some inaudible cue, all four were lined up at the water's edge, their heads bowed. Quanah heard the tongues lapping the cool water and suddenly Nocona drew the bow all the way, loosed an arrow and whipped the one from his teeth and notched it in a single fluid motion.

The first arrow struck home, catching the big buck below the left shoulder and burying itself all the way to the fletching. The buck fell as if it had been pole-axed and the second arrow was on its way, the bowstring singing in the shadows. The second target, the larger of the two does, was hit in the chest as she turned. The buck went to its knees with a curious noise that sounded like a cough, its head bobbing as it tried to figure out what had happened to it.

The brush exploded as the remaining deer bolted across the creek, their hooves splashing in the water, and in a flash they were gone.

But Nocona had aimed well. His two targets lay on the creek bank, the buck already dead, the doe struggling to get to her feet. The chief snatched a third arrow from his quiver, nearly tugging it from Quanah's hands, notched it, and let it fly. Again the bowstring hummed, and this time Quanah heard the thud of the arrow as it drove deeply into the doe. She made a strange cry, took a step and then collapsed into the water.

Nocona grunted with satisfaction, then stepped out from his cover, Quanah right behind him. Wading in the creek, the older man walked to the nearer of his two kills. The buck was staring vacantly, its head stretched out on the grass, its hindquarters still quivering. Turning to his son, Nocona said, "Run and get the horses."

He watched as Quanah slipped through the underbrush and disappeared, then turned to the business of butchering. Drawing his knife, he knelt on the sandy bank and started the grisly work.

By the time Quanah returned, the horses tethered together and following in his wake, the water was red with blood. The buck had already been gutted, and Nocona was working on the doe. Quanah turned away, but couldn't help peeking over his shoulder to watch Nocona eviscerate the doe. Normally, he would have brought the entire carcass home, but he didn't want to overburden the pack horse. The liver was a delicacy, and he would pack it separately, using a parfleche he'd brought for the purpose.

"We'll have plenty of meat," he said, grunting as he bent over the limp form of the doe.

He wiped his knife on the grass, then dipped it into the current and swished it clean before drying it on the grass and tucking it back into its sheath.

The carcasses were heavy, but Nocona handled them easily, his broad back and shoulders taking the heavy load easily as he hoisted the buck onto the pack horse. He lashed it in place with buckskin thongs, then did the same with the doe. Together, the two deer made for a heavy load, but he had chosen the pack horse carefully, and didn't want to ride double. If they ran into trouble, it would be better if he and Quanah had separate mounts. He could always hunt another deer, and cutting the pack horse loose would be a small price to pay for survival.

When the deer had been securely lashed, he turned to his son, who kept looking at the deer, then at his father, then at the swirls of blood still curling away from the clotted mound of viscera murkily visible under the surface of the creek.

Nocona patted him on the head. "Patience," he said. "That's the secret."

"Will we go home now?" Quanah asked.

Nocona nodded. "We don't want the meat to spoil, do we?"

"But the other deer got away."

"We don't need them. A good hunter always leaves some game for the next hunt."

"When we hunt the buffalo, we kill a lot more. Why not the deer?"

"We hunt the buffalo to feed ourselves all winter. Besides, there are many more buffalo than deer. You know that very well. You have seen the herds of buffalo, haven't you?"

"Yes."

"Have you ever seen that many deer at one time?"

The boy shook his head.

"There you are, then. Let's go."

Nocona hoisted the boy onto his horse, climbed onto his own mount, and nudged it through the brush and out into the broad, green valley. As they started up the gentle slope toward home, they were forced to move slowly, the pack horse laboring under its heavy load. Nocona was watchful. An enemy would see how slowly they were moving, and would know they were vulnerable to attack. Surprise would give the enemy a distinct advantage, and the worst he would have to show for his effort would be a pair of freshly killed deer and a good horse, reason enough to take on a solitary warrior and a small boy.

The sun was well on its way toward the meridian now, and the late morning was hot. The meadow was full of flowers, and there seemed to be a dozen bees for every bloom. The whole valley throbbed with the collective humming of a million tiny wings.

When they reached the ridge, Nocona stopped to scan the floor of the next valley. Like the one behind, it was full of bluebonnets, but there was no creek and no cottonwood stand. That meant there was little cover, small enough problem if they hadn't been hampered by their catch. Satisfied the valley was deserted, Nocona started down, turning to wave for Quanah to follow him, when he spotted something moving among the trees near the creek.

At first, he thought it might have been more deer, coming late, waiting until the interlopers had left. But he wasn't sure, and he couldn't afford not to be. Tilting his head toward the valley ahead, he said, "You go on." Handing the lead rope of the pack horse to Quanah, he realized the boy wouldn't be able to hold it if the pack horse bolted, and fashioned a quick loop in the long lead and draped it over the neck of Quanah's pony.

"What's the matter, Father?"

Before Quanah could answer, a sharp crack shattered the stillness. A moment later, three horses burst through the underbrush along the creek, and Nocona yanked on the pack horse's lead, swung it free of Quanah's pony, and slapped its rump with the free end. To Quanah, he shouted, "Ride. Ride home. I'll follow you as soon as I can."

"But what . . . ?"

Taking the bow from his shoulder and jerking an arrow from his quiver, he snapped, "Do it!"

As soon as he was sure Quanah had obeyed, Nocona turned his horse and notched the arrow. The three horsemen were charging uphill straight toward him. They were Anglos, probably Texans, and he saw immediately that all three were armed with rifles. The one who had fired the shot was trying to reload on horseback, not the easiest thing to do, and he was lagging a bit behind. The other two men were waving their rifles and shouting.

He wondered how long they had been watching him, then, knowing it didn't matter, he drew the bow. The first arrow sailed long, and he quickly notched a second at the same time he kicked his pony and started downhill toward the attackers.

A second rifle shot cracked the silence, and Nocona heard the whistle of the bullet as it sailed past his head, high and to the left. More used to firing from horseback, the chief had a slight advantage. He could also fire several arrows for every bullet from the clumsy muzzle loaders, but there were three of them, and the men probably had pistols, as well.

His next arrow struck the lead horse dead center in the chest, and the horse broke stride, stumbled and fell, spilling its rider over its mane. The man shouted something, rolled over several times and scrambled to his feet as his companion fired.

Once more the bullet sang nearby, and the unhorsed rider tugged at his waistband. Nocona drew the bow once more, this time holding for a split second to be sure of his aim. He heard the moist whack of the arrow as it struck the white man in the ribs. He was using hunting arrows, rather than war arrows, and the placement of the arrowhead made it harder to find a gap in the ribs, but this one managed. The man fell backward, his hand clutching at the arrow half buried in his left side.

The man in the rear had reloaded now, and Nocona watched the bobbing muzzle of the long gun as the attacker tried to hold his aim. The other horseman was still charging ahead, and Nocona jerked the bridle of his mount and dashed downhill at an angle, causing the charging men to turn and disrupting their aim . . . but not his own.

Launching a fourth arrow, he saw it narrowly miss the nearer of the two horsemen, who ducked sidewise as it flew past close enough to scrape his shoulder with its feathered fletching. Another arrow and another, neither finding a mark, and another gunshot.

Nocona was downhill now, circling around behind. The two survivors were trying to wheel their mounts, but the big American horses were less maneuverable. The slope didn't help matters, and Nocona was now on their tails, urging the pony back uphill, an arrow drawn all the way to the head. He let it go and saw it strike one of the men in the biceps and pin the arm to his body as it pierced the fleshy part of the arm and burrowed on into the right side of his chest.

Instinctively, the man jerked his arm and yelped in pain as the arrow came free, tearing a hunk of flesh loose with its barbs. It flapped now as the man waved his wounded arm, snapped the arrow off with a shriek of rage, then jerked it free, sending the blood-smeared shaft in a tumbling arc as he tossed it away.

Nocona already had another arrow nocked, drew and fired in one fluid movement as his pony narrowed the gap. Preoccupied with his wound, the man looked surprised when the second arrow hit him, this time dead on, just below the collarbone on the left side. He fell backward off his horse, his lips pursed as if to shape a question. But he said nothing as he fell, then let out a whoosh of air as he landed flat on his back, just in time to receive a third arrow as Nocona galloped past. This one pinned him to the earth.

The third man had already turned tail, but Nocona thundered after him, drawing his bow once more. He held the arrow at full draw until fifty yards became forty, then thirty. Only when he had closed to within twenty yards did he snap the string.

The arrow struck bone with an audible crack as it shattered a shoulder blade and knocked the last of the three attackers from his horse. Nocona closed hard, leaping from his horse and drawing his knife while in the air. The man lay on his stomach and was crawling through the grass, one hand curled around the arrow shaft, his legs and remaining arm clawing, making him look like a crippled insect.

Nocona landed on the man's back with his knees, snapping the arrow as he grabbed the man by a fistful of greasy hair and hauled the head back far enough to jerk the knife once across the exposed throat. The taut tendons parted with dull snaps and a horrible gurgle gushed in a spume of bloody froth from the severed windpipe. Slicing once more, Nocona lifted the scalp, jumped to his feet and held the bloody flap of skin and hair high overhead as he shrieked in triumph.

Moving quickly, he raced on foot to another of the attackers, took a second scalp, then darted toward the third body. He had the hair in his hand and the knife poised when something caught his eye on the ridge. He looked up then, frozen, to see Quanah watching. He looked down at his victim, hesitated a moment longer, then took the scalp.

This time, though, there was no shriek of triumph. Only a grunt of grim satisfaction.

Chapter 16

Summer 1858

TEXAS WAS VAST, so vast that the Comanche had been relatively secure in the Llano Estacado. They had been free to wage their kind of war, lightning-fast raids on small settlements, isolated homesteads, the occasional wagon train on the way down the Santa Fe trail. But their own haunts had been relatively free from intrusion except for an occasional raid by a small band of Texans. Although treaties had been signed, and the U.S. Army had received permission in those treaties to establish military posts, the army presence had been all but nonexistent.

But 1858 would be the year that would see all that change. Fed up with the incessant raids, frustrated by the Comanches' ability to strike where and when they pleased and to escape unpunished into the huge, barren void of the Llano, Texans set up a clamor that finally

caught the ear of newly elected Governor
Hardin Runnels. Anxious to please his con-
stituents, he appointed John R. Ford, known to
one and all as "Rip," the supreme commander
of the Texas Rangers, with the rank of senior
captain. Ford was given the authority to raise a
company of a hundred tested men, orders to
wage the war his way, and instructions to punish the Comanche and drive them out of Texas
if possible.

Not one to take so daunting a challenge
lightly, Rip Ford set to work immediately,
exchanging frequent letters with the governor
to make sure that his orders were explicit and
unequivocal, and to ensure that support would
be unwavering. Too often in the past, as Ford
well knew, outrage sputtered out like an
untended fire, and men hastily dispatched to
the field found themselves suddenly cut adrift,
wage commitments revoked, supplies short or
unavailable and support withered and blown
away even before the enemy had been sighted.
Rip was determined that wouldn't happen
again, not this time, and sure as hell not to
him.

Particular to the point of fussiness in his
choice of Rangers, and intent on doing things
right if at all, he made his selections quickly, but
not hastily. By midspring he was ready to go. But
Ford knew that his chances of finding the
Comanche would be considerably enhanced if he
had the benefit of Indian assistance, particularly

with tracking, and he arranged for a contingent
of Tonkawa, numbering more than a hundred,
under the leadership of their chief, Placido, to
join the expedition. The Indian Agent, Ranger
Capt. Lawrence Sullivan Ross, better known as
"Sul," had used his good offices with the
Tonkawa, and his son, Shapley, also a Ranger
captain, was given command of the Indian
forces.

The Tonkawa were mortal enemies of the
Comanche, having been driven out of their lands
by the latter as they drifted south and east from
their original hunting grounds in Colorado. The
Comanche also believed the Tonkawa were can-
nibals, with some reason, and despised them as
they did no other Indian enemies, even the hated
Osage and Apache.

The expedition started up the Brazos River
heading toward Comanche lands, picking up volunteers on the way, angry ranchers and their
hands who over the years had lost thousands of
head of cattle and horses, and more than a few
friends, to the marauding bands of Quohada,
Noconi and Peneteka Comanche.

The punitive force was well supplied and
borrowed more than a little determination from
Rip Ford, who was no more tolerant of failure in
others than in himself. Tonkawa scouts were
sent out well in advance of the main force, with
orders to gather as much intelligence as possible
but not to tip the Comanche as to what was
coming.

Cutting toward the Red River, Ford led his men along the western edge of the Wichita mountains then heading toward the Canadian River and the Antelope Hills, a favorite Comanche camping and hunting ground not far from the Indian Territory border with Texas.

The hills were an ideal defensive position, and the big U-shaped bend of the Canadian River gave them plenty of water and provided a defensive perimeter behind which the Comanche would retreat after a raid into Mexico or eastern Texas. It was to this region that the raiders brought their Mexican captives, of which they had more than a few, and where the stolen horses, cattle and mules were herded. The livestock was often used in trade with other tribes, especially the cattle, which were less highly prized than good horses.

Believing themselves secure in their stronghold, the Comanche were unaware of the approaching army. On May 11, two scouts reported the presence of a large band of Comanche, and Ford sent Anglo spotters out to check on the reports. Establishing a camp on the Washita headwaters, Ford rode out in the company of Ross and several Tonkawa. From a high ridge, they watched as a small hunting party of warriors chased a small herd of buffalo in a valley dead ahead. He had found his quarry. Now all he had to do was run them to ground.

Ford returned to camp, already intent on launching an attack at sunrise the following morning. He still hadn't seen the main Comanche village, and had no knowledge of which band it belonged to. But to Ford, such distinctions were arbitrary and, in the present circumstances, beside the point. Comanche were raiding Texas ranches, and Comanche would pay the price. He knew enough about them to know that they all hated Texans, and made a distinction between Texans and Americans. The Peneteka had honored their treaties with the Americans, but believed Texans were different, worse than the hated Mexicans, and neither party to the treaties nor deserving of their protection.

Up well before sunrise, Ford was giving his plans one final consideration and apprising Shapley Ross of his responsibilities. Satisfied that everything was in order, Ford gave the order to move out, and two hundred and fifteen men, red and white, began their march. Ford wanted to strike just at sunrise, when light would be sufficient to distinguish between Comanche and Tonkawa, but just to make certain, had instructed Ross to keep his Tonkawa force to the left, and made sure that the Rangers knew of the deployment.

Approaching through a shallow valley, the Rangers found a small camp, only five tipis, and immediately launched a surprise attack. In the one-sided confrontation, the lodges were burned and several Comanche killed or captured, but two warriors managed to escape and raced ahead to warn the main camp of the impending assault.

Ford followed as quickly as he could, and when his forces crested the last rise before the Comanche village, he held his breath for a moment. He said later it was the most beautiful Indian village he had ever seen. The tipis, some bleached nearly white by the sun, others still the soft beige of more recently prepared skins, some splashed with bright color, lay in perfect symmetry under the rising sun.

The Noconi, under the chief Pohebits Quasho, were ready and waiting. The old chief, whose name meant Iron Jacket, possessed a full set of Spanish armor, which he donned for the occasion, and in which he had implicit faith. Backed by dozens of warriors, he approached the deployed Rangers and Tonkawa, taunting the latter with insults and challenging them to single combat.

Unable to resist the challenge, several of the Tonkawa broke ranks and moved into the open. Like the Comanche, they were in full regalia, brightly smeared with bands of red, yellow, blue, black, and green paint, the feathers fixed to their bows, shields and lances fluttering in the morning breeze.

Ford and Ross watched with mouths agape, almost unable to comprehend what they were seeing. Time and again, a pair of warriors, one

Comanche and one Tonkawa, would goad their
mounts and charge headlong, lances lowered,
and earsplitting war cries shattering the morning
stillness. Beyond the combatants, women and
children were retreating while the rest of the
Comanche, following Iron Jacket's lead, arrayed
themselves in a defensive wall between their
families and their enemies.

As yet another pair of warriors closed, Ford
said, "For God's sake, Ross, it's like something
out of medieval times. Like knights in shining
armor."

Sensing that the advantage of surprise was
rapidly dissipating, he ordered a volley, and the
sudden sputtering of pistols and rifles drowned
out the thunder of hooves. Designed to ward off
the blows of swords, the armor failed and Iron
Jacket, riddled with rifle balls, fell to the ground.
As if the old man's death had been a signal, the
Rangers and Tonkawa charged ahead, and the
Comanche warriors rushed into the field to
avenge him.

The initial attack was furious, and the
Comanche, armed only with their traditional
weapons, were seriously disadvantaged. Their
bows were no good at long range against the far
more accurate, and far more deadly, rifle fire of
the Rangers. Iron Jacket's replacement knew
instinctively that the best he could hope for was
to cover the retreat of the women and children,
raced back and forth along the line of battle,
shouting instructions to the warriors, command-

ing them to hold as long as they could.

Slowly but surely, the Comanche retreated under the unrelenting pressure. Soon their backs were against their lodges. The retreat of the women and children was paramount, and the Comanche fought valiantly, trying to hold the better-armed attackers and sending runners to nearby camps for reinforcements.

One of the runners reached Peta Nocona's camp, four miles away, with the news that the Texans had come, and that Iron Jacket had been killed. Nocona was now the principal chief of the Noconi band, and he started rallying his warriors. Quanah, not quite thirteen years old, was one of the first on his pony, and in a matter of minutes, nearly five hundred warriors had assembled and followed Nocona out of the village, leaving just a small detachment behind for defense.

Ford, sensing that he had the upper hand, pressed his advantage, driving the Comanche back through their camp and beginning to lay waste to the lodges. Some of his men split off and began to torch the tipis while the balance continued pursuit, as women and children, unable to get to the horses, most of which had been driven off by the Tonkawa, fled on foot, leaving everything behind.

Bodies lay everywhere, almost all of them Comanche, and more than a few of them women and children. In the hail of arrows, the Rangers were not particular about their targets. If something moved, it drew a bullet.

Smoke started to fill the valley as the lodges and supplies burned, settling just above the ridge line in a dark gray pall.

Resistance had all but vanished a little after noon, and Ford, reluctant to push too far from his camp, called his men back. The Tonkawa were less willing than the Rangers to respond to the order to stand down, but exhaustion made them tractable enough that Placido and Ross were able to get them in line.

Taking a breath, Ford looked over the campsite and gave orders for the few Texas wounded to be tended to. A small unit went through the village, picking its way among the burning lodges and scattered belongings, for a body count. Nearly seventy Comanche lay dead, while Ford had lost only two killed and a handful of wounded. The firepower he had at his command, coupled with the suddenness of the attack, had done its work.

But as he surveyed the ruins, a sergeant noticed something on a far ridge, and raced back to Ford. Taking field glasses, Ford looked in the direction the sergeant was pointing and saw more than five hundred Comanche massing for a counterattack.

Men and horses were exhausted, and Ford was unwilling to risk losing the advantage he had gained, but the Tonkawa were rowdy, and a few of them charged out to meet the newly arrived Comanche horde.

Nocona, seeing that there was little he could

do to punish the heavily armed Rangers, was reluctant to engage. But he couldn't turn his back and ride away, either. He led a charge downhill, and the Tonkawa turned tail, running under the umbrella of the Ranger rifles, then turning to taunt the Comanche with displays of bravado and shouted insults.

Ford, realizing that his men were perilously close to collapse after seven hours of incessant combat, decided to fall back and regroup. The men needed rest and food, and their ammunition was nearly exhausted.

Riding behind his father, Quanah watched as the Texans pulled out. He felt confused, knowing that Iron Jacket had fallen because he was a Comanche, that his father was now chief of all the Noconi Comanche, and that, like the men who had killed Iron Jacket, his mother was white. He felt as if a giant fist were squeezing him, trying to crush the breath from his lungs. He wanted to run and hide, or to charge blindly downhill into the muzzles of the Ranger rifles. But Nocona, sensing his son's confusion, ordered him to stay by his side.

For his part, Nocona felt his heart sink as he watched the burning lodges. This was what he had always feared. Not just a raid—a war, a war the way the white man made war. It had come for certain, just as he had always known it would, and there was no turning back.

Chapter 17 ═══════════

Autumn 1860

PETA NOCONA HELD UP HIS HAND, and Quanah
reined in beside him. Gesturing toward some
cottonwoods, Nocona nudged his horse into a
walk, and Quanah fell in behind him. The sun
was high overhead, but it was late in the year,
and the shadows long and pale.

Nocona slid from his pony, grabbed the bridle
and tugged it into the shade, tethering it to some
brush. He watched Quanah dismount, told his
son to tether his own mount, then walked
through the brush to sit beside the small creek
bordered by lush grass. Quanah followed him
through the brush and when he reached the
grassy bank, Nocona was already sitting down.
He patted the ground beside him.

"Sit," he said. He looked up at his older son,
realizing almost with shock how tall he had
become. And so soon.

Quanah was baffled, but did as his father told

him. He leaned toward the ground, felt it with one hand, then turned and looked at the sky for a second, almost as if he expected to find in the sky some explanation of his father's strange behavior.

"Is something wrong?" he asked, as he folded his long legs beneath him and lowered himself to the ground.

Nocona shrugged. "Everything is wrong," he said. He cleared his throat the way he always did before he spoke around the council fire, and Quanah knew something very serious was about to be discussed.

"I don't understand."

"It has not been easy for you, growing up not sure whether you were Comanche or Anglo."

"I haven't minded. You have been good to me. So has my mother. I don't think I would change anything, even if I could."

"That's easy to say now, but someday, not too far away, everything will be different. You know how the whites feel about the Comanche."

"But as long as we are free, what difference does it make what the white man thinks?"

"We might not always be free. Every year, there are more and more Texans. Up north, the whites are increasing like grasshoppers in summer, more and more and more . . . Soon, it will be the same way here."

"The whites don't want the Llano Estacado. There is nothing there for them. Life is hard for them where there is no water. They are not hunters like we are. They like to put down roots in one place, like a tree, and hang on even when the wind is strong. The Comanche knows when it is time to bend, to move, but the whites don't know. They are different."

"But every year, there are more of them. They want our land, and they will do anything to have it. That is why they are always putting their papers under the nose of some Indian, telling him to make his mark. They tell him the paper means one thing and then, after the Indian makes his mark, they tell him it means something else. It happened to the Keechi and to the Kickapoo. It happened to the Osage and the Tonkawa. It happened to the Peneteka Comanche, too. One day it will happen to us all. Because one day the choice will be to make a mark on the paper or die, and no man wants to die."

"No man wants to give away his land, either, Father. You taught me that if you taught me nothing else. I will never make a mark on the white man's paper. And neither will you. So what difference does it make how many papers he brings, or how many times he sticks the pen in an Indian's hand?"

"It is different now. When we fought against the Mexicans, they always ran. They ran from the Apache and the Comanche, because they were afraid. We fought them bravely and they went away. But these Anglos are different. You see how it is. They make their soldier forts, and their army comes. Once that happens, they don't go away."

"But . . ."

"Let me say what I want to say, Quanah. Still, you haven't learned the value of patience. You are like all the other young hotheads, sometimes."

"I'm sorry."

"I am getting old. The buffalo are getting scarce, and for every buffalo that goes away, three white men come in its place. Soon, there will be more white men than buffalo, and one day there will be more white men than all the buffalo that ever were."

"I don't believe that."

"It is so. When the Texans attacked the Penetka last summer, I understood that they would not rest until all the Comanche were dead or on a reservation. But you see what it is like on the reservation. You have seen how the agents lie and cheat and steal from the Indians. You have seen how the Cherokee and the Choctaw live, wearing white man clothes and living in white man houses. That is what it will be like for all of us one day. But I don't think I will live long enough to see it. At least I hope not."

"I won't either."

"I think you will. I think the time is not that far away. And I think you ought to give some thought to what it will be like when that day comes. You are young yet, and these are hard things to think about and to understand, but you have to start, because one day you will be a chief, and these questions will need your answers. I want you to think about these things and we will talk. And I want you to explain to Pecos, too, because when you are a chief, you will have to lean on him the way an old man leans on a stick. He will help you the way you will soon help me."

Quanah shook his head. "I understand," he said. "I will do anything you ask of me. You know that. I will even learn patience."

"Good. Now we should return to the village, because tomorrow we will be leaving on a hunt. We have to spend much more time looking for the buffalo now that the white man has started to kill them for their skins. But we will talk more while we are away. I don't like to talk about such things when your mother can hear. It upsets her."

Nocona got to his feet heavily, heaved a sigh, and stretched his arms, then bent at the waist to relieve the stiffness that increasingly plagued him. He looked at the creek for a long moment, bent to pick up a small twig lying in the grass and tossed it into the water. The impact made a splash, sending a sheet of translucent gold and ruby fanning out from the point of impact for a brief moment. When it was gone, the twig spun once on the current then started to move.

"You see that?" Nocona asked. "You see how that stick moves?"

Quanah nodded.

"The stick does not decide where it wants to go. The water decides and the stick goes because it has no choice. The water is like the white man flooding into our land, and we are like that stick."

"I don't believe that," Quanah argued.

"Neither does the stick," Nocona said, with a sad smile. "But it is so."

The next morning they left early, taking most of the warriors from the small camp. The main village was two hundred miles away, and the small hunting camp was little more than a way station, fewer than fifty lodges. Pecos was along on his first buffalo hunt, and Quanah was given the assignment of keeping a close eye on him, charged especially with making sure that the younger boy's youthful enthusiasm, sometimes a virtue and sometimes a danger, didn't lead him into peril.

As they headed out, fifty miles to the south, other men were heading north. Sul Ross, given his instructions by no less a figure than Sam Houston himself, had been charged with smoking out the scattered hornets' nests of Comanche. To help, Houston had gotten a unit of the 2nd Cavalry assigned to Ross, under the command of Capt. N.G. Evans. The idea was to make a strong showing and convince the Comanche by a show of force that Texas was serious about putting an end to depredations, using force if persuasion proved inadequate.

They traveled for two days, heading toward

the Pease River, the bane of southern cattlemen.
Its alkaline waters were almost useless, and the
treacherous quicksands which migrated across
its bottom seemed to swallow almost as many
cattle as the northern appetite for beef.

The Ranger unit and cavalry had traveled up
the Brazos, and picked up nearly seventy angry
cattlemen as volunteers. Ross, concerned that the
irregulars would be undisciplined, had tried to
keep them on a tight leash, but they were spoiling for a fight, and the Ranger captain knew he
would have his hands full once the expedition
struck Comanche sign. He was hopeful that they
could accomplish their purpose without a battle,
but he had been on the frontier too long to think
it likely.

On the first morning of their second week out,
they entered the southern end of a long valley
and were halfway up when they heard the thunder of buffalo hooves, hundreds of them, stampeding their way. Ross knew the most likely
explanation for the terrified flight of the huge
animals was a hunting party, as like as not
Comanche, somewhere behind them, and he sent
scouts out to find the trail.

The captain himself headed for a nearby ridge,
where he found marks in the dust. Dismounting,
he examined them closely, another ranger kneeling across from him. "One pony, unshod," Ross
said.

"Indian for sure," the ranger agreed. "Just one
pony, near as I can tell."

"Not too long ago, either. Maybe an hour, hour and a half at the most." The center of the scuff marks was still damp with morning dew, despite the sun. Looking down into the next valley, he scanned the floor for sign of the solitary warrior, but he was nowhere in evidence.

"Probably not too far away," Ross said. "Buffalo don't run that far when they get spooked. They usually play out in an hour or so."

"Could be a small hunting party on their tail," the ranger suggested. "They'd run longer, then."

"Yeah, they would. Guess we'll have to wait until the scouts get back."

"Captain," the ranger asked, getting to his feet and brushing off his knees, "suppose it's a big village. I don't know if we ought to take 'em on with them goddamned cowhands along. They'll shoot us as like as not, once things start to heat up."

Ross shook his head. "Sometimes folks get in their own damn way, but there's nothing you can do to stop it. All you can hope for is that they keep their heads on straight, and that it's over quick. With any luck, we can parley with the head man and just send them packin' and nobody has to get shot."

"If they're Comanche, and I'd bet my Sunday hat they are, there won't be no parley. We'll have to shoot some sense into 'em."

Ross nodded. "You're probably right, Roy. But that's why the good Lord invented prayin'. We do it right, maybe he'll listen."

Roy laughed. "Captain, I ain't been a Ranger that long, but I don't recall nothing at all about prayer being part of the arsenal."

Ross grinned. "What the governor don't know won't hurt him, will it, Roy?"

He sprang back into the saddle and moved on back to the main force. Harley Beauchamp, the nominal leader of the cowboy volunteers, was sitting his horse alongside Captain Evans. He was chewing tobacco, and an unsightly trickle of amber juice leaked from the corner of his mouth. He spat a stream into the dust, then wiped his jaw with one sleeve. "Find anything, Cap'n?"

"One set of pony tracks is all. Most likely a scout."

"They'll know we're here then," he said.

"Maybe not."

"We'd best push on, anyhow," Beauchamp urged. "Just in case . . ."

"We will, Mister Beauchamp, we will," Ross assured him.

But it was two days before they found the camp, nestled in a shallow bend of the Pease. Surveying the camp through glasses, Ross concluded that it would be lightly defended. Handing the glasses to Captain Evans, he said, "You ever fought Comanche, Captain?"

Evans shook his head. "No, sir, I haven't, but I'm looking forward to it."

"You won't say that again tomorrow, Captain, I assure you. Fact is, you better hope and pray you live to look back on it."

"Doesn't look like we can expect much opposition."

"All the better." As he was taking the glasses back, Ross heard a shout somewhere to the left, and glanced up in time to see a solitary Comanche dashing for the small village. One of the cowboys was drawing a bead, and before Ross could stop him, the man fired.

The shot fell way short, the ball making a small geyser in the water barely fifty yards short of its target. But the damage was done. There was no chance of having a peaceful talk, not after the unprovoked gunshot.

"Damn it to hell," Ross barked. "I ought to skin your ugly ass for that."

"We come here to kill redskins, Cap'n. I don't know about you, but I ain't about to try and scare 'em to death," the cowboy snapped.

Ross nudged his horse closer, then reached out and grabbed the man by the shirtfront, half lifting him from the saddle. "Listen to me, mister! You so much as breathe from now on without my permission, and as God is my witness, I will put a bullet through that thick skull of yours. This ain't no picnic, and I got two hundred men to worry about. One less will be just fine with me."

Chapter 18

WITH THE POSSIBILITY OF SURPRISE gone, Ross ordered a charge. The Rangers and the cowboy volunteers swept up through the valley and over the ridge. Already, the Comanche had started to scatter. The few warriors on hand had mounted their ponies and charged out of the village, desperately hoping to delay the assault long enough for the women and children to get away.

As at Antelope Hills, the Comanche were armed only with bows and arrows, lances, and war clubs. Ross and his men had rifles and revolvers, and there was little the warriors could do to repel the attack. There was no help within a short ride as there had been two years before. A small hunting camp, it was a hundred miles from the nearest village. The Comanche could not use overwhelming numbers to offset the superior firepower of the Texas raiders. Their only chance was to slow them down long enough to let their families escape.

A handful of warriors moved in a wide arc, as

if trying to slip around the left flank and get in behind the Rangers. Captain Ross sent a small detachment to cut off the flankers and drive them back. He slowed his assault long enough to make certain he wasn't encircled. Clouds of arrows were arcing high in the air, as the Comanche fired as fast as they could notch and draw.

But Ross was too far away for the arrows to do much good. Most of them fell short and those few that managed to reach the attackers were spent, rattling harmlessly in the tall grass. Ross reached out and snatched one from the air, admiring the craftsmanship in spite of the circumstances. He wondered what it must be like for Stone-Age savages to face modern weapons. But the thought didn't last long, and he flipped the arrow over his shoulder and pushed his horse toward the left flank, his pistol drawn as he dashed toward the would-be flankers.

The Texans laid down a heavy fire, and the Comanche were forced to pull back, cursing in their fury and sending wave after wave of harmless arrows. Several dismounted and took cover in a clump of brush.

Ross led a charge toward the embattled warriors, and as the Texans thundered down on them, they stood their ground. One Ranger was hit in the shoulder and fell from his horse, but waved Ross on when the captain turned to see if he needed help. "Go," he shouted, "go on!"

The thunder of the big American horses flushed

the Comanche from their cover, and they sprang back onto their ponies and dashed back toward the camp.

Ross could see women and children scattering in every direction, and when he noticed the small herd of Indian ponies, knew he had to capture them before the refugees managed to mount up.

Leaving the small unit to chase the fleeing defenders, he shouted to Lt. David Anderson. "Bring some men and follow me," he yelled, wheeling his mount and making for the horses down by the river.

Some of the animals were already scattering, and three young Comanche were trying desperately to keep the herd together. Firing his pistol in the air, Ross frightened the ponies still further, and several of them broke free, knocking one of the boys to the ground. The boy scrambled on all fours, narrowly avoiding the bolting ponies.

Anderson and his men were right behind him now, and Ross circled around the far side of the herd, driving several of the strays back toward the main body. The rest of his men had already broken toward the camp, and a ragged line of Comanche on foot was falling back, trying to force the Texans to take cover. But several had already fallen, and the incessant firing of the Texans' weapons pushed the defenders harder and harder.

It was a hopeless situation for the Comanche, but they refused to break. Several charged forward on foot, trying to drag the charging rangers from their saddles, but a flurry of gunshots sent three of the warriors sprawling in the dust and the rest were forced to break off their charge.

Ross shouted for the men to cease firing, but if they heard him, they ignored him. He knew the cattlemen would be undisciplined, but it seemed to have spread to the Rangers, as well. The entire assault was teetering dangerously close to anarchy.

Beyond the camp, he saw a woman running awkwardly, a child in her arms, and two warriors right behind her, running backward and firing arrows as fast as they could draw the strings of their bows. Ross charged toward them, waving his pistol. He didn't want to shoot if he didn't have to, for fear of hitting the woman, but the warriors refused to yield.

Aiming his pistol, he pulled the trigger, and the hammer fell with a dull click. He pulled the trigger again, and this time nothing happened. The gun was jammed.

One of the warriors cut loose with an arrow, and it caught Ross in the side, just above the hip. As his horse charged on, Ross ducked away from an outthrust lance, but it caught him a glancing blow and knocked him from the saddle. He sprawled in the grass, trying to get to his feet, but the pain was intense, and he watched helplessly as the woman ran on, toward some horses standing against a clump of trees.

Jerking the arrow free, he felt blood seeping

inside his shirt and glanced at the arrow, where a chunk of his flesh was impaled on the razor-sharp head. One of the warriors had retrieved a rifle from the ground and was pointing it at him. He heard a shout and then a flurry of gunshots and the warrior fell, two bloody holes punched in his chest.

Anderson rode past, and Ross waved him on. "Get the woman," he shouted.

The charging Rangers overtook the squaw, and two of the men dismounted, grabbing the woman by the arms and spinning her around, then dragging her, shrieking and flailing her legs back toward Ross who sat on the ground with one hand pressed to his side to stop the bleeding.

"This one looks like a white woman, Captain," Anderson said. "Look at her eyes."

Ross struggled to his feet. Bending at the waist and propping his weight on one knee, he leaned toward the woman, conscious of the blood oozing between his fingers. "They're blue," he said. "By God, her eyes are blue."

"Never yet seen a Comanche with blue eyes," Anderson said.

"Are you white?" Ross asked.

The woman spat at him, then lashed out with a moccasined foot, catching him in the knee.

"Wildcat, more likely," Ross grunted. Once more, he asked, "Are you a white woman? What's your name?"

But Naudah just glared at him, and he shook his head. "We'll have to take her back, see maybe somebody knows her. Could be that Parker woman."

"Not likely, Captain," Anderson said. "She's been missing a long time. Twenty years or more."

"Isaac Parker would know. He's her uncle. We'll see if we can get him to camp to take a look at her."

The firing behind him had dwindled away and he turned to survey the camp. Several Comanche lay in the dust, one or two moaning and most deathly still. Pools of blood glistened in the sunlight, and flies already buzzed around the fallen warriors, filling the camp with a steady hum as Ross limped back toward the river.

Behind him, Anderson and his men brought along the woman and her child, whom she refused to surrender to the Rangers.

"You'd best sit down, Captain," Anderson said. "We'll get you bandaged up soon as we can."

Ross nodded. "See to the wounded, Lieutenant. We'll have to get a couple of wagons up here to carry them."

"What about the redskins?"

"Bring them, too. I don't want any massacre here. You see to it, Lieutenant."

"Yes, sir, Captain," Anderson said.

Ross moved to a patch of tall, green grass under some willows, and sat down, propping his back against the rough bark and chewing on his lower lip to keep his mind off the pain.

Two Rangers who had Naudah by either arm followed him, unwilling to let go of her arms.

He closed his eyes for a moment, taking a deep breath and letting out a low moan. When he opened his eyes again, Naudah was sitting beside him, her hands tied and her ankles hobbled. The child, and Ross saw now that it was a baby girl, sat in her lap, head buried in her mother's shoulder.

Ross watched the woman, trying to decide if she could possibly be Cynthia Ann Parker, and thinking that if she were, then this camp must belong to Peta Nocona, now the most feared and certainly the most hated, of all Comanche chiefs. He studied the woman's face for a long time, but she ignored him, busying herself with trying to calm the infant girl.

He saw Anderson glance his way and waved him over.

"Captain?" he said, when he reached his commander.

"If that woman is Cynthia Ann Parker, then Peta Nocona is somewhere around here."

He watched the woman's face as he spoke, and saw her eyes flicker toward him then away. The movement was so quick and so slight, he wasn't sure it meant anything. "Check the dead and wounded. See if anybody in the company knows for sure what he looks like. I saw him once, but it was a long time ago. I'm not sure I'd recognize him."

Anderson nodded. "Yes, sir. I'll check."

"And Captain?"

"Sir?"

"If he's alive, I don't want him harmed. Understand?"

Anderson looked skeptical, but nodded. "Yes, sir, Captain Ross. I understand."

Ross turned to the woman again as Anderson moved off. "We don't mean you any harm," he said.

Naudah looked at him with blank eyes, her lips curled in hatred. She spat once more, and Ross shook his head. Twenty years, he thought, twenty years. Even if she is Cynthia Ann Parker, she's more Comanche now than she ever was white.

He closed his eyes again as a wave of nausea swept over him. He didn't come to again until he felt hands lifting him into a wagon. He felt the hard wood under him, and opened his eyes. The woman captive was in the wagon behind him, her back against the back of the wagon bed.

Once more, the pain overcame him, and he drifted off to sleep.

The Rangers reached Camp Cooper, with nearly two dozen captives, in addition to Naudah and her daughter, Prairie Flower. Isaac Parker was sent for, and he hurried to the camp, hoping the white woman captive was his niece, but not willing to believe it. Twenty-four years was just too long a time.

When he reached the camp, Naudah had been taken under the wing of the wives of the military men, bathed and given a new calico dress, not unlike a larger version of the one she had been wearing so long ago, when Peta Nocona had carried her away.

When Isaac was ushered into the office of the camp commander, Naudah looked at him blankly.

"Is that your niece, Mister Parker?" Colonel Ellington asked.

Isaac, uncertain, moved closer, peering at her as if through a pair of spectacles, blinking his eyes and trying to see through a quarter-century's mist. "How are you, my child?" he asked.

Naudah shook her head. She no longer understood English, hadn't used the language in so long the words had rusted and crumbled away.

"It looks like her. It could be, I just don't . . ." Isaac said, leaning still closer.

Then, shaking his head sadly, he said, "No. That's not Cynthia Ann." He turned to go.

Naudah, something triggered in her memory, thumped her chest. "Cynthia Ann," she said, patting her breast. The alien words were little more than a croak in her throat. "Cynthia Ann."

Chapter 19

THE HUNT HAD GONE WELL. The buffalo were plentiful, and Peta Nocona had organized his warriors well. Despite their small numbers, they had worked the surroundings to near perfection. Encircling the herd was not easy to do, because the buffalo, especially the big bulls, had a keen sense of smell. One had to watch the wind and make sure that he didn't get too close until everyone was in position.

Only then could they be sure of getting enough meat for the coming winter. On the signal from Nocona, the warriors had closed in, riding around the herd and keeping them off balance, taking the biggest bulls first, often with a single arrow. If a warrior was strong enough, and his bow good enough, he could often send an arrow clean through his target and someone would lean from his pony and pluck it from the ground without even slowing down, to use again and again.

For Pecos, it had been the adventure of a lifetime. Quanah was already an old hand, and had been given the responsibility of seeing that his younger brother did nothing foolish. That had hampered Quanah somewhat, but he had been good-natured about it, and shared his recently gained knowledge with Pecos without missing out on his own kills.

Now, with the buffalo downed and the pack horses loaded with fresh meat, it was important to make good time and get them back to the hunting camp so the women could begin the drying. The skins, too, had to be scraped and dried before they spoiled. There was plenty of work now for everybody, and even though the warriors were tired, they could not look forward to real rest for a few days. But at least they would eat well during the winter, and there would be plenty of new buffalo robes to keep the worst of the cold and snow at bay.

Nocona was worried. Normally, the women would have come along, to be there when the herd was struck, but circumstances had disrupted the usual practice. It had taken longer to strike a herd than it usually did and, rather than risk losing it, the warriors had decided to surround and strike. The herd hadn't been that large, and it seemed a foolish risk to wait for the women to catch up.

Quanah was nearly exhausted, but when Nocona sent him on ahead to alert the camp, he was delighted. He knew from previous hunts the excitement news of success would generate, and he was looking forward to a chance to be the cause of such celebration.

He saw the smoke from the camp, and something seemed odd. There wasn't as much smoke as there should have been, and it was thick and black, as if people were burning wet, greasy wood. He pushed his pony hard to get to the ridge line, from where he might be able to see the camp. But when he broke over the rise, he was disappointed. There was still another valley between him and the camp. For a moment, he debated whether to ride back and tell Nocona that something was wrong, but he wasn't sure, and if he made such a mistake, they would laugh at him all winter and all the following summer. He was too proud for that, and had too much sense to generate alarm where none was called for.

Instead, he kicked his pony hard, and raced down the long, gentle slope into the valley, then up the far side, from where he knew he would be able to see everything. Then he could decide whether anything was wrong and whether it was necessary to run for his father.

And as soon as he reached the ridge, he knew. He pulled up sharply, leaning against the ropes which helped him stay on the pony, and which let him lean far over one side or the other when hunting or raiding without danger of falling off.

The smoke was not from campfires, and trickled toward the sky from a hundred mounds of burning trash. Lodges, knocked on their sides and collapsed, had been torched. Stacks of buffalo robes had been set ablaze, and the air was full of the stink of burnt hair. He saw bodies, too, and felt his heart hammer against his ribs.

Nocona's own lodge was one of those unburned, but it had been knocked over and collapsed. Quanah could see the long, dark place where a burning branch had been thrown on the skin and burned away without setting fire to the lodge itself, leaving an ugly scar nearly a yard long.

But it was the bodies that held him. He had seen dead people before, but never this many, never this close and, except for Antelope Hills, always they were enemies. Now it was his own people who lay sprawled in the pasty mud of their own bleeding, and as he nudged the horse downhill, he could smell the stench of death. He knew the disaster couldn't have been that long ago, because the ruins were still smoldering. And they had been gone only five days. But the wreckage was so complete, it seemed to him as if it had happened in one fell swoop, as if a thunderbolt had laid waste to the camp, flattening it and burning its ruins all in one instant.

He pushed the pony harder and harder, until they were traveling at breakneck speed toward the valley floor and river beyond. He raced to Nocona's lodge and leaped from his pony, calling, "Mother? Mother?"

But there was no answer. He grabbed the edge of the overturned lodge, straightened, and peered inside as far as he could see, but he already knew that it would be empty, and let it fall again as he turned away, his eyes picking out first one body then another. There was Blue Elk, and Runs Fast, and over there was White Mustang. One after another, he ran to the bodies, checking to see whether they were alive, knowing they would not be, and turned from each bloated face, its black tongue lolling lewdly over a bloody jaw or straining upward as if to lick away the flies crawling on the staring eyes and buzzing angrily when Quanah came too close.

There were women and children, too, but no sign of Naudah or Prairie Flower.

Again, he called out, "Mother?"

And again his voice fell dead, a single dead leaf on a windless day. Not even an echo bothered to mock him.

There were dead horses, too, and he realized that all the arrows lying on the ground were Comanche arrows. This had not been a raid by Osage or Tonkawa or Apache. This had been done by Anglos. The mangled bodies lay beside a broken bow, a shattered lance, a handful of arrows. One, that of Green Horse, still had its fingers curled around the shaft of a war club, its face, even distorted by bloat, wearing an expression of outrage mixed with surprise.

One by one, he examined the bodies. He knew them all. But Naudah was nowhere to be seen. Nor was Prairie Flower.

Shaking his head as if to rid it of the horror he

had just seen, he raced back to his pony, sprang onto its back, and slipped his legs under the ropes, slapping its side even before he was ready to ride.

Quanah started lashing the pony with his bow, striking it again and again and again. The pony was straining as it tried to comply, but Quanah no longer realized what he was doing. Again and again, he smacked the pony on the flank as he charged uphill away from the devastated camp.

By the time he reached the hilltop, each slash of the heavy bow scattered an arc of small rubies, and Quanah didn't notice the blood flecking his chest and thighs as he drove on, yelling until his throat was raw and the words, if they were words at all, no longer meant anything to him.

Once, he glanced back, half afraid that the ghosts of the dead were following him. By the time he spotted Nocona and the heavily laden hunting party, he was gasping for breath, despite the fact that it was the pony that was doing all the work. He felt his chest pounding, as if each rib wanted to pull away from his body, to get away from the madman whose skin restrained it.

Nocona saw him coming, and his first instinct was annoyance at the boy, playing when there was such serious business to be tended to. But as he watched Quanah, still slashing at the hapless pony, he knew something was wrong. Goading his own mount, he dashed ahead of the others, heading straight for his son and yelling to Black Snake to keep Pecos with him.

He met Quanah on the valley floor, the son panting, choking with tears, the father stunned and helpless as he waited for an explanation.

"What's the matter? Quanah, what happened?"

All the boy could do was shake his head, trying to get rid of the thick paste that clogged his throat. Words fluttered from his lips, but they were unintelligible, and Nocona shook his head in frustration. "Tell me what happened!"

Taking a water bag from the back of his horse, he handed it to Quanah, holding it while the boy sucked greedily, the heavy bag throbbing with every gulp. Then, licking his lips, Quanah rubbed a wrist across his cheeks and only then saw the flecks of blood on his skin.

He stared at them as if not quite certain what they were, until Nocona pointed to the bow. Quanah looked down at the blood-soaked bow and bowstring, then at his pony's flank. He took a deep breath, whirled the bow three times overhead, then threw it as far as he could. Only when it landed in the grass, did he try once more to speak.

"The camp . . . they're dead . . . gone . . . everyone. I . . ."

Realizing what his son was trying to say, Nocona gave a great shout, "Naudahhhh . . ." Then he kicked his war-horse furiously, prodding it again and again with his heels. Quanah was left behind. His pony was spent, and he wasn't sure he wanted to return to the camp, so he turned about and sat there, watching his

father disappear over the ridge and down into
the next valley.

He could hear shouts now from behind him,
turned and waved frantically. Several warriors
had already sped ahead of the main party, and he
saw Black Snake at their head. His father's friend
was jerking a spare along in his wake, and
Quanah freed his legs from the ropes of his pony
and slipped to the ground.

As Black Snake and the others thundered past,
he grabbed the war rope and bounced onto the
back of the spare. He saw Black Snake looking
back over his shoulder and waved, shouting
something that neither he nor Black Snake
understood. Pecos was in the rear, his face a
mask of confusion, and Quanah told him to wait
with the others, then kicked the new horse, urging it to catch Black Snake and then on ahead.

When they broke over the ridge, the camp
was just as Quanah had last seen it, and he
heard the gasps as the others took in the dev-
astating sight, then began to shout and wail,
venting at one time their sorrow at the loss
and their rage at its perpetrators.

Nocona was standing in the middle of the
camp, his arms spread wide, his head tilted back
as if to inquire of the sky why this horror had
visited him yet again.

They could hear him screaming, but it wasn't
until they were halfway down the hill that
Quanah realized Nocona was calling Naudah's
name.

Before they reached the flats at the valley bottom, Nocona was running for his horse again and swung onto its back as the others rode up.

"Come with me," he shouted, heading back the way they'd come. He led a mad charge back to the main body of hunters, told them what happened in as few words as possible, and told most of them to follow him. He left just a few behind to tend to the dead and, if there were any, the wounded, and to guard what was left of their belongings.

"Where are we going, brother?" Black Snake asked. His voice was tight, but he sounded fearful that Nocona might do something foolish.

"To find the ones who did this. They can't be far. We will catch them soon."

"But . . ."

Nocona raised his face to the sky again. "No!" he snapped. "I don't want advice. I don't want an argument. I want my family back. And I want revenge for all those who have been taken from us."

He started toward the camp, his eyes scanning the ground for signs. It wasn't hard to find the tracks left by the iron-shod American horses and, like Quanah, he had noticed the absence of enemy arrows, leaving no doubt as to who had wreaked such havoc on the camp and its inhabitants.

They followed the trail for three hours before the sky began to darken. Quanah had spent his rage and settled now into an icy calm, not quite as arctic as that which enfolded his father. He looked at the sky, surprised that the sun should be setting so early, and saw the huge mass of boiling black clouds speeding toward them from the west.

Ten minutes later, the first drops of rain, large as sparrow eggs, spattered men and horses, each one feeling like a spent rifle ball, stinging the skin and hitting like a closed fist.

Puffs of dust mushroomed around those that hit the ground, and soon it was pouring steadily. Nocona raged against the weather, knowing that if it kept up very long, all trace of the raiding party would be wiped away.

It rained steadily, darkening continually until the sun was gone and two hours later there was no hope of following the trail in the stygian darkness.

Nocona told his warriors to rest, and sat all night, his back against a rock, the rain pouring down over him until he shivered and began to cough.

By sunrise, it was still raining, a drizzle now, but the damage had already been done. Nocona sent scouts in every direction, and paced anxiously while he waited for their return. It was nearly an hour before they were all in, and none had been able to find a trace of the Anglos.

Nocona ground his teeth, walked to his horse and climbed onto its back.

"Where are we going, Father?" Quanah asked, voicing the questions the others shared but were too nervous and demoralized to ask.

"To the camp," he said.

"But, Mother . . . Prairie Flower . . ."

Nocona nodded. "I will look until I find them or until I die. But right now, we have to bury our dead."

Chapter 20

Autumn 1862

IN CAMP, PETA NOCONA SPENT more and more time alone with his sons. When he went into battle, he was courageous almost to the point of recklessness, as if he wanted to make up for the loss of Naudah with as much blood as he could spill. But Quanah was worried. Nocona seemed not to care whether he lived or died. The raids he led were still as carefully planned as always, but the greater the odds, the more Nocona seemed to relish the fight.

In the summer of 1861, with the Rangers occupying Camp Radziminski, recently vacated by the army, skirmishes were frequent, sometimes planned, sometimes the accidental fallout of circumstance. And Nocona hated the Anglos now more than ever, even more than he hated the Osage. It was as if the loss of Naudah and Prairie Flower, so uncertain, not knowing whether they were alive or dead, was harder to bear than the loss of White Heron and Little Calf. Quanah sometimes thought there was a great abyss deep inside Nocona, one that had to be filled with blood to make him feel whole.

Pressed by the Rangers, Nocona kept his village on the move, even though he stayed deep in the Llano Estacado, where even the Rangers were reluctant to go. When he learned of the outbreak of the War Between the States, Nocona smiled, but it was a terrible smile, ghoulish and inward looking, as if the news satisfied some dark wish.

"Now," he said, "the Anglos will help us. They will kill each other, and there will not be as many of them for us to kill. We will have our lands to ourselves."

Quanah wasn't so sure. He knew that some of the tribes already on reservations, especially the Caddo and the Wichita, favored the North, while others, especially the Tonkawa, favored the South. Because of his hatred for the Tonkawa, Nocona inclined the least little bit toward the North, and when word reached him that war against the hated Tonkawa was being planned, he attended the council to offer his help.

The Tonkawa heard rumors, and made a run for it, heading south and east, deeper into country firmly controlled by the Texans, but it did them no good.

Caddo scouts kept track of them, getting word back to the alliance of chiefs planning the attack, and when it seemed the Tonkawa had stopped running and established a permanent

village, a great war party of Caddo, Wichita, and
Comanche assembled in a river valley near
Anadarko. They moved quickly, and in three
days had surrounded the Tonkawa village.

The hope was that the Texans would be too
busy with their own war to worry much about
their Indian allies. Surveying the Tonkawa village under the cover of darkness, Nocona saw
that it was so. Clutching Quanah by the shoulder, he said, "See, the Anglos don't care about
anyone but themselves. The Tonkawa sold themselves to the Texans and now that they are of no
use, the Texans don't care about them. These are
the ones who killed Iron Jacket. These are the
ones who roast our brothers over the fire and eat
their flesh. These are the ones."

Slipping away from the vantage point above
the valley where the village lay, Nocona rejoined
the main war party and told what he had seen.
The attack was for the next night. It would be
swift and it would be sudden. "If we are careful," Nocona told them, "we can get them all."

The following day was spent in preparation.
More arrows had to be made, lances relaced, war
clubs repaired. No one spoke much. Each man
was busy seeing to his own weapons, knowing
that the coming of night would present him with
an opportunity to settle old scores, to get revenge
for loved ones lost and to punish an enemy too
long hiding behind the power of the Anglos. But
this time, the Tonkawa were alone. They would
have no one to turn to, nowhere to run.

As twilight began to darken the sky, Nocona
pulled Quanah aside. "If anything happens to
me," he said, "I want you to promise me that you
will look after Pecos."

"You know I will."

Nocona nodded. "I know. But I want you to
promise me."

"Nothing will happen to you."

"Perhaps not. All the same, promise. I have
lost too many people to go easily to the other
side if those left behind are in danger."

Quanah sighed. "I promise." He was troubled
by the request, because Nocona seemed resigned,
as if he foresaw some terrible doom that he
believed he could not escape. Even the morose-
ness of the last two years was nothing compared
to the heavy sadness that seemed to surround the
great chief now.

When darkness fell, the war party moved
out. They had ten miles to go, and rode in a
long file, whispering among themselves until
the war chiefs passed the word that surprise
depended on complete silence. From that
point on, Quanah, riding beside Nocona, listened only to the drum of unshod hooves on
the dry turf. He knew the white soldier
columns always made noise, because the
leather of their saddles squeaked, and the
metal fittings of the bridles and the soldiers'
spurs jingled. Peering over his shoulder into
the darkness behind him, he could make out
only a handful of gray shapes, and could not

have guessed the size of the war party from the little he saw.

When they reached the last hill before the ridge overlooking the valley where the Tonkawa village lay, the warriors spread in a long line, waiting for the word to advance up the hill. When it came, the line moved almost like a sidewinder, small groups getting out ahead a bit, then lagging, waiting for the others, who moved a little ahead. The battle line wriggled up the hill and stopped once more on the ridge overlooking the Tonkawa village. Large campfires, tended by shadows, filled the valley with light. The Tonkawa lodges were splashed with orange and black, the colors of the designs pale and dull in the flicker.

With an earsplitting shriek, Great Bull, a Caddo chief, led the charge, and then it was every man for himself as the war party swept down on the unsuspecting enemy. Quanah saw Nocona pull away, getting out in front of the small Comanche contingent, and he was among the first to reach the edge of the village. The Tonkawa spilled out of their lodges, jumping on the ponies tethered beside the entrances, grabbing bows and lances and trying to get their bearings as the war party swarmed over them.

Despite the alliance with the Anglos, the Tonkawa were not well armed. A few had pistols and old muskets, but after the first flurry of gunfire, the combat was too close and too furious for reloading. Comanche, Caddo, and Wichita thundered through the village, knocking lodges over, upending meat racks and sending defenders sprawling in the dust.

The shrieks of the warriors mingled with the wails of women and children as the furious battle surged like a flood among the lodges. Quanah leaped from his pony feet first, hitting a burly Tonkawa in the middle of the back and knocking him to the ground. He tumbled over once, sprang to his feet and turned to face the enraged defender, who charged with a lance held at his hip.

Quanah ducked under the thrusting tip, knocked the shaft aside, and closed with a war club held in his right hand. He swung wildly, nearly losing his feet as the Tonkawa whipped him with the lance, catching him on the hip with the flame-hardened wood.

Pulling the lance back, the Tonkawa made another vicious thrust, but this time Quanah closed a hand over the shaft and jerked the warrior off balance. The man stumbled toward him, letting go of the lance and flailing his arms. Bringing the war club down in a sharp arc, Quanah caught his opponent on the shoulder. He heard the crack of breaking bone, and the Tonkawa's left arm went limp. Pulling a knife, the burly warrior charged into the slender Quanah, slashing back and forth with the broad blade. The knife caught the firelight and left smears of gold behind it after each vicious slice.

Timing the passes of the blade, Quanah danced backward, turning slightly, then brought the war club down again, this time striking the knife hand just below the wrist. The Tonkawa yelped as the knife flew from his hand, made a dive for it and closed his fingers around the hilt just as Quanah's foot reached it, pinning both hand and knife to the ground.

With his other arm useless, the Tonkawa tried to wriggle free, then curled the wounded arm around his head as the war club whistled toward him.

Once more, there was a loud crack, this time sounding as if a tree limb had snapped in two. Blood poured from a ragged wound on the Tonkawa's temple, and Quanah, feeling a rage he didn't understand, slashed once more and then again with the heavy club, hitting the same place both times, and leaving the side of the warrior's head a mush of red and gray.

Panting, Quanah backed away, turned and saw another Tonkawa racing toward a Comanche warrior whose back was turned. Shouting, Quanah charged, but the defender reached the Comanche first, thrusting the lance deep into the lower back above the right hip. The Comanche groaned, reached for the lance as he tried to turn, and only then did Quanah realize the target was Nocona.

Hurling himself at the Tonkawa, Quanah clawed at his bare back, whipped an arm around the warrior's neck, and reached for the knife on his hip. In a single blinding arc, the knife slit the Tonkawa's throat, and Quanah felt the rush of warm blood flood over his forearm and hand. He let the man fall and turned to Nocona, who had already snapped off the head of the lance, in front of his hip.

He lay on his side, and when he saw Quanah, he rolled onto his stomach. "Pull it out, Quanah, quickly!"

He gritted his teeth as Quanah grasped the lance, wincing with the pain. Pressing his foot right beside the wound, Quanah jerked the lance free, and Nocona groaned.

He knelt then to tend to Nocona, but his father waved him away. "Pay attention to what matters," he said. "I'll be all right."

Reluctantly, Quanah turned back to the battle swirling around him on every side. It was apparent that the Tonkawa were getting the worst of it, and many of them were already dead or wounded. The Caddo, especially, were fiercely determined, and each time the battle seemed about to flag, they mounted a charge that rekindled the flames.

Lodges were in ruins, horses lay dead and wounded and bodies were strewn everywhere. Quanah threw himself back into the thick of the battle, as much to get his mind off Nocona's wound as for the joy of the fight itself. For another hour, the combat raged, breaking down into smaller and smaller groups of hand-to-hand contests, and as the numbers of Tonkawa warriors able to resist continually dwindled, the pockets of resistance grew fewer and fewer.

Quanah managed one more combat, this time against a Tonkawa not much older than himself, but the defender had little heart for the battle, and it was over quickly, with Quanah once more victorious, whirling to look for his next challenge. But by then, it was over. He saw the Comanche gathering together, chattering among themselves, and noticed that Nocona was among them.

With a great howl, Nocona held his right arm high overhead, and the circle of Comanche around him echoed the howl with furious shrieks of their own. As Quanah approached, the Comanche parted to make room for him, and he saw a body lying on its back at Nocona's feet, its arms limp, its legs twisted as if broken, and the glitter of orange light on naked bone where the scalp lock should have been.

One of the warriors noticed the baffled expression on his face. "Placido," he said. "The one who led the fight where Iron Jacket was killed." He laughed, and twisted his face into a smile that was so maniacal it frightened Quanah.

And it was time to go home, time to celebrate the victory. There were so few Tonkawa left that, for all practical purposes, they had ceased to exist as a separate nation. Gathering their horses, the Caddo, Wichita, and Comanche chattered incessantly about the great battle, singing their own praises and those of friends. Endless waves of shrieks and howls rippled through the warriors as they mounted up and dug their knees into their ponies.

Quanah took his place beside Nocona, who was nearly doubled over on the back of his mount, and obviously suffering from the lance wound in his hip. Quanah wanted him to rest, but Nocona was anxious to get back home.

"I want to see Pecos," he said, "to tell him of the great battle, and how his brother saved my life."

Quanah tried to wave the praise away as if it were a swarm of gnats, but Nocona, through clenched teeth, went on and on. The ride home took four days, and Nocona's condition worsened with every mile. He had difficulty sitting erect on his horse, and the shock of the thudding hooves made him grimace now and then.

He had stopped bleeding, and the wound had been packed with herbs and mud, but Quanah was worried. By the time they reached the Comanche village, Nocona had to be helped from his horse. His skin felt hot and stiff, like the white man's paper. He was mumbling incoherently, and Quanah rushed him to his lodge and sent immediately for the medicine man.

Pacing outside while the shaman worked his magic, Quanah tried to explain to Pecos what had happened, downplaying his own role in the battle. The difference in their ages had never seemed so great. Quanah felt that they were standing together looking over the edge of a deep pit into which Nocona was falling, and when he closed his eyes, it was as if he could see Nocona sailing, drifting lower and lower, swooping in great circles as he shrank in size.

And when the medicine man finally left the lodge the following morning, he clapped a hand on Quanah's shoulder. "I don't know if my medicine is strong enough to help him," he said. "He wants to see you and your brother. You'd better go in quickly."

Quanah ducked through the flap with Pecos on his heels and rushed to Nocona's side, where the great chief lay on a buffalo robe beside the fire. He was wrapped in another robe, and his teeth chattered as he opened his eyes.

"I am very cold, my sons," he said. "So very cold."

Then, with a shuddering gasp, he closed his eyes.

Chapter 21 ═══════

PECOS DIED THAT SPRING. Stricken with cholera in one of the waves of the deadly diseases that were sweeping the plains, along with smallpox and typhoid, he lingered only two days, and Quanah spent every minute with his younger brother, alternately swearing revenge on the Anglos for bringing the plague and promising anything and everything if only the boy would be spared.

When it was over, Quanah was alone. With Naudah and Prairie Flower taken away by the Texans, Nocona dead, and now Pecos, he had no one. Chieftainship was not strictly hereditary, but with Nocona's help, Quanah knew he would have been a chief one day, but now there was no hope of that.

He drifted aimlessly, from the Noconi to the Peneteka to the Quohada. He even spent some time among the Kiowa. He was welcomed everywhere, not only as the son of one of the greatest of all Comanche chiefs, but as an outstanding warrior and hunter in his own right. But it was cold comfort. He missed his father's gentle lectures, the teasing of his brother. He missed Naudah's comforting words when things went wrong. He felt as if he were alone on the plains. No amount of friendship could take the place of his family, and it seemed like he were looking for something to fill the void.

In 1863, he decided to join a band of Comanche led by the famous chief Yellow Bear, and quickly became one of the leading warriors in one of the most active of all Comanche raiding bands. With the Texas Rangers preoccupied with the Northern Army, and homesteads and ranches ripe for the picking, the Comanche swept over half of Texas, hitting and running, leaving little but death and embers in their wake.

Stealing cattle and horses, they roamed at will over the plains, seldom staying in one place for more than two or three weeks. The buffalo were beginning to dwindle now, and food was harder and harder to find. Whites had been slaughtering the great beasts in numbers, taking trophies and skins and leaving the meat to rot in the sun. Time and again, a Comanche hunting party would break over a ridge only to see the next valley full of bloated carcasses. The stink of the rotting meat swirled in clouds, and the drone of flies seemed to fill the whole valley. At a distance, it looked as if the carcasses were glistening with some sort of iridescent cloth. Only on closer approach could the individual maggots be seen, swarming over entire carcasses, writhing in the putrescent fluids of the rotting buffalo.

But Quanah didn't mind the long days on the trail. As long as he kept moving, he didn't think about the fact that he had no real home. On the trail, all warriors were homeless. Only in the breathtaking excitement of a hit-and-run raid on a cattle herd or the breakneck thunder of an attack on a wagon train did Quanah feel comfortable.

There were some who thought he was courting death, as they had thought Nocona had done after Naudah was taken. Others just thought that he was trying too hard to live up to Nocona's reputation. Still others, those few he allowed to get close, knew that he was mourning in the only way he knew how—living the life his father had taught him, the life he loved, and the only life he really knew.

He seemed to care nothing for the accumulation of possessions. Even the hundreds of horses taken on raids were given away. He kept only what he needed. He hunted as much for the solitude it brought him as for the meat, killed more game than he needed, and gave most of it to the needy, the old women with no one to hunt for them, or the old men whose sons were dead and gone and who could no longer wield the bow or the lance to feed themselves.

It was a harsh life, but Quanah didn't seem to notice. He wasn't morose, but he was seldom

cheerful, either. It seemed almost as if he wanted to be there without being there, to blend
into the background, as if he'd rather not be
noticed.

But there was one who noticed. And he found
himself paying more and more attention to her.
Weakeah herself was noticed by almost everyone, but she seemed to live only for Quanah.
With her, he could be himself, tell her what he
thought about, even what he dreamed about. The
more time they spent together, the more time
they wanted to spend together.

But Quanah was not the only one who fancied
Weakeah. Tennap fancied her, too, and Tennap
had a wealthy father, Ekitacups, a man who
owned a hundred horses and more, and who
could make a gift to Weakeah's father that
Quanah could never hope to match.

The more they saw of each other, the more
they wanted to see. But Tennap was not prepared to give up easily. While Quanah and
Weakeah sat by the river, spinning the silky webs
of a glorious future, Tennap was working hard to
ingratiate himself with Yellow Bear.

Tennap was a good warrior, hardly Quanah's
equal, but still a courageous fighter and good
hunter. Yellow Bear had been friendly with Peta
Nocona, and he was fond of Quanah, not just
because of that friendship, but because of the
qualities he recognized in Nocona's son. As
chief, he was concerned not just about the man
who might one day marry his daughter, but also

about the man who might one day lead his people, and there was no doubt in his mind that Quanah would be a worthy successor.

That Quanah was half white was an issue that Yellow Bear chose to disregard, and Tennap, full of himself and confident that his father's wealth would make up for any discrepancy in reputation, went out of his way to cultivate the chief's affection.

But Quanah was impatient, and fearful that wealth would win what character might not. Rather than approach Yellow Bear directly, and risk getting a definitive answer not to his liking, he hatched a plan that was not without risk, but seemed the surest way to win Weakeah for himself.

One evening, with the moon full and flooding the plains with silver light, he told her that he had something very important he wanted to discuss with her.

"Tell me now," she said.

Quanah shook his head. "Not yet. We're too close to the village."

"Is it a secret?"

"Not for long," he said, giving her a cryptic smile.

He tugged her by the hand, moving down toward the river and past the last lodges. When he could no longer hear conversation from any of the tipis open to the evening breeze, he sat on the grass. Tugging her down beside him, he held her hand. Weakeah was surprised that he would be so demonstrative, since it was frowned upon and was not his way.

"What do you want to tell me?" she asked.

"I have been thinking . . ." He hesitated.

"That will come as a great surprise to just about everyone," she teased.

"I'm serious." He seemed nervous, and she decided to let him have his say with no interruption.

"I'm listening."

"You know that Ekitacups has many horses."

"Yes."

"And that I have only those I need for hunting and for war."

She nodded, wondering what he was getting at.

"Tennap is a good warrior."

"Not as good as you are. And not as good looking, either."

"Please, be serious, Weakeah."

"Well, please tell me what you have to tell me. You are making this as long as one of my father's stories, and you know how long-winded he can be."

"I am afraid that Yellow Bear will look favorably on Tennap, if he asks for you."

She shrugged. "Maybe. But Yellow Bear will ask me what I want, and I will tell him."

"And what will you tell him?"

"What do you think?"

"I don't know. That's why I am asking you to tell me."

"I will tell him that I do not wish to be married yet. And that when I do, I will tell him."

Quanah seemed crushed. "Oh," was all he managed to say.

"Why, was there something else you would want me to tell him?"

"No."

They sat in silence for nearly a minute. Finally, Weakeah leaned over and tugged on his ear. "I am teasing," she said. "Naturally, I will tell Yellow Bear that I prefer you."

The news did little to lighten Quanah's mood. "Suppose he doesn't listen?"

"What else can we do? If you have a better idea, I'd be happy to hear it."

"I thought we might run away together."

"Alone?"

He shook his head. "Not alone, no. There are many warriors who will go with us."

"And what do you think Tennap will do, if we run away?"

"I don't know. I haven't given that much thought."

"You know he will feel cheated, and then Ekitacups will bend my father's ear, and twist his arm. He will say that you didn't play fair."

"But if we are already gone, it will make no difference."

Once again, silence filled the night around them. Quanah watched the current, and tugged at the grass beside him, tossing blades one by one into the river and watching them glide away. Once a fish, tricked by the grass, broke the surface, then arced through the air and fell back with a splash, a blade no doubt clenched in its jaws.

Once more, it was Weakeah who broke the silence. "When can we leave?"

Quanah, as if he were uncertain of her words, said, "What?"

"I asked you when we could leave."

"Do you mean it?"

She nodded. "Yes."

"Tomorrow night, as soon as the sun goes down. We can be far enough away by morning that no one will catch us."

"I wouldn't be so certain of that. But I'm willing to take that chance. There is just one thing . . ."

"What?"

"If Tennap is prepared to fight, I want you to promise me that you won't hurt him."

"I won't, unless he gives me no choice."

"All right. I will be ready as soon as it gets dark."

"Meet me here. I will have a horse ready for you. Bring only what you need. We will want to move fast."

He leaned over and pecked her on the cheek, then said, "Promise me you won't change your mind."

"I promise."

"Good. Then we should go back. There is no point in making anyone suspicious."

He got to his feet, helped her up, and walked

her to Yellow Bear's lodge, where he said a quiet good night.

Back in his own lodge, he lay awake all night. In his mind, he kept revising the list of whom he would tell and what he would need to bring along. Each time he thought he had made the final choice, something or someone else occurred to him. He knew pretty well which of the young firebrands would follow him, and which ones he could trust. But he wouldn't be able to sleep until they were well away from the village, so he stoked the fire and packed his meager belongings, then covered them with a buffalo robe in case a visitor should pay a call during the day.

Chapter 22

QUANAH AND HIS ALLIES TRAVELED nonstop for more than twenty-four hours. Several of the warriors who accompanied him had wives and children of their own, and brought them along. Without intending to do so, Quanah had established himself as the leader of a separate band of Comanche. It was a small group, and when they made camp after the flight, most of the warriors stayed up all night, talking about their plans for the future.

"We can do anything we want, now," Fast Panther told Quanah. "You will be our chief, and we will follow wherever you lead us."

"I am not ready to be a chief," Quanah argued. "All I want is to be with Weakeah and be left alone."

Fast Panther shook his head. "You know we won't be left alone. The Anglos will never leave the Comanche alone. One reason we came with you is to continue to fight them. The old chiefs are getting soft. Yellow Bear thinks all the time of how to live in peace. He doesn't understand that the Anglos will not let us live in peace. They say the only good Indian is a dead Indian. You know that as well as I do."

Quanah nodded. "What you say is true, but maybe Yellow Bear knows something we don't. Maybe his years have taught him things we don't yet know."

"Peta Nocona would never think of peace with the Anglos," Fast Panther argued.

Quanah smiled sadly at the mention of his father. "Peta Nocona thought of peace often. He thought that the old ways were going to change, whether the Comanche wanted them to change or not. He believed that it was better for the Comanche to decide for himself how to change, and when."

"But that time has not yet come," Fast Panther insisted. "There are plenty of buffalo. We can still hunt where we wish and live where we wish. I don't want to be like the Cherokee and wear white man clothes and live in white man houses. I want to be free."

Quanah agreed. "I want to be free, too. I want to live as we have always lived. But we have to think of the future. Right now, the blue coat soldiers are not here, and it is easy to talk of what we wish to do, and say brave words about how we will fight to the last warrior. In my heart," he said, thumping his chest, "that is what I want. But when there are children to worry about, and old ones who need help, it is not so easy to be free."

"Did you run away so that you could make peace with the white men on your own?" Fast Panther asked.

"No!" Quanah glared at his friend. "I ran away to be with Weakeah, to have a family of my own, to live the kind of life I want to live."

"You can't live that life and make peace with the Anglos," Fast Panther insisted. "Because the Anglos won't let you."

"I know." Quanah sighed. "I understand. But we need to think about what we want to do. We need to plan carefully. If we are full of ourselves and reckless, and walk around thumping our chests to show everyone how strong we are, we will make fools of ourselves and we will lose everything. Better to be cautious, to decide what we want and get it our way."

"We need horses," Fast Panther said. "We will have to raid the Anglos, and soon. That will bring the Rangers after us, maybe the blue coat soldiers, too. Are you prepared for that?"

"I am prepared for anything but surrender on the white man's terms," Quanah said. "I have thought a great deal about what my father believed, and I think he was right that the Comanche have few choices. But I think there is another way, too. It might mean a lifetime of war, but I am prepared for that, if it is necessary. But I don't know about the others."

"The others will follow you. They know you think more than they do, and they respect that. They know, too, that you learned much from

Peta Nocona, and that he was not afraid of the Anglos."

"What we need first is rest," Quanah said. "Then, if we are to fight the white man, we need white man weapons. You have seen, as I have, how the white man's long guns are more powerful than our bows and arrows. They can sit far away and kill us one by one, as their hunters do the buffalo, without ever getting close enough for us to fight back."

"But where do we get such weapons? The whites will not sell them to us. You know that."

"Yes, I know that. And I know that we will have to get them from those who already have them—Anglos. And that will be the first thing we do, once the horses are rested."

By morning, Quanah had decided that he would continue Nocona's fight, not because he wanted blood, but because it was the only way to preserve the freedom he had been raised to love, and because the Texans were determined to put an end to that freedom, no matter what the cost.

As the sky turned gray, he looked up at Double Mountain and watched the sun rise over the twin peaks, thinking that it was more than the beginning of a new day. It was the beginning of a new life, one that he would defend with every drop of blood.

They spent several weeks in hiding, picking up a few more warriors, as word of Quanah's defection spread. Sporadic raids added more horses to their herd, and soon they were ready to move again, even farther south, away from Yellow Bear's village.

But Tennap did not take his loss lightly. And as his resentment simmered, he made up his mind to make one final attempt at winning Weakeah. Gathering a few trusted friends, he headed south, painstakingly hunting the run-aways. It was several weeks before one of his scouts stumbled on a returning band of raiders and tracked them to Quanah's camp on the Rio Concho. Once they were certain they had found Quanah, they raced back to Tennap and told him of their discovery. Resentment boiling over into rage, Tennap sprang onto his pony and led his small band to the camp.

But what he found was not a frightened Weakeah cowering by Quanah's side in some makeshift tipi, but a strong, well-armed band of Comanche, and discretion prevailed.

He paid a visit to Quanah's lodge, and barely recognized the man he had for so long painted in his own mind as a skulking weakling. There was no mistaking Quanah's courage, or his determination, and Tennap bowed to the inevitable. He returned to Yellow Bear's village full of admiration for the young warrior even he could now see was destined to become a formidable chief, if he wasn't one already.

For the next few years, Quanah swept across the Texas plains like the wind, raiding where and when he wanted to, adding more and more warriors to his band as tales of his exploits spread from camp to camp, not just among the Comanche, but among the Kiowa and Arapaho, too.

The great chiefs of the last generation were getting old, and had had their fill of bloodshed. Most of them were beginning to see what Nocona had seen so long before, that the days of the wild Indian on the great plains were coming to an end. But the younger men were not willing to surrender just yet. As long as there was someone willing to lead them, they would follow. Just as Crazy Horse was building a devoted following among the Sioux, Quanah was accumulating influence, hard won, and not consciously sought, by his insistence on his right to live the way he saw fit.

But as the Civil War came to an end, the defeated Confederates and the Union Army began to see eye to eye on at least one thing—the Comanche were an obstacle to settlement, and something had to be done about it. During the war, with both armies currying favor among the plains tribes for their own ends, and with neither side having time for a second war, the Comanche had managed to push back the western edge of settlement by more than one hundred miles.

Ranches had been overrun, the stock commandeered or driven off, the buildings burned to the ground. Many were little more than patches of tall weeds sprouting from the ashes, vines creeping over the few stones of ruined foundations still remaining.

But the pressure from the East was growing as hordes of settlers headed west to claim their piece of manifest destiny. The railroads probed westward like inquisitive fingers, cutting the huge buffalo herds of the great plains in two, then cutting the halves apart into smaller and smaller herds. The Buffalo hunters were doing their share, felling the great beasts by the hundreds of thousands, and as the herds shrank, more and more of the plains Indians were forced to face the inevitability of their future.

Within two years of the end of the war, the clamor from the East for an end to Indian depredations, with substantial sympathy among Easterners in general for the plight of the plains tribes, led to the creation of a Peace Commission, sponsored by Senator John Henderson, the chairman of the Senate Committee on Indian Affairs. Senator Henderson was sympathetic to the Indians, and the report commissioned for him blamed almost all of the difficulties on the white settlers.

The commission was to be comprised of seven men, three military leaders, and four civilians. The military contingent included Gen. William Tecumseh Sherman, the highest-ranking man in the army, Gen. W.S. Harney, who had significant Civil War accomplishments on his impressive résumé, and Gen. Alfred H. Terry, at that time the commander of the Department of Dakota.

Two of the civilian members were themselves retired generals, John Sanborn, practicing law in

Minnesota, and C.C. Augur. The other two were a Methodist minister, Nathaniel Taylor, and a third former army man, Col. Samuel Tappan.

The commission had explicit instructions, straight from the White House, to settle the Indian difficulties once and for all, and to concentrate on four specific objectives: eliminating the causes of Indian unrest; convincing the plains tribes to settle down and take up farming; persuading them to leave the railroads alone; and making it clear that attacks on white settlements had to stop.

They met for the first time in St. Louis on August 6, 1867, and embarked on the riverboat *St. Johns* for their trip to the first stop, which was to be a council with the Indians of the northern plains, primarily the Sioux. They came away with a treaty that few believed the Indians genuinely understood, and fewer still expected to be observed, and headed then for Medicine Lodge, Kansas, on the southern branch of the Arkansas River, for their second big council, this time with the southern plains tribes.

They expected to meet representatives of the Kiowa, Arapaho, Kiowa-Apache and Comanche, and had more than ten thousand dollars' worth of "gifts" in tow, which they expected to go a long way toward creating the bargaining flexibility they needed.

For the sake of security, they were accompanied by a contingent of the Seventh Cavalry under Maj. Joel Elliott, and had a gaggle of jour-

nalists, including no less a personage than Henry
M. Stanley, in tow. The army, to make a bold
impression, was dressed in full uniform at the
council's opening, and paraded to the small tent
city erected for the commissioners at the site of
the council.

Not to be outdone, the southern tribes, numbering more than five thousand warriors, staged
a parade of their own, in full regalia, each brave
in a war bonnet, mounted on his horse, and both
horse and rider in full paint and feathers.

As they approached the site, they broke into
formations and surrounded the main meeting
area in five concentric rings, each tribe's members with his fellows, and singing in his own
language.

The commissioners had never seen anything
like it, and the soldiers were more than a little
uneasy. Despite the cavalry's reputation and
modern weaponry, they were badly outnumbered, and not one of them believed he would
see the next morning if things were to get out of
control. More than a few of them believed exactly that was bound to happen. Some of the more
militant among the chiefs were already haranguing their own people, and even though there was
only one interpreter present, who had fluency
only in Comanche, it was soon apparent that
negotiations were not going to go smoothly.

When he had received word of the council,
Quanah was skeptical, and wanted no part of
any settlement with the white man on the

white man's terms. He believed that any lasting peace had to be won on the battlefield, but he was enough of a pragmatist to know that he should be present to learn firsthand what the white men proposed.

He arrived on the first day of the council, alone, and took his place toward the rear of the Comanche contingent. Not yet regarded as a chief by the other Comanche leaders, he was highly respected for his accomplishments in battle, and they tried hard to get him to take part.

But Quanah would have none of it.

Chapter 23

October 1867

THE COUNCIL GOT OFF to a bad start. Major Elliott had taken a small group of officers and enlisted men to a nearby valley when word reached the waiting commission that a herd of buffalo was grazing.

The soldiers killed several of the animals for the sheer pleasure of shooting something and watching it die. They had no interest in eating the meat, and they were not interested in trophies. The Indians, already angered by the increasingly wanton slaughter of the animals on which they depended for most of their food and much else they needed to live, from clothing to shelter, were angry, and Satanta, the Kiowa chief who was known for his explosive temper and his contempt for all things the white men held sacred, protested.

He cornered General Terry. "Your blue coat soldiers killed many buffalo. They killed them and left them to rot. They didn't take the skin to make robes, and they didn't take the meat to feed themselves. Now the buffalo are covered with white worms and they are good for nothing. You wonder why the Kiowa don't want the white man in Kiowa country. This is one reason why."

Terry, unaware of what had gone on, was at a loss to explain it. "I'll look into it, Chief," he said. As soon as Satanta was gone, he called Major Elliott to his tent.

"One of the chiefs was complaining that soldiers were hunting buffalo. Look into it, would you, Major, and report back to me."

Somewhat flustered, Elliott cleared his throat. "No need, General."

"The hell there isn't, Major. I want to know what happened. And I want to know yesterday. Now hop to it, Mister Elliott. That's an order."

"I know what happened. I was there."

"You what?"

"I was there."

"You mean to tell me you knew about this and didn't stop it."

Elliott loosened his collar, twisting his head from side to side. "I was part of the hunt, General. In fact, it was my idea."

Terry exploded. "Damn you, Elliott! Are you out of your mind? We have five thousand redskins out there, half of them spoiling for a fight, and you go and hand them goddamned ammunition?"

"I didn't see the harm in it, sir. There were thousands of the buffs, and we only shot a few."

"How many?"

Elliott shrugged. "Twenty . . . maybe a few more. Not more than thirty, for sure."

"And what did you plan to do with the buffalo once you shot them?"

"Nothing. Like I said, there were thousands of them. I didn't see the harm."

Terry took a deep breath. "Mister Elliott, I want the name of every man who participated in this outrage, and I want it now." He pointed to his camp desk. "Sit down and make a list. And I want a full written report, as well. Then we'll see about this."

"Yes, sir. Sorry, sir, I didn't think that . . ."

"I know you didn't, Mister Elliott. And we'll be lucky if we didn't all waste our time coming out here, thanks to you. In fact, we'll be lucky if we get to leave."

Terry stormed out of the tent and grabbed the first soldier he saw. "Sergeant, I want you to get the rest of the commissioners and tell them to meet me in Taylor's tent in ten minutes."

It took less than that to explain to his colleagues what had happened, and less time still to decide that all of the men had to be punished. They were confined to quarters pending disciplinary consideration, and Elliott was placed on report and relieved of his command for the duration of the council.

Later that morning, after the elaborate opening ceremonies and the usual diplomatic flourishes had been dispensed, the council got down to business.

Senator Henderson laid out the intentions of the great Father, as the Indians had come to think of the President. His speech was long-winded, and tried the ability of the sole translator present, Philip McCusker, who spoke only Comanche, leaving the Kiowa, Arapaho, and Kiowa-Apache to depend on those of their number who had a smattering, however inadequate, of the Comanche tongue. The language barrier alone was a significant impediment to the commission achieving its aims, but no one seemed to notice.

By the time Henderson was through explaining that the Great Father wanted to build schools and churches on reservations set aside for each of the tribes in attendance, teach them agricultural skills and provide them with annuities for an extended period as well as all the necessary farming implements and seed and livestock for their herds, the Indians were completely baffled.

Satanta, still angry over the buffalo slaughter, was the first speaker, and it was evident that he was in no mood to consider such absurdities as Henderson suggested.

"Two years ago I made peace with Generals Harney, Sanborn and Colonel Leavenworth at the mouth of the Little Arkansas. That peace I have never broken. When the grass was growing in the spring, a large body of soldiers came along the Santa Fe road. I had not done anything, and therefore I was not afraid. All the chiefs of the Kiowa, Comanche, and Arapaho are here today; they have come to listen to good words. We have been waiting here a long time to see you and are getting tired. All the land south of the Arkansas belongs to the Kiowa and Comanche, and I don't want to give away any of it."

That statement struck a responsive chord, and the entire throng of Indians seemed to press closer to the main council tent as Satanta continued.

"I love the land and the buffalo and will not part with it. I want you to understand well what I say. Write it on paper. Let the Great Father see it and let me hear what he has to say. I want you to understand, also, that the Comanche and the Kiowa don't want to fight, and have not been fighting since we made the treaty. I hear a great deal of good talk from the gentlemen whom the Great Father sends us, but they never do what they say."

He paused to wait for McCusker to translate and, once again, his words seemed to stir the crowd. There was a steady buzz as word spread, and a sudden hush descended when he resumed.

"I don't want any of the medicine lodges within the country. I want the children raised as I was. When I make peace it is a long and lasting one—there is no end to it. We thank you for your presents.

"All the headmen and braves are happy. They will do what you want them to do, for they know you are doing the best you can. I and they will do our best also. When I look upon you, I know you are all big chiefs. While you are in this country we go to sleep happy and are not afraid. I have heard you intend to settle us on a reservation near the mountains. I don't want to settle. I love to roam over the prairies. There I feel free and happy, but when we settle down we grow pale and die."

The mention of reservations provoked a ripple from the Kiowa, who understood the reference immediately. The rest had to wait for the translation. It seemed as if a black cloud were slowly passing over the assembly as faces darkened.

"I have laid aside my lance and bow and shield," Satanta went on, "and yet I feel safe in your presence. I have told you the truth. I have no little lies hid about me, but I don't know how it is with the commissioners. Are they as clear as I am?

"A long time ago, this land belonged to our fathers; but when I go to the river, I see camps of soldiers on its banks. These soldiers cut down my timber; they kill my buffalo; and when I see that, my heart feels like bursting; I feel sorry. I have spoken."

The commissioners waited for the last words to be translated, but could sense already that Satanta had made considerable impact on the assembled Indians. Ripples continued to spread through the five thousand warriors as word of what Satanta had said made its way toward the rear.

Quanah, far in the back, nodded his head. He understood exactly what Satanta feared, and he feared it for himself and his own people, as well. He knew the record of treaties made, and treaties broken. He knew there were concessions made and every year more were demanded. He knew the trickle of Anglos into the plains was slowly but surely rising to a flood. And he knew that, if it weren't stopped, that flood would sweep them all, Comanche, Kiowa, Arapaho, away. To weaken now, to give in at all, would only swell that flood, and hasten the day when the only choice was that between living on the reservation or dying on the run.

Better to run now, he thought.

But there were some among the chiefs who did not feel so strongly as Satanta. Another Kiowa chief, Kicking Bird, rose to speak, and the excited hush settled down to a silence in which only the cry of birds could be heard, and the whisper of the wind in the tall grass as it swept across the valley.

When the first day's session had ended, Quanah drifted from one council to another. He was welcome everywhere. His years of wandering from band to band, village to village, had won him friends not just among the various

Comanche groups but among the Kiowa and Arapaho, as well.

When he entered the Kiowa council lodge, Satanta was just winding up a long articulation of his position, and Kicking Bird was shaking his head sadly.

"No," Kicking Bird said, "you are wrong. The white man will honor the treaty because it is his treaty. He wants it. He has nothing to gain by not honoring it."

Satanta nodded to Quanah, then spat in disgust at what Kicking Bird was saying. "You know nothing. The Cheyenne are here, those who are left. If you think the white man honors his treaties, ask the Cheyenne about Sand Creek. Black Kettle trusted the white man, and the blue coats attacked his village for no reason. But still, Black Kettle wanted peace, and so he forgave the white man. Then Chivington came to Sand Creek, and when he was finished, there were women and children thick as leaves dead on the ground. The women had their private places butchered by the blue coat soldiers. Is that your idea of peace? Because that is the white man's idea of peace."

"Then why did you say you were peaceful?" Kicking Bird demanded. "You said you had no little lies hidden about you. That was a lie."

"It was a lie, maybe. But no more a lie than the lies the white men always tell us. I think Kicking Bird will make a foolish mistake if he signs this treaty paper. He will touch the pen and the commissioners will go to Washington and show the paper to the Great Father and say, 'See, here is where Kicking Bird touched the pen. That means we can take his land. And we will give him what we feel like, when we feel like giving. And if we don't feel like giving, well, then, Kicking Bird will not care because he doesn't know any better.' That is what happens when you make a treaty with the white man."

The debate raged on into the small hours, and Quanah sat quietly, listening. It was not his place to speak in a Kiowa council lodge.

When the argument, still as unsettled as it had been when he arrived, finally adjourned for the night, Quanah spent some time with Satanta and the other skeptics, discussing what might be done if some of the chiefs signed the treaty.

"You know," Satanta said, "that if just one Kiowa touches the pen, then the commissioners will say he speaks for all the Kiowa. They will say the treaty is made, and that all Kiowa have to move to the reservation. They will try to pen us up like they pen their sheep and their cattle. And if we let them, then we will be fit for nothing else. They can shear us for their wool and squeeze our teats for their milk because we will be like their livestock."

"I would rather die on the open plains," Quanah said. "It is no life to live like the white man lives. And everybody has seen how he

treats the Indians on the reservation. The
Cherokee are not free men. They think they are,
but they are not. I don't want to be like a
Cherokee and wear cloth leggings and go to a
wooden medicine lodge. I can stand under the
stars and speak to the Great Spirit. But the Great
Spirit does not hear the Indian anymore when he
speaks. You have seen the pictures of the white
man's Great Spirit. He has white skin and blue
eyes and wears his hair long on his face, just like
the old white men do. But that is not *my* Great
Spirit."

Satanta nodded his agreement. "You are right.
I will not believe this treaty. I will not touch the
pen, and I will not live in a corral like a sheep.
Kicking Bird can live in a cage like the ones the
white women keep their little singing yellow
birds in. But I will not."

After much similar conversation, in which it
was clear to Quanah that many among the
Kiowa thought as he and Satanta did, the Kiowa
chief led him outside. Taking him away from
the lodges, he said, "I have seen a friend of
yours."

"Who?"

"Little Belly. He asked me if you were here
and I said I did not know. I think he wants to see
you about something important. You should find
him. He is with the Kiowa of Kicking Bird, of
course."

Quanah, puzzled by the message, nodded. "I
will," he said.

"Quanah," Satanta said, as the younger man was about to walk away. "Whatever the other Comanche chiefs do, don't touch the pen. It will mean nothing but trouble for you. You will have trouble either way, but at least you will not die of a broken heart."

Quanah nodded, but he was starting to think that was exactly what he would die of.

Chapter 24

QUANAH SPENT A SLEEPLESS NIGHT. He had listened to all the things the commissioners had said, and he was not impressed. It was not just the distrust of the Anglos that he had learned at Nocona's knee, although that was a major part of his concern. It was that what the white men were proposing seemed designed to make the Indians into white men. And yet, no matter how many white ways they adopted, Quanah knew the Indians would always be Indians. He had been near some of the white man's forts. He saw how the Anglos looked at the Indians, their eyes full of contempt, even hatred. This was something that no piece of paper could change, no matter how many names were on it. Not even if the Great Father himself came and sat in the lodge and put his own name on the paper in front of all the chiefs would that look go away.

And as he sifted through the details of the previous day's discussion, he found one reason after another not to sign the treaty. The white men

wanted the Indians to learn to farm. And when
he saw how the white man farmers lived, tied to
the earth, breaking their backs in the hot sun,
knowing that too little rain, or too much rain, or
a cloud of grasshoppers or a prairie fire could
wipe out a year's work in a matter of hours, it
didn't seem any way to live. Why scratch the
ground and make yourself a slave to it. The
Indian could go anywhere for his food. He carried his house around with him. Everything he
needed to live was already out there on the
plains, and there was enough for everyone. Or
there had been, until the white man started
killing the buffalo for no reason, taking thousands for as simple a thing as the tongue, leaving
the rest of the meat to the buzzards. The killing
was indiscriminate and, worse than that, it was
utterly wasteful.

Quanah knew things weren't that simple. He
knew the Indian sometimes had hard times.
Sometimes the buffalo were difficult to find.
Sometimes the water holes dried up and left
nothing but bitter mud behind. Sometimes a bolt
of lightning set the grass on fire, and left miles
and miles of ashes and scorched earth behind.
But when that happened, the Indian had the
option to move, to go where there was enough
buffalo, where the grass was green, where the
water was cool and clear and good to drink. If
the white man had to do that, he would have to
leave his house behind, and maybe everything
that was in it. Why, he kept asking himself, was

that way to live better than the one the Comanche already had?

And he didn't have to look too hard to find the answer. The simple truth was, it wasn't better at all. It was different. Maybe it was even good—for white men. But Comanche weren't white men. Neither were Kiowa or Arapaho or Cheyenne.

And Quanah knew all the stories about the Indians who had agreed to give up their right to roam where they pleased, to settle down on the white man's reservations. Always it was the same. The goods the treaty promised were late, if they came at all. And more often than not, when they did come, they were worthless. The grain had worms, the cattle were skin and bones and only half of them even reached the Indians at all. The agents were mostly thieves and liars, lining their own pockets with stolen profit, selling the goods and keeping the money. And always someone came to the reservation and found something the white man wanted, gold or timber, sometimes even something as simple as good land for farming. And always the Indian had to sign another paper that made the reservation smaller, and he got nothing in exchange. Signing a treaty was jumping off a cliff. There was no place to go but all the way to the bottom once you jumped.

No, there was no reason that made any sense at all for any Indian to touch the pen to the white man's treaty paper. And by the time the sun came up, he knew that he would not sign and that he would do everything he could to convince the others not to sign. He hoped that the Comanche would listen to him, and that others opposed to the treaty, like Satanta, could convince their own peoples not to sign. Once the pen touched the paper, the Indian way of life would be doomed.

He knew all the arguments about the treaties, especially how they would keep the Indians from fighting among themselves. But it was not much more than two years since the white men had been fighting among *themselves,* and he had heard stories about battles in which more white men died than there were Comanche and Kiowa put together. If the treaty would keep the Indians from killing each other, why couldn't the men who wrote the treaties keep from killing one another?

He went outside the lodge as the sun rose, and saw that the soldiers were already up and about. A line of them was heading into a tent, and another line was coming out, holding tin plates of food. Many of the Indians were already gathering in small groups, and he looked for Satanta, but there were so many Kiowa lodges that it took him nearly twenty minutes to find his friend.

Satanta was already hard at work, haranguing the Kiowa and some Arapaho against the treaty. But opinion seemed to be divided. The hardliners, like Satanta, were contemptuous of those disposed to sign, and Quanah wondered if maybe they were being too inflexible.

When Satanta saw him, he waved him over. "We will have trouble sending the commissioners home without a treaty," he said. "There are many Indians, even Kiowa, who have lost their hearts. They are tired of worrying about the white man and want to sign his paper so he will leave them alone."

Quanah nodded. "I know. I have been thinking all night about it."

"You won't sign, will you?"

"No. But I understand why some will, no matter what we tell them. I'm afraid that one day we will all be forced to live on reservations. My father was afraid of that, too, and I think he was right, even though I disagreed with him when he would talk that way."

"Peta Nocona thought so?" Satanta seemed surprised. "I would have thought he would be opposed to the treaty. I know how he felt about the Anglos."

"No, he wouldn't have signed, but he knew there were many who would. Every year more and more."

"Ah," Satanta said. "I think he was right. Did you see Little Belly?"

"Not yet. After the meeting today, I will look for him."

Satanta spat into the dust. "The meeting," he said, his voice dripping acid, "will be much wind and little sense. Talk, talk, talk. I know people think I talk all the time, that I like to hear the sound of my own voice. But it isn't so. I talk all the time to keep bad words out of the air. If I keep the wind filled with my words, there is no room for foolishness." He grinned, and Quanah laughed.

"They say you are the Orator of the Plains."

Satanta shrugged. "Somebody has to be. If you have ever spent much time around the council fire in a lodge full of Kiowa, you know where I learned it. I have to spend more time trying to convince these fools not to sign," he said. "I will see you at the meeting."

Quanah drifted around, hanging on the perimeter of one conversation or another for the better part of an hour. And everything he heard convinced him that there would be some kind of treaty to come out of the great council. He was depressed and angry, and tried not to let his ill temper show, but he was having a hard time of it.

By the time the meeting got underway, the commissioners were sitting at their long table, papers in front of them. It was nearly nine o'clock. The ceremonial passing of the pipe took nearly another hour.

And finally, at a little after ten o'clock, Kicking Bird stood. Commissioner Taylor recognized him, and the Kiowa chief spoke at length about the treaty, and what he thought it would mean for his people. There were murmurs of approval, and a few shouts of contempt every time he paused, and Kicking Bird seemed aware that he was speaking for a majority, if not of the most influential, at least in terms of the overall attendance.

The Kiowa chief had had a meeting six months before, with General Hancock, and he spoke once more as he had spoken then. And it was obvious to Quanah that Kicking Bird had become the leader of the peace faction, determined to have the treaty signed at all cost. He wondered whether Kicking Bird understood just how high that cost would be, and what he would have to say when the white man acted as if the paper had never been signed, when the soldiers came, and the buffalo hunters and the settlers.

By the end of the day, though, the commissioners were pushing for a signing the next morning.

Quanah watched as the meeting broke up, and drifted off looking for Little Belly. Finally finding his lodge, he called to his old friend, whom he hadn't seen in more than three years, and Little Belly came rushing out.

He threw his arms around Quanah and dragged him into the lodge. "There is someone I want you to meet," he said.

Quanah, once his eyes adjusted to the dim light, was surprised to find himself staring at a white man, whose red hair looked like fire, and whose face was hidden behind a full, dark red beard.

Quanah recognized him immediately. It was the interpreter, Philip McCusker.

Little Belly introduced the two men, then chattered excitedly. "Mac has come to the council as an interpreter. He has news for you. I have been looking for you ever since I heard you were here."

Quanah shook hands with the white man, who got to his feet.

And Little Belly broke in even before the hands had separated. "Mac has news of your mother!"

Quanah looked stunned.

McCusker measured him with his gaze. "You're Cynthia Parker's son?" he asked.

"You know what happened to my mother?" Quanah asked, ignoring the question put to him. "Where is she? What happened to her?"

McCusker raised a hand. "Hold on, one at a time," he said. Dropping back to the buffalo robe on the floor of the lodge, he patted the ground beside him. "Sit down," he said.

When Quanah was seated, McCusker took time to roll a cigarette. Quanah wanted to grab him by the shoulders and shake the information out of him, but he forced himself to be polite. When the cigarette was finished, McCusker asked if he wanted one, but the impatient Quanah just shook his head.

Taking a deep breath, McCusker paused, looked at Quanah with a mixture of sadness and pity. "I can only tell you what I heard," he began. "I wasn't there, and I didn't see any of this with my own eyes, but I believe it to be true."

He waited for that preamble to sink in, then nodded. "Naudah, I think she was known as among your people. At least, that's what I've heard."

"Naudah, yes," Quanah said, leaning forward.

"Well, there was a Ranger attack on a camp at Pease River . . . your camp . . . and Naudah was captured, along with a baby girl."

"Prairie Flower," Quanah said, trying to keep his voice from cracking.

"Right. Anyway, the wives of the army officers at Camp Cooper took good care of her. They cleaned her up and gave her something to eat. She hadn't been hurt. Neither had the baby. And Captain Ross, he was the Ranger who was in charge of the raid, he sent for Isaac Parker. That was her uncle. Your great-uncle, I guess, I'm not too sure of how that works. Anyway, Isaac Parker came to the camp. Whenever a white woman was recaptured from the Indians, even if they weren't Comanche, Isaac would always go, hoping to find Cynth . . . Naudah. When he got there, she was sittin' in a rocker, holding the baby. He didn't recognize her right off, and the longer he looked at her, the less sure he was. Finally, he was about to leave, and said it wasn't Cynthia Ann, and she ups and says she was. She was afraid of him at first, but I guess when he said her name, it reminded her of something."

"Then what happened?" Quanah asked, his voice barely a whisper. "Where is she?"

"Isaac Parker took her and the baby home with

him. She had a little sister, just a baby when she was taken away, and she lived with the sister. She was all the time worried about you and your brother and your father, though. At first, she tried to escape, to come back to the Comanche, but they always caught her. Finally, she figured she'd never find you anyhow, so she tried to fit in. But it didn't work out so good. She couldn't get used to the white man's ways, and she was pining away for her family. The baby got sick and died. It seemed to take everything out of your mother. Not long after, she passed away herself."

McCusker had made the entire narration without looking at Quanah. Now, his own voice barely audible, he looked at the Comanche for the first time. "I'm sorry," he said. "But I thought you'd want to know."

Quanah nodded.

"She was well taken care of," McCusker said. "She had people around her who loved her, but I guess . . ." His voice trailed off.

"Thank you," Quanah said. Then without another word, he got to his feet and walked out of the lodge, leaving McCusker and Little Belly to stare after him.

By the time the Kiowa could get himself into motion, Quanah was already lost in the crowd.

That night, he rode away from the council, not knowing and not caring whether the treaty was to be signed.

Chapter 25

Spring 1868

ON THE LONG, LONELY RIDE from Medicine Lodge, Quanah had plenty of time to think. He was barely twenty-two years old, and he was as alone in the world as he had ever been. Peta Nocona was dead. Naudah was dead. Pecos and Prairie Flower were dead. And his way of life was slowly dying. He had Weakeah, but somehow it seemed not to be enough, because she was as trapped in the downward spiral as he was.

What he had seen at the great council had done nothing to reassure him. He knew that Satanta, and the others like him, would fight until they could fight no longer. But they were already great chiefs, and they had substantial reputations as warriors. It was easy for such men to get others to follow them. But who was Quanah? A Comanche orphan. Worse, a Comanche orphan with blue eyes.

He had no sense of where he belonged in the world, if, indeed, he belonged anywhere at all. All he could be sure of was that the Anglos had to be resisted at all cost, and it was into that resistance that he resolved to pour every bit of his strength and intelligence. The Staked Plains were Comanche land, always had been and, if he could do anything about it, they always would be.

By the time he reached his camp, he had made up his mind. The white men sent soldiers to talk about peace. What they really meant was give us peace on our terms or we will give you war. If war is what they want, Quanah thought, then war is what they will have.

Weakeah was pleased to see him. She worried about him every time he left the small village, and when, as increasingly happened, those absences were solitary, she worried still more. She was haunted by the possibility that something would happen to him and not only would she never see him again, she would never know what had happened to him.

The thought of Quanah lying somewhere in the vast emptiness, his body food for wolves and crows, was almost more than she could stand, and her dreams were haunted by one ghastly scenario after another. She was not naive. She was, after all, the daughter of Yellow Bear, a great chief, and she knew that the life of a Comanche warrior ended more often than not in sudden violence. But this was no ordinary man who slept beside her, this was Quanah, a man who had it in him to lead his people, not just the small band of refugees, but all the Comanche. He could make war against the white man, or he could find a way to lead his people along the path of peace. But she feared that the choice would not be hers to make. And that it would not be Quanah's.

It was near sundown when he rode in, and she couldn't help but notice the grim set of his jaw.

"What happened?" she asked.

He shook off the question. "I don't want to talk about it," he said. "Not now."

"But . . ."

He shook his head once more. "I have much to tell you, but I don't want to talk yet. I want to think. There is so much that I have to try to understand, and I don't know where to begin."

"At least tell me if the treaty was signed. Is there going to be peace? Will we have to go to a reservation like the Caddo and the Wichita?"

With a labored sigh, he moved to the fire and lay down, folding his arms behind his head and staring at the smoke hole at the top of the lodge.

Weakeah walked over to sit beside him. He reached out one hand and turned onto a hip to look up at her. She took the hand in both of her own and held it in her lap.

"You want to know everything, don't you?" he asked. There was no anger in the statement, but his voice seemed to come from a great distance, as if he were barely aware of her, perhaps even talking to himself.

She smiled. "Of course I do. I didn't run away from my father's lodge to have you keep secrets from me. I did it because I want to share everything with you. Good and bad. Is that so hard to understand?"

He shook his head. "Yes, in some ways it is. I don't have very much to share. The life I have is not one that many people would even want to share."

"I don't . . ."

He reached up to hold a finger to her lips. "Wait," he said. "Just give me a little time to . . ." He stopped, sat up, and looked at her intently. "I don't know if the treaty was signed," he said.

"But, I thought you went to the council to see what happened."

"I did. But there was so much going on. There were thousands of Indians—Comanche, Kiowa, Arapaho, Kiowa-Apache, Cheyenne— it seemed there were as many Indians as there are blades of grass. But then I thought about how many Anglos there are, and it seemed suddenly that there were so few Indians that we could never hope to . . ."

"Did they sign the treaty then, because they were afraid of the numbers, is that what happened?" Weakeah was trying to understand, but his mind seemed only to skip from one stone to another, when she was asking him about all the water between them.

Sensing that he was not making himself understood, he sighed, lay back, and stared again at the top of the lodge. He saw where the lodge-poles were lashed together, and he thought that is what he and Weakeah were like. They were lashed together, with something stronger than rawhide, and if he were to be fair, he would have to try to tell her what he was going through. If she didn't understand, at least he would have done his part.

"I don't know if the treaty was signed because I left before the council was over."

"But why? That is why you went. Why did you leave? What was the point in going, if you were not going to stay until the very end?"

Closing his eyes, he swallowed hard. "Naudah," he said. "Prairie Flower."

"What? What about them? You saw them? You saw your mother?"

He shook his head. "No," he whispered. "But I met someone, a white man named McCusker, who knew what happened to them."

"What? What happened? Tell me, Quanah . . ." She lay beside him then, resting on her stomach, propping herself on her elbows and raising her head to look at his face. "Where are they? Can you bring them here?"

"Dead," he said. "Both of them. I . . ."

She noticed the tears squeezing out through closed lids, saw the lids tremble as he tried to squeeze them tighter still, to hold back the tears. Inching closer, she leaned over him, kissed him on the forehead, and rested her head on his shoulder. His arm encircled her, and she felt the strength of his hand as it stroked her back.

He told her then, everything that McCusker had told him, leaving out nothing and relating it almost word for word as McCusker had told it to him.

When he was finished, Weakeah was crying, too. "I'm sorry," she said. "I'm sorry, Quanah."

He nodded that he understood. But understanding wasn't enough to stop the pain.

He drifted off to sleep, Weakeah in his arms, and when he awoke, it was the middle of the night. She was awake, sitting by the fire, watching him.

"You were very tired. It was a long journey. You should go back to sleep."

Shaking his head, he sat up, then got to his feet. Moving toward the entrance, he turned. "Come for a walk with me," he said.

She followed him outside. Overhead, the stars were brilliant points in the cold early November air. He looked up at them, then pointed. "Like drops of water in the grass," he said, "they sparkle."

She mumbled agreement, and moved close to

him, taking the extended arm and draping it over her shoulder. "This is the way it should be," she said. "Just like this. Always."

Quanah shook his head. "It won't be. Peta Nocona knew that it was all changing. He tried to stop it, and when he understood that he couldn't stop it, he tried to find a way to control it. But he failed at that, too. And I know that I will also fail. There is no stopping it."

"You worry too much about such things," she said.

Instead of answering, he changed the subject. "When I was a small boy, Nocona took me for a walk at night. We were at the Laguna Sabinas, where I was born, and it was the same time of year I was born. There was so much to see, even at night, and he kept pointing at things, things I didn't know were there until he showed them to me."

He stopped to stare up at the sky, and she wondered if instead of looking at the brilliance of the stars he might be looking at the vast, empty blackness between them.

"There were stars then, just like now, bright like these are. It was cold and very still. Then Nocona pointed. At first I didn't know what he had seen, but he kept watching, and then he pointed again. 'There,' he said, 'do you see it?' The second time, I noticed something, but I wasn't sure what it was, just a black shape. I could see it only because it passed in front of the stars, but I still didn't know what it was."

He paused and she glanced up in time to see the last vestige of a sad smile slip away.

"The third time," he continued, "I saw it much better, but I still didn't know what it was. So I asked him."

"What was it?"

"He didn't tell me. 'Wait,' he said. 'Watch.' And then it was coming right at us, so close I could hear the wind of its passing. Then I heard a noise behind us and I turned. I saw something on the ground, just movement, and then it was climbing into the sky again. I asked him what it was again, and this time he told me. It was an owl, and it had come down to strike a rabbit."

He laughed. "And then I remember that he told me that the night was full of owls, but you had to know to look for them. And then he said something that I will never forget. He said that we live in the dark, never knowing when the owl might come for us. 'But it will,' he said. 'It will.' And I don't think I knew what he meant until now. I think he meant that it is impossible to know when death will come. Thinking about Naudah and Prairie Flower, I realize that death will come and we can't know where or when. I think that was why he lived the way he did, especially after Naudah was taken. I think he was looking for the owl."

"You think more than that," she said. "You think he found it. You think he wasn't willing to wait for the owl to come find him so he went looking for it. You think he wanted to die, don't you."

Quanah nodded. "Yes, I think he did. I think after Naudah was taken he didn't have a reason to live."

"He had you, and Pecos."

"It wasn't enough. He had lost too much, suffered too much. When Naudah was taken, it brought everything else back, White Heron, Little Calf, all of it. . . ."

"White Heron?"

"The woman before Naudah. And Little Calf was their son. My brother. They were killed by the Osage. Nocona lived alone for a long time after that happened. And he would never tell me anything about them. Most of what I know, I know from Black Snake, Nocona's friend."

"They say you are like Nocona, that you are fierce, and that you take chances in war. Are you looking for the owl, too? Is that what you're doing? Do you want to die?"

Quanah shook his head. "I don't know. I don't think so, but maybe when that is what you're doing, you don't know it. Maybe that not knowing is part of it."

"Are you sure?"

"I'm sure. But I'm sure of one other thing."

"What?"

"That war is coming, and that it will be bad, and that I may not live to see it end."

Weakeah leaned still closer. She said nothing
because she realized there was nothing to say.
The night was full of owls, just as Peta Nocona
had said.

Chapter 26

Summer 1868

JARED WILKINS LAY ON THE HILLTOP, a long duster trailing on the ground behind him. Three hundred yards to his left, Joseph Hanley lay on the ground and, beyond him, another four hundred yards, Felton Peters did the same. Wilkins watched the valley below him, where a herd of buffalo was grazing peacefully. Turning to look behind him, he waved a hand to two more men, Anthony Chambers and Donald Duncan, who sat in the shade of one of four huge wagons parked in a row, their teams bobbing their heads lazily, and switching their tails to keep the flies at bay.

Wilkins shifted his position to get more comfortable on the hard ground. He had a canvas carryall on the ground beside him and tugged it closer, pulling down one side to expose several boxes of ammunition for his Sharps buffalo gun. The .55-caliber cannon with its octagonal barrel was the cleanest thing about the man, who stank of sweat and buffalo grease. Flies swirled overhead but seemed frightened to come too close, whether kept off by the smell of the man or his movement would have been difficult to tell.

He raised his hand high in the air, then dropped it, and turned his attention to the box sight of the big Sharps. Wilkins was a good shot, one of the best. He swore he could hit the center spot on the ace of spades at five hundred yards, but that might have been pushing it, although he was confident enough over a bottle of whiskey, when he usually made his announcement, that no one had yet taken him up on his five-hundred-dollar wager.

Wilkins was a buffalo hunter, and he was pushing deep into Comanche territory, chasing the big beasts into a region where most of his fellow buffalo hunters were reluctant to travel. "Got to go where the buffs are," he liked to say. "No point goin' where everybody and his brother's already been. Sides, with that big Sharps, ain't no Comanche gonna get half close enough to lift my hair." It was a barroom line, the one he'd used to convince Peters and Hanley to throw in with him, and he chuckled now, repeating it out loud for the benefit of the wind and the flies.

The first echo of one of the hunters' big guns rolled toward him, and he glanced sideways before squinting through the sights once more and taking aim on a big bull which had lifted and turned its head. The animal seemed to be looking right at him, but Wilkins knew the buffa-

lo had poor vision and wouldn't be able to see
him if he were even closer than the five hundred
yards that currently separated man and beast.

He squeezed the trigger, feeling the kick of the
big gun all the way down his right side, jerked
the empty out and shoved another round in. He
was starting to feel it now, the thrill of dispens-
ing death at long range, hurling thunderbolt after
thunderbolt down into a big herd, watching the
bulls fall to their knees, then rolling over on
their sides. One by one, they fell. Peters and
Hanley were good shots, too, but not as good as
Wilkins, and the boom of the big guns started to
sound like distant thunder as one or another
seemed to be firing before the echo of the last
shot had died away.

It had taken them three weeks to find the
herd, and Wilkins had been getting antsy, sus-
pecting that maybe there had been something
wrong with his logic. Maybe nobody bothered to
come this deep into Comanche territory because
there were no buffalo to bother with.

For two hours, the three hunters banged away.
The mound of shells by Wilkins grew deeper and
broader, each one clinking onto the heap still
hot, still giving off a little wisp of gunsmoke. The
stench of gunpowder swirled around him, soak-
ing into his duster and giving the flies further
pause.

The animals below, terrified by the gunfire,
didn't know which way to turn. And because the
sounds came from such a long way off, and were

joined by echoes, they were unable to settle on a direction for flight. As a result, they milled around helplessly. Wilkins was particular, and didn't shoot just any buffalo. Each time, he picked a good specimen, going for the ones with the best skins, because that's where the money was.

Back east, they were paying a fortune for good skins, and Wilkins meant to get his share. He wished there could be some way to mark each kill with his personal sign, so he could segregate the skins and make sure that his discriminating eye was fairly rewarded. Since that wasn't possible, the profits were pooled, then shared out according to a formula Wilkins had outlined to the other two hunters. Duncan and Chambers were just skinners and wagoneers. Their cut would be smaller, but still a goodly sum.

When the barrel of the Sharps began to grow too hot, Wilkins put the gun aside and rolled onto his back, watching the clouds drift by for a while.

But Wilkins and his friends weren't alone. The first sound of the big guns had drawn a pair of Comanche, who had heard them often enough to know exactly what they were. But they had been surprised to hear them here, so close to their camp, and they wanted to be certain what was happening.

They had hidden their horses in a willow break and walked nearly a mile before catching sight of the wagons. It took them a half hour to find out exactly how many men were in the hunting party, because they knew only too well the accuracy of the big guns, and couldn't afford to get too close.

But soon enough, they had all the information they needed, and they knew the hunters would be there for a long time. It took a lot longer to skin three hundred buffalo than it did to shoot them. And since it was too late to save the herd, there was no hurry.

Sneaking back the way they'd come, they leapt onto their ponies and headed back to their small village, their anger at the slaughter boiling into a fury at the violation of their territory. By the time they'd reached the camp, they were in a towering rage, and word spread quickly about the hunters.

Fast Panther was the first one into Quanah's lodge.

"Buffalo hunters," he said.

Quanah looked up, startled. "Where? How far?" But he didn't wait for an asnwer. Running out of the lodge, leaving Fast Panther to follow him, he raced to where the two scouts were retelling their story for the fourth time.

"How many guns do they have?" Quanah asked.

Swimmer, one of the two who had seen the hunters, shrugged. "I don't know. Three hunters, and two other men. That means at least five."

"Often the buffalo men have more than one gun," Quanah said. "They shoot so many buffalo the guns get hot and they switch to another while the first one cools."

"We should go while they are still there," Swimmer said.

Quanah nodded. "We will go, but we won't attack them. Not now. The buffalo guns are too strong for us. If they know we are there, we will never get close enough. The hunters are not like the soldiers, who have bad guns and don't even know how to use them."

"We can't let them go," Fast Panther said. "If we do, then others will come. We have to show them that Comanche land is for Comanche only."

Quanah nodded. "We will show them. But we will show them in our own good time."

"When?"

"Tonight."

"Suppose they finish their skinning?"

"If they do, they will still stay where they are for the night. They don't travel after dark. And even if they leave, we can follow them, now that we know they are here. Go to your lodges and get ready. If you have a gun, bring it."

Quanah went back to his own tipi and went inside. He had a gun of his own now, a Springfield carbine, but he had very few bullets. There were so many different kinds of guns the white man used, and the bullets for some did not fit others. He knew of some Comanche who fired bullets too small for the guns they had, and the bullets would not go where they were supposed to. But Quanah had the feeling that bullets were not going to be necessary this night.

The war party was ready to go in less than twenty minutes. Fourteen were already on their ponies by the time Quanah came back out of his lodge. He had learned from what happened at Pease River, and never took more men than necessary on any raid, always leaving enough behind to protect the camp.

They reached the valley where the wagons had been with less than an hour of daylight left. Quanah led the way on foot up the hill, following the wagon tracks to the top of the ridge. He lay down and crawled to the crest, where he found a pile of shells from one of the buffalo guns and several broken pasteboard boxes. There were even a few good shells in the grass. As he stuck them into his shirt, he thought how wasteful the white man could be, that bullets, which were like jewels to the Comanche, could be left unspent in the grass as if they were worthless.

Looking down into the valley ahead, he saw the wagons, just as he had expected. They were spread out across the valley floor, and as he watched, he saw one of the skinners straighten up and carry two fresh skins to the wagon, throw them onto a heap of other skins, and trudge back to his next carcass.

All across the valley floor, the great mounds of red flesh that had been buffalo just a few hours before, lay scattered, barely recognizable for

what they were. They might as well have been
mounds of red clay, for all they resembled buffalo.
Quanah felt the rage boiling up inside him now,
and he knew that he had to control himself. He
would like nothing more than to leap to his feet
and lead a charge down into the valley. But that
would be suicide. Stealth was the only hope he
and his warriors had, the only ally. To punish
these men for their invasion of Comanche land,
he would have to get close enough, and rage
would not help.

He scanned the valley from end to end, counting five men, then scanned it again to make sure
that he hadn't missed one bent over his work
and hidden by a buffalo carcass or a wagon. But
he had missed none.

Already, the men had a fire built at one end of
the valley, and one of the wagons sat beside it,
the team already unhitched. He knew that is
where the men would camp for the night, away
from the stink of the rotting carcasses, and he
backed away from the ridge line until he could
stand without risking being seen by the hunters.

He led the men at a trot, wanting to be in
position before sundown. As he ran, he heard
the whistle of one of the wagoneers, followed
by the sharp crack of a bullwhip. When he
reached the far end of the valley, not a quarter
mile from the ridge overlooking the hunters'
campsite, he could hear the creak of wagon
wheels, and he nodded with satisfaction.

"They are coming," he said, when he had

gathered the warriors around him. "They are making camp on the other side of this ridge. There are five of them."

"Only five?" Swimmer said. "We should attack them now, while there is still light."

Quanah shook his head. "No. They are not all in the camp yet. And once it is dark, the only light will be their campfire. There is no moon tonight, and their long guns will be of no use in the dark. Even the best shooter can't hit what he can't see."

He smiled but it was a cold smile, speaking more of the revenge to come than of any pleasure felt at the moment.

The Comanche waited for sunset, watching the sun as if the weight of thirty determined eyes would drag it down sooner. Quanah waited impatiently until the sky darkened, then went black, and he could see the stars.

It was time.

Leading his warriors carefully up the hills, he stopped at the top and crawled forward to take a look. The men were sprawled around the fire, eating from tin plates like the ones the soldiers used. He could see all five of them, and they were careless enough that they had parked their wagons all in a row instead of arranging them for protection. This would be easier than he had feared.

Quickly, he backed away and explained what he wanted done, then crept back to the hilltop and waited for the warriors to get into position.

Instead of launching an assault from this high up, he was going to move in close, and he would communicate with the others by birdcalls and animal sounds, as few as possible and using only those appropriate to the time of day, because the hunters often had a keen ear for any sound that did not belong.

He could see that some of the men were drinking. They passed a bottle back and forth, and the more they drank, the louder their voices became. He was glad to see that it was not only Indians who made fools of themselves with whiskey.

When the others signaled they were in position, he started down the hill. They had encircled the camp, but since they numbered only fifteen, there was considerable distance between each pair of warriors. Only when the noose closed around the camp would they be close enough to see one another.

It took nearly an hour. But finally, Quanah was so close that he could smell the burnt meat from the meal, and the stink of the white man clothes. As prearranged, he made the first move, notching an arrow and pulling the bow to full draw. Sticking his tongue between his teeth as he often did when shooting, he held his aim for a split second, then let the arrow go. He followed its flight, saw it strike his target just a little higher than he had intended, but not enough to matter, and saw the man clutch frantically at his back where the arrow had lodged, getting to his feet and spinning around several times.

Suddenly a hail of arrows poured into the camp, and he knew that all of the hunters had been hit at least once. There was a single gunshot from a pistol as one of the wounded men drew it from his hip and fired blindly into the darkness.

Quanah's second arrow was on its way, and he saw that several of the others had chosen the same target, because the man was hit by half a dozen shafts almost instantly, as if he were sprouting quills.

And just that quickly, it was over. Quanah moved close, another arrow drawn, keeping a wary eye on the five bodies, just in case one of them was not already dead.

But there was no movement, and the only sound was a ghastly rattle as one of the hunters tried to breathe once more, then trembled and lay still.

As if in a frenzy, the other warriors charged in and riddled the bodies with arrows, then ransacked the supply wagon for anything of value. Quanah reached into the fire for a brand and tossed it onto one of the wagonloads of skins, and soon all three were in flames and, when the fourth had been pilfered, it joined the others in flames.

Quanah drew his knife, knelt beside one of the hunters, and grabbed a fistful of stringy hair that was slippery under his fingers. He brought the knife down, held it at the dead man's forehead for an instant, remembering Nocona doing the same so long ago, then sliced the scalp and held it aloft, offering it to the dead chief.

He felt no joy, and as the warriors fell on the others' bodies, their scalping knives flashing in the firelight, he walked off into the darkness. Already, he knew that the war would be long, and he thought he knew how it would end.

Chapter 27

Autumn 1871

KIOWA RESISTANCE WAS ALL BUT BROKEN by the middle of 1871. Earlier that year, Gen. William Tecumseh Sherman had been visiting Fort Richardson when news reached him that a wagon train led by Henry Warren, bringing supplies of feed corn to Fort Griffin, had been attacked near Salt Creek, between Richardson and Griffin. Seven men had been killed and five more badly wounded. The supplies of corn were dumped on the ground and the dead savagely mutilated by the raiders, widely believed to be Comanche.

Outraged, Sherman ordered a punitive expedition under Major Alton Woods, but the cavalry was unable to find the raiders and returned empty-handed. Many of the Kiowa and Comanche were by this time nominally settled on the Kiowa and Comanche reservations in the Indian Territory, with Fort Sill at the hub.

Sherman then sent for some of the Kiowa chiefs, and when Satanta, Big Tree and Satank came in, they were arrested, jailed, and held for trial.

Satanta was still one of the fiercest of the plains chieftains, as was Big Tree, but Satank, the oldest of the trio, was another matter. He had lost his favorite son and, when he went to recover the body, found nothing but bones, which he gathered up, washed, and wrapped in a blanket. For the rest of his freedom, he traveled everywhere with the blanket-wrapped remains in trail on a second horse. He was a broken man, and seemed to accept the confinement without protest.

But that left the matter of the Comanche, and Sherman was less certain what to do about them. Quanah had been elected chief of all the Quohada Comanche at the remarkable young age of twenty-five, and his determination to resist the whites had drawn others to his band, including remnants of the Yamparika and Katsoteka Comanche and some die-hard Kiowa.

And Sherman knew that it was Quanah Parker who held the key to pacifying the Plains of Texas. As long as Quanah remained free, he would be a lightning rod for the disaffected, regardless of tribe, and he was determined to bring Quanah into the reservation or kill him, and made no secret of his preference for the latter.

But finding Quanah was no easy task. After the three Kiowa chiefs were tried and convicted in early summer, and confined to prison,

Sherman ordered the commander of Fort Richardson, Col. Ranald Slidell Mackenzie, to enter the Llano Estacado, find Quanah, and put an end to his resistance, by whatever means necessary.

In September of 1871, Mackenzie assembled a formidable force, consisting of four units of the 4th Cavalry, two units of the 19th Infantry, and twenty of the few remaining Tonkawa as scouts. His expedition overall consisted of six hundred officers and men supported by a train of one hundred pack mules. Joined by Major Woods, Mackenzie left Fort Richardson on September 19, and headed up the Fort Griffin road until he reached the Clear Fork of the Brazos River. From here, they were ready to brave the Llano in search of Quanah and the Quohada, and entered the Staked Plains on September 25th.

Mackenzie was no fool. He knew that the Comanche would get word of his presence, and would scout every inch of his march, but there was nothing he could do about it. He was in territory familiar only to the Comanche, and was more than a little concerned about meeting so fierce an enemy on that enemy's home ground, but there was no other way to bring the Comanche to heel. Quanah was too smart, and too good a general, to relinquish an advantage voluntarily.

They traveled thirty miles the first day, camped for the night and Mackenzie watched and waited to see what Quanah would do. The following

morning he had his answer. The Murphy ranch on
the edge of the Llano had been raided during the
night, with more than one hundred cattle and
more than a dozen horses captured. But the cavalry didn't take the bait, believing that it was simply
a diversion, an invitation to divide their force and
weaken the expedition.

The next day, the expedition left the Clear
Fork and marched toward Double Mountain,
near where Quanah had hidden out after leaving
Yellow Bear's camp. The army crossed the Paint
and California creeks and camped at Cottonwood
Springs. They were in the heart of Comanche
country now, and Mackenzie was determined
not to make a mistake. He ordered extra
restraints on the horses, and posted heavy security. He was no stranger to Indian fighting, and
knew that one of the first goals of the Comanche
would be to reduce his men to foot, if at all possible. And if the Comanche should succeed in
that, the entire expedition would be at their
mercy.

Once the preparations had been made, the
men lay down to sleep. Shortly after midnight,
Mackenzie was awakened by a thunderous din
sweeping down on the camp. He dashed out of
his tent to find buffalo stampeding toward him,
and quickly organized parties of men with
blankets to try and deflect the stampede. They
couldn't use guns for fear of signaling their
precise location to the Comanche and the men
ran around in desperation, shouting at the tops

of their voices, dividing the herd in two and sending it streaming past on both sides of the camp and off into the darkness.

When the dust had settled, and the thunder of the buffalo subsided, Mackenzie found himself wondering whether the stampede had been organized by the Comanche. But there was nothing to be done about it and after doubling the guard, he and the men returned to bed.

The next day's march brought them across the Salt Fork of the Brazos, where a supply base was established, and most of the pack mules left behind. The deeper they probed into the Llano, the more alien and inhospitable the terrain became. Vast plains studded with cactus and mesquite were broken by towering buttes. This was the country of the Comancheros, the renegade traders, mostly Mexican, who made their living supplying guns, ammunition, and other supplies to the recalcitrant Comanche, in exchange for stolen horses and cattle, and whatever else the raiding bands might turn up in their attacks on settlements, wagon trains, and homesteads.

Mackenzie was certain now that his expedition was being watched, and decided to march at night, in hopes of getting the jump on the Comanche by slipping past scouting parties. He followed the Clear Fork of the Brazos to where it flowed into Blanco Canyon. The following morning, a party of Tonkawa scouts stumbled on a large Comanche village several miles farther up the Brazos. The expedition was now in Blanco Canyon, surrounded by its towering walls, and to protect the horses that night, Mackenzie ordered double sentries posted. His constant fear was that the horses would somehow be captured, rendering the column little more than a helpless string of sitting ducks.

In the middle of the night, the Comanche roared down on the camp, using everything from guns to cowbells to make enough noise to frighten the cavalry mounts. The uproar terrified the horses, and despite being hobbled, nearly a hundred of them broke free and were driven off.

By morning, Mackenzie was convinced that an attack was imminent. The presence of the village meant large numbers of warriors nearby, and the military force could not be ignored. If the Comanche followed their usual practice, he knew, they would attack at least to cover the removal of the village and allow the women and children to escape to safety. And if the Comanche band was large enough, there might be an all-out attack in hopes of crushing the army.

Colonel Mackenzie sent a small horse unit upriver, with the purpose of tempting the Comanche to reveal their plans. Captains Robert G. Carter and John Gregg were at the head of the small detachment when they stumbled on a small band of Comanche warriors. Excited by the first contact with the enemy, the cavalrymen charged and the warriors turned tail and fled.

Sweeping around a bend in the canyon, the Comanche disappeared, and Gregg rallied his men, getting out in front and urging them to catch the fleeing warriors. But when he raced around the bend, he found himself confronted by a large contingent of warriors in full charge. At their head, Captain Carter recognized Quanah Parker on a coal-black mustang, Nightwind, his favorite war pony.

The cavalry was badly outnumbered, and fell back, firing to cover their retreat. But the Comanche kept on coming. Quanah charged Gregg and his men at full speed. He was painted for war, wearing a war bonnet and armed with a pistol in addition to bow and arrows. Heading straight toward the retreating soldiers, he dashed past the stragglers and fired at Captain Gregg, catching him in the center of the chest and killing him instantly.

Carter rallied his men, refusing to let them turn their backs to the charging Comanche, knowing that their only chance was to fire and fall back, fire and fall back, trying to slow the charge by accurate fire.

Some of the men panicked and made a break for it, and Carter watched helplessly as the warriors thundered after them, picking them off one by one.

Then, as suddenly as it had started, the fight was over. Quanah wheeled Nightwind around and led the Comanche back up the canyon toward the village, already disassembled and

starting to move. It seemed clear that the battle
had been joined less to defeat the expedition
than to delay it long enough to permit an orderly
escape.

Carter regrouped, then raced back to
Mackenzie, informing him of the fight.

"We've got them now," Mackenzie said. "We
can't afford to lose them. If they make it out of
the canyon and onto the plains, we'll have a hell
of a time catching them again. And if we do,
they'll have the upper hand."

"But we can follow them wherever they go.
There's no way they can conceal their route,
Colonel," Carter said.

"Do you want to be out in the open with a
thousand Comanche around you, Captain?"
Mackenzie asked.

When Carter shook his head, Mackenzie said,
"Well, neither do I. Let's get going."

It didn't take long to get the expedition moving, and by the time they marched on through
the canyon, they could see the remnants of the
villagers leaving the canyon's other end.
Mackenzie ordered a burial detail for Gregg and
the other casualties, and pressed his men hard to
close the gap. But before the army could get out
of the canyon, they were attacked again. Quanah
had organized several small parties of warriors
and deployed them in ambush along the canyon,
choosing sites which were easily defended by
small groups of warriors and that allowed them
to harass the column, which would have to

choose between exposing itself to heavy fire or
dig in.

Mackenize did his best, but Quanah had gotten the upper hand. It took the rest of the day for
the expedition to fight its way through the
canyon, and by the time they were able to get out
onto the plains, the Comanche were nowhere in
sight. Pushing his men to their limit, Mackenzie
pressed on. The tracks of the hundreds of travois
were easily followed, but the lead was considerable, and Mackenzie's men were exhausted.

Slowly but surely, the army narrowed the gap.
But the further Mackenzie followed, the deeper
into the Llano Estacado he went, the further
behind he left his supplies. His men were well
armed, but their ammunition had been seriously
depleted in the running battle through Blanco
Canyon, and he was starting to doubt the wisdom of further pursuit.

But before he had a chance to change his
mind, the weather changed dramatically. The
sky darkened and the wind picked up. Freezing
rain started to slash across the plains, and there
was no place to take cover from the worst of the
storm.

By nightfall, Mackenzie had ordered the men
to stand down and make camp. It got colder, and
the wind continued to howl. The storm was
coming out of the north, and Mackenzie knew
that such weather often dropped the temperature
by thirty or forty degrees in a matter of hours.

And this time was no exception. The freezing

rain changed to sleet and then to snow. They knew they were close, and they knew the Comanche were as exhausted as they were. All along the line of march, abandoned goods, lodgepoles, dead horses had marked the Comanche flight. But the weather was just too oppressive to push on any further.

The temperature had fallen below zero now, and the snow was so heavy that visibility was reduced almost to nothing. But Quanah was leaving nothing to chance. Out of the snow roared a large contingent of Comanche, Quanah at their head. They encircled Mackenzie's exhausted command and managed to drive off still more of the cavalry mounts before vanishing into the blizzard.

By daybreak, the storm had lifted. Mackenzie found himself in the heart of a frozen wasteland. The ground was frozen solid, but he knew that when the temperature climbed, it would turn to mud. It would not be hard to follow the trail of the refugees, but supplies were short and the men worn down to the point where further pursuit would have been unwise if not outright suicide.

Reluctantly, Mackenzie had to admit he was beaten. He waited much of the morning, less to think through his options, which were few and equally unpalatable, than to give his men a chance to rest and recover some of their strength. The horses, too, were near the breaking point, and in the back of his mind was the horrible possibility that Quanah might return, and force his men to flee on animals that no longer had the stamina to outrun the Comanche, who almost certainly would have switched to fresh mounts from the considerable herd they were driving ahead of them.

It was nearly three in the afternoon when the sun finally came out, and suddenly the Llano, as far as Mackenzie could see, had turned into a blinding sheet of white that made it almost impossible to see. Squinting against the glare, Mackenzie surveyed the horizon then, dejected, gave the order to pull out. With their backs to the blinding sun, the men headed back toward Blanco Canyon.

And Quanah headed west.

Chapter 28 ══════════

Summer 1874

DESPITE THE ESCAPE from Mackenzie, Quanah knew that his days of freedom were dwindling. Secure in the Llano Estacado, he waged a relentless guerrilla war on the Texas settlers, but his band was small, and the army was everywhere. Raiding was getting to be a tiresome and dangerous life. And he had changed his tactics. Believing that it was important to stop the settlement of Comanche land, and knowing that he was unable to kill all the Anglos who were pouring into Eastern Texas, pushing relentlessly against the barrier the Comanche presence had created, he started concentrating his efforts on destroying homesteads and sparing the settlers.

On raid after raid, he would ride up to the house, alone, his hand raised in truce, and use the little English at his disposal to warn the residents to flee. Then, even before they were out of sight, he would give a whoop and summon the rest of his band, who would descend on the homestead, run off the stock, and burn the buildings to the ground. He had never been disposed to brutality and torture, like some of the other Comanche chiefs, but now he seemed even more restrained.

At first it baffled his warriors, but they had too much respect for him to challenge his approach. There were whispers that he had seen a little girl who reminded him of his mother and, realizing what her ordeal must have been like, chose not to inflict it on another child, or leave another grieving family wondering what had happened to a son or daughter. And he knew there was nothing to be gained by pointless killing.

Soldiers and buffalo hunters were another matter, however. He had no qualms about waging war against men who could defend themselves, especially the hunters.

Even though Quanah had not signed the Medicine Lodge Treaty, he knew of its provisions from those who had. He knew that buffalo hunting by whites had been outlawed in Texas. But the hunters, anxious for the two dollars and fifty cents a good hide would bring, flooded into Texas by the hundreds.

The buffalo were dwindling, and in 1871 alone, by conservative estimates, more than a million hides made their way east. And Quanah was not alone in his hatred for the buffalo men. Some of the Kiowa chiefs who had refused to stay on the reservation, especially Satanta, newly pardoned by the Governor of Indian Territory and released from prison, were determined to drive the hunters from the plains by any means necessary. And if they resisted, so much the better.

One evening in early May, a medicine man named Isatai, who had been building a following with his teaching that the white man could be driven from Comanche land, came to Quanah's lodge.

After smoking a pipe, the two men began to talk. "You know," Isatai said, "that I have seen the Father of all red men."

Quanah nodded. He had heard the story from many warriors, some of whom believed the medicine man, and some of whom were skeptical. "So it is said," Quanah answered.

"And you know that I have strong medicine. I can swallow the white man's bullets, and I can cough up bullets for the Comanche guns. I can stop bullets from hitting our warriors."

Once again, Quanah nodded.

"I have had a vision," Isatai went on. "I have seen a great battle between white men and red men. In this battle, the white men, buffalo hunters, are trapped behind stone walls, and the red men come and kill them all, and the buffalo return to the plains. The white men leave Indian land, and the Comanche go back to live in the old way with no white men to interfere with their living."

"You believe this vision, Isatai?"

It was the medicine man's turn to nod. "I believe it," he said. "I think we should have a council. I think we should invite the Kiowa and the Arapaho, and the Cheyenne. We should invite all the red men who hate the buffalo hunters and want the white men to give us back our lands."

"This battle," Quanah said, "do you know where it is fought?"

Isatai described the vision in detail, and by the time he was through, Quanah thought he knew the place the shaman was talking about. There was an old fort, built by William Bent and long abandoned, known as Adobe Walls. It had been a fort for three generations, abandoned, rebuilt and abandoned again. Now, it was drawing buffalo hunters, who were using it as a staging area for their illegal hunts. Stores had been built inside the ruined walls, and the hunters came there for their supplies and to drink whiskey between hunts. They shipped their skins from the fort and it was a place where they all met to exchange stories and information about the location of the huge herds on the Texas Plains.

Quanah was more than willing to agree to a council with the express purpose of attacking the hunters and driving them from the plains. Word went out, and in the middle of May, nearly a thousand warriors gathered at Elk Creek on the North Fork of the Red River. Comanche hosted

Kiowa, Arapaho, and Cheyenne, and among the chiefs in attendance were Satanta, White Horse, Lone Wolf, Howling Wolf, and White Shield. Along with Quanah, Para-o-coom represented the Comanche.

Isatai was not bashful, and as soon as the Kiowa Sundance was celebrated, he got down to business. He explained that the united tribes had three main goals. "First, we must take revenge of the white men for our Comanche brothers who have been killed in Texas. Then, we must kill the last of the Tonkawa, the eaters of human flesh who still give themselves to the white man and fight against their red brothers. And last, we must take our revenge on the white men who hunt our buffalo and slaughter them for nothing but their skins. The Great Father promised us in the Medicine Lodge Treaty that white men would not hunt buffalo on our lands, and still they come by the hundreds and kill every buffalo they see."

The assembly grew excited as he continued to rage against the hated enemy, and by the time he explained how he could swallow the white man's bullets, he had the listeners in the palm of his hand.

A war party was assembled, and Quanah, as host and as the most celebrated of Comanche chiefs, was given the honor of leading the raid.

Adobe Walls was quiet in the middle of the night of June 27, 1874. The three main buildings inside the fortification were Hanrahan's saloon which catered to the thirsty hunters, Rath's supply house, which provided them with most of their needs, including ammunition, and Leonard's store, where they could get everything missing from Rath's shelves.

Most of the twenty-odd men inside were sleeping when a sharp crack woke them. No one was sure what it was, but a quick search soon revealed that a beam in Hanrahan's saloon had snapped. The inhabitants pitched in to replace the beam before the heavy adobe roof could collapse, and it turned into an all-night affair, with Jim Hanrahan catering to the thirsty band of would-be carpenters.

It was near dawn when Billy Dixon went outside to tend to his pony, tethered at the riverbank. As he started back toward the fort, he spotted a huge war party racing toward the fort. Firing his pistol and shouting to wake the hunters and merchants, Dixon raced to the fort with the war party closing on him.

Men spilled out of their bunks still groggy from lack of sleep as Quanah led the warriors right through the gates of the fort, instead of resorting to the usual Indian practice of riding in circles trying to pick off defenders luckless enough to expose themselves at the wrong time.

All of the defenders rushed to one of the three buildings, which were separated one from another by fifty or sixty yards. The Indians stayed on horseback, charging the buildings and returning the sporadic fire of the defenders. In the first

onslaught, the warriors destroyed every window
in all three buildings, and opened fire on the
dodging hunters, who were armed with their
long-range buffalo guns as well as a variety of
repeating rifles and pistols.

The hunters, although outnumbered almost
twenty-five to one, had the advantage of the sturdy adobe walls and their superior marksman-
ship. There was plenty of ammunition in the
stores, and as the Indians raced around the
inside of the fort, the buffalo hunters chose their
targets carefully, determined to make it last.

Two men were trapped outside the walls, and
the Comanche fell on them with a vengeance,
venting their accumulated rage, and the addi-
tional anger at their surprise attack being thwart-
ed. Both men were killed and scalped before the
attackers dropped back to regroup.

Quanah knew that success had depended on
complete surprise, because his warriors were no
match for the big buffalo guns. At the range of
nearly a mile, one of the warriors was killed as
he prepared to join the second assault.

"It is important that no one escapes to go for
help," Quanah warned. "If any of the hunters get
away they will bring the army, and we will be
forced to break off."

Leading the second wave back into the fort,
Quanah ordered supply wagons burned, along
with several wagons full of buffalo hides. The
stench of burning hair swirled in thick black
clouds as the attack resumed. Trying to get into

the buildings by hacking through the roof, three warriors were killed, and the defenders had used the lull to redistribute ammunition, replenishing the supply at Hanrahan's. The defenders had briefly considered consolidating their forces into one of the three buildings, but decided that the placement of the structures gave them an advantage by allowing them to fire at the Indians anywhere in the fort from one of the three.

One of Quanah's warriors dismounted and charged Hanrahan's on foot, brandishing his rifle, but was hit in the chest, and knocked to his knees by a pistol shot. Quanah, still on his horse, charged straight toward the wooden porch on which the wounded warrior lay, calling to him to get to his knees. As Nightwind rumbled up onto the wooden walkway that ran the length of the saloon, Quanah leaned far over, caught the warrior under the arms and hauled him to safety before dashing away from the muzzles of the Sharps and Spencer rifles.

One of the younger hunters, the not yet widely known Bat Masterson, suggested that he would try to make a break for it and go for help.

"Are you crazy?" Jim Hanrahan asked. "The closest help is Dodge City and that's two days' ride. You'll never make it. There must be a thousand redskins out there."

"We can't let them starve us out," Masterson argued. "We have to do something."

"There's plenty of food in Leonard's. Besides, word'll spread all by itself, and we'll have help pretty soon without you taking a fool chance like that."

Masterson was skeptical, but several of the hunters ganged up on him and their combined arguments convinced him to wait.

Quanah pulled his men back again, frustrated at their inability to crack the defense. He knew that he was waging the most important battle of his life and, if he failed, that Comanche dominance in the Llano would be at an end.

Once more, he ordered an attack, and once more the huge war party swept through the shattered and yawning gates of the old adobe battlements. Once more, the defenders laid down a withering fire that kept the warriors at bay. It was near dark, and the attack was short-lived. Quanah pulled back to wait for dawn.

During the night, one of the hunters, Henry Lease, slipped out the back of Hanrahan's, climbed over the walls and disappeared into the darkness without being seen. He headed for Dodge, knowing that it was just a matter of time before the attackers managed to overwhelm the fort.

On the way, he met a party of hunters, told them what was happening, and pushed on for the border and Kansas. The hunters spread the word, and raced to the fort. All night long, the buffalo men streamed in, fighting their way through the small bands of warriors patrolling the area.

By dawn, there were nearly a hundred men inside, and virtually every one of them was armed with a buffalo gun. But Quanah could not afford to give up just yet. There was too much at stake, and if this attack failed, there would never be another chance.

As the sun rose, the Comanche led the war party back into the battle, but this time they were unable even to get inside the walls, since the defenders now had enough men to line the walls with sharpshooters. Again and again, the thunder of one of the big guns rolled across the plains, and another Indian fell.

Knowing it was useless, Quanah called off the attack and led the war party back into the Llano. By the time relief forces arrived from Dodge, there was no sign of the attack except for a dozen Comanche heads arranged in a row of stakes driven into the ground beside the gates.

Heading back into the vastness of the plains, Quanah knew that he had failed. He knew, too, that it was now only a matter of time before every Quohada warrior was either dead or confined to a reservation.

There had to be a way to change that, he kept thinking. There had to be. But there was none, and he knew it.

Chapter 29 ═══════════

Autumn 1874

GEN. WILLIAM SHERMAN WAS CONVINCED that an all-
out war on the remnants of plains Indian resistance was the only way to bring the Indian wars
to a successful conclusion. He knew that many of
the hostile bands were using the reservations as
hiding places, raiding at will, and returning to
the protection of the various agencies afterward,
where they would mingle with those who had
never left. They were being fed by the government, Sherman believed, to make war on that
very same government and its people.

Accordingly, he argued vigorously with the
administration in Washington for permission to
put troops in the field full time until the last hostile bands were forced to come in and sue for
peace. It was a difficult battle, because there
were many in the nation's capital who understood that even though the conflict between red
and white was costly, and had taken a consider-

able toll in settlers' lives, ravaged property, and untold millions of dollars, all the wrong was by no means perpetrated by the Indians.

The peace faction recognized that the Indians had been double-dealt, that treaties had been broken almost at will and often before the ink had dried. They argued that fair treatment was the only way to end the wars permanently.

But Sherman prevailed. By the beginning of autumn, he had gotten the authorization he sought, and immediately passed word to Gen. Philip Sheridan to proceed. The first part of Sherman's grand design called for all Indians, peaceful and hostile alike, to be told that any Indian found off a reservation without permission would automatically be considered hostile and would be fair game for the military.

As soon as the message was disseminated, many of the chiefs who were ambivalent about further resistance recognized that while there was little to be said for life on a reservation, there was little or nothing to be gained by continuing to prosecute a war they could not win. The continual hostilities were taking their toll on women and children. With the incessant slaughter of the buffalo, which saw more than two million hides shipped eastward in 1873 and 1874 each, food was increasingly hard to find. It was apparent to many of the holdouts that their best chance was surrender.

The next step for Sheridan was to dispatch troops to the field, and he devised an elaborate, five-pronged pincer campaign designed to surround the hostiles and gradually contract around them. From Camp Supply in the northern reaches of Indian Territory, one column headed into action under the command of Col. Nelson A. Miles. A second column was commanded by Col. John W. Davidson, and departed from Fort Sill, heading west.

Maj. William Price followed the valley of the Canadian River from New Mexico, with orders to prevent flight to the west. Fort Griffin was the point of departure for a fourth deployment, under the command of Colonel G. P. Buell and the last was led by Colonel Mackenzie, still smarting from his last encounter with Quanah and his Quohada Comanche band.

In the vast wasteland surrounded by these units, bands of Comanche, Kiowa, and Cheyenne still managed to fend for themselves, striking occasionally at small military units, harassing homesteads and saving the worst of their fury for the hunters who continued to flood the plains and ignore the provisions of the Medicine Lodge treaty.

The overall commander of the campaign was Colonel Mackenzie, and he was determined not to allow another fiasco like Blanco Canyon to prevent him from completing his mission. Each of the five columns had intermediate objectives, and Mackenzie's first concern was the Blanco Canyon vicinity. He intended to flush out all of the hostiles between the parallel valleys of the Pease and Red rivers.

Miles was operating in the vicinity of Antelope Hills when he stumbled on a trail that led him into a Comanche maelstrom. But his men were well supplied and heavily armed, including several gatling gun units, which gave him overwhelming superiority in firepower.

Buell and Richardson also encountered scattered bands of hostiles, but the Indians, realizing the insuperable odds, chose to hit and run rather than stand and fight a pitched battle they could not win. They knew the terrain far better than the army, and they were more mobile, but they were hampered immeasurably by the fact that they had their families along. Any battle fought on Indian land exposed the women, children, and old people to the indiscriminate fire of the attacking soldiers, so the hostiles resorted to life on the run, sending small bands of warriors in a dozen directions, swooping down on detachments to exchange scattered gunfire, run off a few horses and vanish back into the emptiness of the plains.

But time was running out, and the chiefs knew it. One after another, they faced the inevitability of their destruction if they continued to resist, and chose surrender to annihilation. But no one had seen Quanah and his Quohada. They seemed to have vanished off the face of the earth.

It wasn't until late September that Quanah made his presence felt, and then nearly defeated Miles and his column in a surprise attack during the middle of the night. But Price was nearby, and Miles had had the good sense to arrange his supply wagons in a defensive perimeter, and Quanah broke off the engagement and disappeared once more.

Everyone knew that the Comanche had a hiding place, one that was large enough to accommodate hundreds of people, and remote enough that no white man had ever seen it. But no one had any idea where it might be. Mackenzie was convinced that the key to subduing Quanah and his Quohada was finding that redoubt. But the ceaseless wanderings of his scouts turned up not a hint as to its whereabouts.

Mackenzie knew he needed a stroke of luck, and when the weather started to turn cold, he despaired of getting it. It was the beginning of the coldest Texas winter anyone could remember, and snow and freezing rain began in mid-September and continued on week after week. The men alternately froze and slogged through impossible mud whenever there was a momentary thaw. Morale was crumbling, and the horses were being worn to the nub by the incessant pressure and grueling conditions.

But Mackenzie had been right, he needed luck, and he got it from an unexpected source. A patrol had stumbled on a group of Comancheros, and after a stiff fight, managed to capture José Tafoya before the rest of the Comanchero band made its escape.

Lt. Byron Mitchell, who commanded the

squadron, immediately took Tafoya to Mackenzie's tent.

"What have we got here, Lieutenant?" Mackenzie asked, looking up from his camp desk.

"Comanchero, sir."

"Oh really?" Mackenzie put down his pen, stood up, and circled the desk to stand in front of the defiant Comanchero.

"Do you speak English, señor?"

"Si," Tafoya replied.

"What is your name?"

"José Tafoya."

"Is this true, what Lieutenant Mitchell just told me? Are you a Comanchero?"

Tafoya shook his head in the negative.

"Speak up, man, are you?"

Once more Tafoya shook his head no.

"Do you know where the Comanche are holed up, señor?"

Tafoya refused this time even to shake his head.

Mackenzie rocked back on his heels. "I'll ask you one more time, Señor Tafoya. Do you know where the Comanche are holed up?"

Once again, Tafoya declined to respond.

"Very well, then. Lieutenant . . . ?"

"Yes, sir?"

"Hang him."

Tafoya opened his eyes wide, but still said nothing.

"Excuse me, Colonel," Mitchell said, not certain he'd heard correctly.

"Hang him, Lieutenant. Now!"

"But there aren't any trees tall enough, Colonel."

"You'll think of something. Use a wagon tongue if you have to, but when I come out of my tent, I want to see this man swaying in the breeze."

"Yes, sir." Mitchell snapped a salute and dragged Tafoya from the tent. Once outside, he detailed half a dozen men to rig a gallows with a wagon tongue lashed to the metal hoops of a pair of wagons. It took fifteen minutes to set up the makeshift gallows, and another two to get a rope around Tafoya's neck. He was hauled off his feet and suspended in the air, gagging and gasping for air.

His hands were free and he clawed at the rope, but couldn't manage to get his fingers inside the noose.

In desperation, he waved an arm to Mitchell. The lieutenant approached slowly while Tafoya, his tongue lolling, signaled that he had changed his mind. With the rope still around the prisoner's neck, Mitchell had him dragged back to Mackenzie's tent, where he proceeded not only to tell where the Comanche hideout was located, but to draw a detailed map of the layout. He spent more than an hour with the colonel, and when he was finished, Mackenzie not only knew the location, he had a fairly clear idea of the surrounding terrain, including the limited escape routes available to the Comanche who, as it happened, were camped in Palo Duro Canyon.

Mackenzie dispatched scouts to verify Tafoya's intelligence, and when they were gone, he told the Comanchero, "Señor Tafoya, I certainly hope you've been honest with me. Because if you haven't, I will personally haul your greasy ass into the air and this time you will not come down from that gallows alive. Do you understand me, señor?"

Rubbing his neck, which still bore scrapes from the rope and glowed a bright red in the lamplight of Mackenzie's tent, Tafoya nodded. "Si, Colonel. I understand."

Scouts confirmed Tafoya's story, and Mackenzie wasted no time. Two days' forced march brought him to the brink of Palo Duro Canyon. The precipitous pink walls ran for miles along the river, and the canyon floor was thick with cedars and lush grass. It was an ideal position to defend, because the only access was down dangerous trails a quarter mile in length, and any troops attempting the descent would be easy targets. They would have to move slowly and in single file.

But for some reason, perhaps lulled into a false sense of security by the seemingly impregnable defense provided by the canyon walls, the encampment was unaware of the army's approach. Mackenzie started down immediately, having reached the rim just after daylight. Scouts found a buffalo trail that wound down the walls, and the troops started down on foot, leading their horses.

Tipis lined the river, but the camp seemed to be asleep. The column managed to avoid discovery until it was on a grass-covered plateau on the canyon floor. Finally, an Indian sentry saw them and fired his rifle to sound the alarm. Almost immediately, dozens of Kiowa, Comanche, and Cheyenne warriors spilled out of their lodges and the fight was on.

But with a significant army force already on the canyon floor, the battle had already been lost. The Indians fought fiercely, using every rock and cedar tree for cover as they pinned the soldiers down. More troops were still making the descent, and Mackenzie was forced to slow his assault to cover them.

But the only way out for the defenders was up the canyon walls, because the mouth of the canyon was cut off by troopers, and the Indians realized they were in a desperate situation. Their herd of more than two thousand horses was useless, and they were forced to abandon it as they fell back, fighting desperately to allow the women and children time to climb up and out of the cul de sac.

The huge village, and everything in it, was abandoned to the advancing troopers. Mackenzie did not wait for the fight to finish before ordering everything burned. He knew the fleeing Indians were on foot, and that they had nothing. He also knew the weather would work against them. Food, clothing, lodges, everything was burned.

Taking control of the captured herd, Mackenzie then made a bold decision.

"Shoot the horses," he ordered. It was almost unheard of for a military commander, especially a cavalryman, to issue such a command. His officers balked initially, but Mackenzie was adamant. "Shoot them all," he insisted.

The troopers set about the bloody business with grim faces and more than a few tears in their eyes. The warriors, clinging to the precipitous trails, saw what was happening, and many of them began to wail horribly at the senseless slaughter. But, hanging on the towering stone walls, helpless to do anything but watch, they saw more than two thousand animals massacred by incessant firing from the blue coats.

When the smoke had cleared, Mackenzie filed his report, and the casualties among the Indians, given the circumstances, were surprisingly few. He reported only four killed. His own casualties were light, and yet, whether he knew it or not, he had accomplished what Sheridan had ordered him to do. He had broken the back of Indian resistance.

Quanah was camped just a few miles away, but was not in the canyon. Had he been there, things might have turned out differently. It is difficult to imagine Quanah permitting such lax vigilance. But the damage had been done, and it was beyond repair, and Quanah knew it.

Still, Mackenzie knew that his principal quarry had eluded him once more. But Quanah knew that the war was effectively over. It was now just a matter of time.

All through the winter, skirmishes continued, but Palo Duro Canyon was the last major battle of the Indian Wars on the plains of Texas.

Chapter 30

Summer 1875

ALL WINTER AND INTO THE SPRING, Quanah and his Quohada managed to evade the increasingly aggressive army units crisscrossing the Llano in search of him. Still waging hit-and-run war, he was merely protracting the bitter end of a war that had already been lost.

More and more frequently, the fugitive Comanche would move their camp, in search of those increasingly rare water holes and hidden canyons unknown to the soldiers. But the constant running was wearing down the people. The women and children were restless and frightened, the old people less and less able to cope with the incessant wandering.

As the spring of 1875 opened, more bands started to come in to surrender, until only Quanah was left. He knew it couldn't continue much longer, and the question now was not whether to surrender but how to do so on the best terms possible for his people.

At one point, he considered heading west to New Mexico, but that would bring him into direct conflict with the Apache, still at war with the American government, and his warriors were too few for such a move. Mexico meant the Mexican army, and that was no better a choice than standing and fighting the Americans.

Surrender was the only logical choice. The women and children were starving, the buffalo were all but gone, and the weather had been brutal. That meant that Quanah could not demand terms. His surrender would have to be abject and complete, and the thought galled him.

The army, not knowing exactly where he was, continued to pursue him, and time was growing short. And Quanah had heard tales of conditions at Fort Sill that deterred him from immediate capitulation. Instead of treaties, as in the past, to establish reservations, now the surrendering bands were treated like outlaws. The leaders were confined to prison cells, the property confiscated and burned. The army was leaving nothing to chance. They wanted those who surrendered to have no recourse but to be totally dependent on the government. No longer would the reservations be used as temporary rest areas, springboards to renewed conflict when strength returned and the weather was favorable.

Fort Sill was crowded, and growing more so. Disease was taking a heavy toll on those confined there, and Quanah's reluctance was heightened by what he learned of the unsanitary, degrading conditions. But still, it would have to happen, and he knew it. Mackenzie sent runners out looking for the last remaining fugitive bands, and one managed to contact a small war party of Quohada and convinced them to come in and talk to Colonel Mackenzie.

Mackenzie, for his part, was conciliatory. He respected Quanah, and understood his reluctance to surrender, but insisted that it was the only reasonable course. He promised there would be no retaliation, and the Comanche would be treated fairly and honorably.

When the war party returned to camp, they explained Mackenzie's position to Quanah, who spent the night thinking about his options, meager as they were. He thought back over the past twenty years. He realized all he had lost and understood that no matter how it had been taken from him, it was gone, and gone for good.

In the interim, emissaries from Mackenzie came to Quanah's camp under a flag of truce. The remaining chiefs were gathered together, but it was clear that it was Quanah who spoke for the Comanche. He listened politely to what they had to say, and promised he would talk to his people and try to convince them to come in.

It took several weeks, and Mackenzie waited anxiously for word.

On June 2, 1875, a sentry at Fort Sill spotted a lone rider approaching, and Mackenzie was notified. The colonel stood on the gallery outside his office as the rider came in through the gates. He recognized Quanah immediately, and stood rigidly at attention, one commander receiving another.

One of the troopers ran over to Quanah and reached for the bridle and Quanah jerked it, turned the horse's head away, and said in his halting English, "No. You no lead me like a cow."

And Comanche freedom was at an end.

Afterword

IMMEDIATELY UPON HIS SURRENDER, Quanah began to work for the future of his people. He knew that, having capitulated to the white man, it was imperative that his people learn the white man's ways. He worked for improved education, urged his people to learn English, and studiously applied himself to mastering the language.

After he had been at Fort Sill for a few months, he started to become curious about his mother's family, and applied for permission to search for them. Because of the work he had been doing, the request was granted, and a search finally turned up a cousin.

Quanah journeyed south, alone on horseback, armed only with a vague map, but managed to find the cousin, who put him in touch with Naudah's brother Silas. Silas took him in, and filled in some details about Naudah's last days, and, much to Quanah's surprise, told him about John Parker, Naudah's brother, who had not been seen since a day or two after the kidnapping of the two Parker children.

Visiting John, he learned that he had been bartered to another band, adopted by them, became a Comanche warrior and traveled into Mexico where he contracted small pox. Because the deadly disease took such a terrible toll on native Americans, the Comanche left him behind, but he had been found by a young Mexican woman who saved his life and later married him.

Quanah also had a chance to visit Naudah's grave, in a remote grove of trees, badly tended and overgrown. The visit saddened him, but seemed to invigorate his determination to seek the best possible future for all the Comanche people.

He spent the next thirty-five years in service of his people, and died on February 23, 1911. He was buried in the Indian cemetery near Fort Sill. A monument was erected by the federal government, and bore the inscription "Resting here until the day breaks and the shadows fall and darkness disappears."

But even in death, he was not free. His grave was vandalized repeatedly and once the bones were disinterred by grave robbers looking for artifacts. Finally, in 1958, Quanah's remains were reburied at Fort Sill along with those of Cynthia Ann Parker.

Quanah's life after his surrender is well documented because as an advocate of Indian rights he was a tireless worker and learned the ins and outs of the alien system that had deprived his people of their way of life. But his life prior to surrender is less well known, and many of the details are missing. Existing biographies disagree more than those of most of the great chiefs, but that of Clyde and Grace Jackson, and the more recent work by Rosemary Kissinger give a good overview of Quanah's life.

A fine general survey of the Indian wars of Texas is *Carbine and Lance,* by Col. W.S. Nye, while *Death Song: The Last of the Indian Wars,* by John Edward Weems, takes a broader view, placing the Comanche struggle in the context of its time and parallels that conflict with those of the Apache and the Sioux. The best and most readily available study of Comanche customs and life in general is *The Comanches: Lords of the South Plains* by Wallace and Hoebel.

▰ HarperPaperbacks *By Mail*

To complete your Zane Grey collection, check off the titles you're missing and order today!

- ❏ Arizona Ames (0-06-100171-6)..........................$3.99
- ❏ The Arizona Clan (0-06-100457-X).................$3.99
- ❏ Betty Zane (0-06-100523-1)................................$3.99
- ❏ Black Mesa (0-06-100291-7)..............................$3.99
- ❏ Blue Feather and Other Stories (0-06-100581-9).......$3.99
- ❏ The Border Legion (0-06-100083-3)..................$3.95
- ❏ Boulder Dam (0-06-100111-2)............................$3.99
- ❏ The Call of the Canyon (0-06-100342-5).............$3.99
- ❏ Captives of the Desert (0-06-100292-5)...........$3.99
- ❏ Code of the West (0-06-1001173-2)...................$3.99
- ❏ The Deer Stalker (0-06-100147-3)......................$3.99
- ❏ Desert Gold (0-06-100454-5)..............................$3.99
- ❏ The Drift Fence (0-06-100455-3)........................$3.99
- ❏ The Dude Ranger (0-06-100055-8)..................$3.99
- ❏ Fighting Caravans (0-06-100456-1)..............$3.99
- ❏ Forlorn River (0-06-100391-3).......................$3.99
- ❏ The Fugitive Trail (0-06-100442-1)................$3.99
- ❏ The Hash Knife Outfit (0-06-100452-9)............$3.99
- ❏ The Heritage of the Desert (0-06-100451-0).......$3.99
- ❏ Knights of the Range (0-06-100436-7)............$3.99
- ❏ The Last Trail (0-06-100583-5).........................$3.99
- ❏ The Light of Western Stars (0-06-100339-5).......$3.99
- ❏ The Lone Star Ranger (0-06-100450-2)..............$3.99
- ❏ The Lost Wagon Train (0-06-100064-7)...........$3.99
- ❏ Majesty's Rancho (0-06-100341-7)....................$3.99
- ❏ The Maverick Queen (0-06-100392-1)................$3.99
- ❏ The Mysterious Rider (0-06-100132-5)...............$3.99
- ❏ Raiders of Spanish Peaks (0-06-100393-X).........$3.99
- ❏ The Ranger and Other Stories (0-06-100587-8)...$3.99
- ❏ The Reef Girl (0-06-100498-7)............................$3.99
- ❏ Riders of the Purple Sage (0-06-100469-3).........$3.99

- ❏ Robbers' Roost (0-06-100280-1)............................ $3.99
- ❏ Shadow on the Trail (0-06-100443-X).................... $3.99
- ❏ The Shepherd of Guadaloupe (0-06-100500-2)..... $3.99
- ❏ The Spirit of the Border (0-06-100293-3)............... $3.99
- ❏ Stairs of Sand (0-06-100468-5)............................ $3.99
- ❏ Stranger From the Tonto (0-06-100174-0)............ $3.99
- ❏ Sunset Pass (0-06-100084-1)............................... $3.99
- ❏ Tappan's Burro (0-06-100588-6)........................... $3.99
- ❏ 30,000 on the Hoof (0-06-100085-X)..................... $3.99
- ❏ Thunder Mountain (0-06-100216-X)........................ $3.99
- ❏ The Thundering Herd (0-06-100217-8)................... $3.99
- ❏ The Trail Driver (0-06-100154-6)........................... $3.99
- ❏ Twin Sombreros (0-06-100101-5).......................... $3.99
- ❏ Under the Tonto Rim (0-06-100294-1).................... $3.99
- ❏ The Vanishing American (0-06-100295-X)............... $3.99
- ❏ Wanderer of the Wasteland (0-06-100092-2)........ $3.99
- ❏ West of the Pecos (0-06-100467-7)....................... $3.99
- ❏ Wilderness Trek (0-06-100260-7).......................... $3.99
- ❏ Wild Horse Mesa (0-06-100338-7)......................... $3.99
- ❏ Wildfire (0-06-100081-7)...................................... $3.99
- ❏ Wyoming (0-06-100340-9)..................................... $3.99

MAIL TO:
HarperCollins Publishers
P.O. Box 588 Dunmore, PA 18512-0588
OR CALL: (800) 331-3761 (Visa/MasterCard)

For Fastest Service
Visa & MasterCard Holders Call
1-800-331-3761

Subtotal..$_____
Postage and Handling...$ 2.00*
Sales Tax (Add applicable sales tax).......................$_____
TOTAL:..$_____

*(Order 4 or more titles and postage and handling is free! Orders of less than 4 books, please include $2.00 p/h.
Remit in US funds, do not send cash.)

Name_____

Address_____

_____

City_____ State_____ Zip_____

Allow up to 6 weeks delivery.
(Valid only in US & Canada)   Prices subject to change.   H0805